The Power Move

Elizabeth Meitzler

First paperback edition November 2023

Edited by Laura Cifelli

ISBN 979-8-9865455-2-3 (paperback)

ISBN 979-8-9865455-3-0 (ebook)

To the Clarion OG's

Thanks for all the memories!

(and the inspiration)

To my family and relatives,

If you choose to continue reading after this page and choose to tell me about it, I highly suggest you only focus on the friendships created at Winger University. Please do not talk to me about any ... activities you read about that aren't related to hockey.

If you are going to turn the page, all I can say is I hope you enjoy this book. Except for you, dad. Stop reading immediately!

Chapter One

The sound of metal scraping metal vibrates through my head as my neck is thrown back against my headrest. I'm sitting at the four-way intersection only a block from my new apartment and someone just ran into the front of my freaking car. I've never been in a crash before and I can't decide if I should scream or cry right now. My head feels dizzy and my vision doubles for a second. Once it's back to normal, I decide that I'm pissed. I look over to the car that hit me and he looks just as mad. Jumping out of my car, I slam my door and walk around to inspect the damage. My bumper has a huge dent and is now hanging slightly lower on one side. Shit! I don't have money to fix this!

"What the fuck?" the guy behind me yells.

I stand up, turning to him with a scowl. Squatting down had my tank top and shorts riding up my not-so-flat belly and thick thighs. I quickly pull my clothes back down into place. "Excuse me? You hit me!"

"Are you crazy? Were you too busy daydreaming to realize I had the right of way?"

Is this guy for real? It's obvious to anyone that he paused instead of actually stopping.

"You slammed into me. Look at my car!"

Horns begin honking and cars full of dorm essentials and frazzled families start pulling around us. It's move-in day at Winger University and we're holding up traffic. Students decked out in blue and yellow – Go, Royals, Go – scream obscenities from their cars at us like that's helping the situation.

I want to punch this stupid human being in front of me, even though I doubt I could hurt him. He looks like his muscles have muscles. Said muscles flex as he runs a hand through his already messy brown hair and that's when I register I'm staring. I quickly blink away, silently scolding myself for finding this asshole attractive.

He walks closer to my car, his shoulders shaking in silent laughter. "Hate to break it to you, but I think you actually improved it. How old is this thing?"

My vision turns red as I briefly wonder exactly what constitutes premeditated murder. "It doesn't matter how old it is, what matters is that you're going to pay for the damage."

"You mean for the bumper falling off or for the countless dents?"

I think my teeth may crack with how hard I'm clenching my jaw.

"Either way," he continues, "I'm not paying for shit. We're creating a scene. Go get your insurance and we'll let them deal with this."

Insurance. Shit. Shit. Shit. I knew this would bite me in the ass. I'm not broke, I just like to budget and save money when I can. Which meant not renewing my insurance because it was super expensive. I've always been a careful driver and never used it before, so I figured I could put the money toward groceries and renew it once school was over.

"Um—"

"You're kidding." He runs a hand over his scruff and this time he laughs out loud. "How the hell do you not have insurance?"

"Move your cars!" Someone yells from behind us.

"Get out of the way!" Another screams.

"This is ridiculous," I tell him. "I'm moving into the apartments off Grand. Meet me in the parking lot and we can talk there."

I turn to head back to my car when his hand locks onto my wrist. "Give me your driver's license. You do have one of those, right?"

I roll my eyes, jerking my hand back. "Of course, I have one, but I'm not giving it to you."

He closes his eyes and inhales sharply through his nose. "It's called collateral. Here's mine."

Reaching behind him, he pulls a money clip out of his back pocket and holds his license for me between his forefinger and middle finger. I reach to grab it, but he holds it higher. I'm 5'3, which I know is already on the shorter side, but I think this guy qualifies as a giant. I stomp back to my car and find mine before we exchange. He looks down, taking note of my name and address.

"How come you don't have an accent?" he asks.

"Excuse me?"

He holds my ID up like I've never seen it before. "This says you're from Kentucky."

"So?"

"So, don't most people from the south have an accent? Or did you happen to give me your fake ID?"

My hands raise of their own volition like they want to strangle this man. Instead, I curl my fingers in and groan. "I'm from the northern part, you know-it-all jerk."

He smiles, which is annoying, looks down at my ID then back up to me. "Well, Kentucky, I'll see you in a minute."

"It's Millie," I spit.

Ignoring the shouting and honking, I get back in my car and head toward my new apartment. I wince when I hear the scraping of my bumper against the pavement. Luckily, the parking lot is close, so I don't think I did any more damage. My phone starts ringing and, knowing who it is, I ignore it. I can only deal with one hot mess at a time. Once parked, I take a minute to look at the license in my hand. Caleb Booker. Born March 16th. Brown hair and gray eyes. His height is 6'0 but I swear he seemed taller.

"You live here?" he asks once I get out.

"No, I'm casing the joint before I rob it later. Yes, I live here."

Using the scrunchie on my wrist, I tie my purple hair up into a bun. Well, semi-purple. It's been a while since I dyed it, so the top of my head is brown and the bottom dark purple. Very Ombre-like. It's pretty long, but I haven't had the itch to cut it yet.

He walks over, leaning his back against my car, crossing his large arms over his chest. Without thinking, I lick my lips at the sight and then drag my eyes to his face. His expression is smug and I think he caught me.

"You don't have insurance."

It's not a question.

"I...No, I don't have insurance. I was trying to save money." My voice quiets at the end of that sentence, knowing how silly it sounds.

Caleb's gaze makes me feel about two feet tall, so instead of letting him make me feel like shit, I walk to examine his car. Of course, it doesn't even have a dent. Stupid car. I want to kick it in frustration, but I feel like that wouldn't be well received.

"You realize—"

I hold up my hand to stop him. "Save the lecture for whatever girl is unlucky enough to date you. You can get off your high horse because I don't need a speech. I need you to pay for my bumper that isn't completely attached to my car anymore."

Caleb shakes his head slowly. "Let me tell you what's going to happen."

"Oh great. I can't wait for you to mansplain it to me," I deadpan.

He pushes off the car — why does that look so sexy? — and stops inches from me.
After a few seconds of silence, I say, "Can you get out of my personal space?"

The corner of his mouth quirks up. "You're going to go get some insurance for your car. Once you have that, call me and we can have the insurance companies sort this out."

I grunt in frustration and this time, I actually place my hands on his chest and push him away. Two mistakes were just made. One, I touched him, getting to feel his hard pecs and two, he didn't even budge. I try again and it's the same results.

"Why won't you move, dammit?" I grunt.

He grabs my wrists, stopping me. He's still smiling, finding this entertaining and I want to push him again.

"Calm down, Kentucky. I'll give you a pass this once. But next time you hit my car, I am calling the cops."

I try to pull away, but he tightens his grip. "Call the cops? I didn't do anything wrong. And how the hell am I supposed to drive without a working bumper?"

His pocket buzzes and he finally lets me go; I hate that my wrists tingle, missing his touch. Without another look, he gets into his car and starts the engine.

"Are you kidding me?" I scream. As his car reverses, and I realize he isn't stopping, I smack the front of his car. His face remains unamused as he speeds away. I freaking hate people.

Chapter Two

Caleb

I deserve an award for not getting out of my car and taking Millie over my knee for smacking my car. I don't give a shit how pissed she is about her bumper, you don't hit a man's car. Besides, if she was paying attention, she wouldn't have hit me in the first place. Yes, my car appears to be fine, but I'm still having my guy check it out as soon as possible. I did not work my ass off juggling hockey and two jobs in high school to bang this beauty up. I'm not a big car guy, but that doesn't mean I can't appreciate my baby.

After I got a text from one of my hockey buddies, I had to walk away before I did something stupid. Millie is fucking hot. And annoying. And she seems ridiculously high maintenance. Ignoring those last two things, we still could've had some fun. I saw her pupils dilate when I grabbed her wrists and pulled her closer. I also caught her checking me out, even if she thought I wasn't looking. Her long wavy hair hung down below her tits, tits that just happened to be pushed up and on display in a tiny little tank top. That top and her shorts showed off her curves and I wanted to take a bite out of every inch of her...until she opened her mouth. It's not really my kink, but if I ever got her naked, I could always gag her. I know some guys who like to do that. Personally, I like access to my girl's mouth, but who am I to judge?

"What took so long?" Jace hollers as he jogs down the sidewalk. Jace is one of my closest friends in the house. He also happens to be one of my teammates. He's tough as shit on the ice and a good guy to have in your corner.

"Some chick hit my car. Sorry it delayed you getting drunk in the middle of the day," I say flatly.

"Your car? It okay?" His head snaps side to side, checking for damage.

I walk around to the trunk, grab the beer, and pass it to him. "I'm fine. Thanks for asking."

He ignores me, helping me unload the entire trunk. Beer, snacks, and more beer. Ballentine House has the tradition of hosting a huge party on move-in day. No school officials are on campus yet, which means the rules aren't as strict. It's my first year living in the house and getting to plan the party has been pretty cool.

"You go and brew the damn stuff yourself?" Kai taunts. A sad attempt at a joke really. I expected better from him.

"Har. Har. Har."

Jocks can be so stupid sometimes.

Ballentine House - or as it's known around campus, Balls Hall - is basically an unsanctioned fraternity. It's a fifteen room house that holds guys from all different sports. It's such a process getting accepted, but it's worth it. The Victorian-style house has been around for generations, run through donations from alumni who have gone on to do better and richer things. Only Juniors and Seniors are allowed in because Freshman and Sophomores tend to be idiots and don't know how to take care of their things. Our kitchen has a breakfast bar with all newer appliances. We have a room designated solely to video games — unless our coaches are riding our asses and we use it to go over highlights from previous games. The best feature is the basement. Only the house occupants get keys and it's where we store all our precious items during parties. Can't have our donors come around to see that we trashed the place. Currently, we have guys from hockey, football, basketball, baseball, and lacrosse in the house. The only rule to living in the house is everyone has to get along. Whatever shit goes on outside, stays outside. It's majority rules here, so if you piss off everyone collectively, you're voted out. Except for a few bad eggs, it's worked out pretty well in keeping the peace across the board.

I'm unloading the last bit when my phone buzzes.

"What?"

"Wow. Is that how you answer the call of your only sister?" She pretends to be hurt.

"Sorry, Bon-Bon," I grunt, propping the phone on my shoulder with my ear and using the arm not holding anything to shut my trunk. "I just got home. We're trying to get ready for tonight."

"Well, can you pause what you're doing?"

I stop walking and sigh. "Why? What's wrong?"

"The old tenants never took their furniture. They were only supposed to leave us the bed frames, but they left way more. Anyway, can you bring some guys over to help move it all out?"

I already know what my answer will be, but it's fun to screw with her.

"I am a strong independent woman. I don't need to live with my brother. I can take care of myself," I make my voice high-pitched to mimic hers and her words from earlier in the summer.

"Caleb," she whines. "Apartment 302."

And then she hangs up. I laugh as I put my phone back in my pocket.

"Zeke, Brooks, and Buzz. You three idiots come with me. Bonnie needs help moving some stuff."

"Bonnie, huh?" Buzz comments.

I stop walking, giving him a death glare. From the moment Bonnie and Buzz met, he's found it funny to mess with me about her. Little does he know, he will never play another sport again if he lays a finger on my sister.

"One day, Caleb's gonna snap," Zeke tells Buzz.

I shrug. He's not wrong.

Chapter Three

Millie

Once my car was officially unloaded, I brought Zola out to show her the damage. "What are you going to do?" she asks.

"I have no clue. I'm royally screwed. I don't have insurance and I don't have the money to just pay and get it fixed. And the jerk that hit me is convinced I was in the wrong."

When Zola doesn't come to my defense, I turn to find her purposely avoiding my gaze.

"What's that look for?"

Zola sighs heavily and asks, "Are you sure it wasn't your fault?"

My eyes bug out of my head. Is she serious?

"I'm just saying," she continues, "you tend to look at stop signs as optional."

My jaw drops. "Are you saying I'm a bad driver?"

"No," she shakes her head while trying to hide a smile. "Never. I'm just saying that—"

"I had the right of way!"

Her face makes me start laughing and soon we're both cracking up. I gently smack her on the shoulder. "I hate you so much."

"No, you don't."

We're walking back to our place when we hear a hoard of boys pull into the parking lot. My smile instantly vanishes when I see a familiar red Acura parked near my car.

"What the hell is he doing here?"

"Who?" Zola turns in the direction of the noise.

Caleb's smirk when he spots me is annoying. "That's the douche that hit me."

Zola's eyes widen. "Oh, the plot thickens. What if he showed up here with his posse to have a showdown or something?"

"You watch way too much television."

Caleb and his group of insanely hot friends are still a few feet away when I ask, "Why are you back here?"

"I missed you, Kentucky," he says with a wink.

I roll my eyes, grabbing Zola's hand and dragging her back to our place. It's only when my hand is on the doorknob that I register the guys are following us.

"Do you need something?"

Caleb sighs heavily, his stupid smile disappearing. "You live here?"

"Am I having déjà vu?" I snap.

He looks like it's taking every fiber of his being to stay calm. It's only at his next words, I realize why. "You're Bonnie's new roommate."

My face falls. There's no way the universe is this cruel. Bonnie's hockey brother is the jerk that hit my car?!

"We going in or just staying out here on the sidewalk," one of his friends asks.

Zola smiles wide, opening the door and gesturing for them to follow her. Caleb and I don't move. Once everyone is inside, he takes two steps toward me. I stand tall, not wanting to back down. This is my apartment. My safe space.

Caleb's eyes quickly trail up and down my body. "This is gonna be fun."

"I hate boys," I mutter to myself as I stomp past everyone and go upstairs to my room. The apartment has a relatively large living room attached to a cute little kitchen with a walk-in pantry. Our furniture is a combination of mine, Zola's, and Bonnie's stuff. Bonnie did bring her big TV which I'm very thankful for. Originally we were supposed to have a fourth roommate, but when she backed out I chose to pay a little extra to have my own room. Zola and Bonnie's is just across the hall with our bathroom in between. The amount of unpacking I have to do already exhausts me, but I don't want to go back downstairs. I suppose it is nice Caleb and his friends came over to help, but he probably only did it because Bonnie's his sister. I doubt he did it out of the kindness of his heart.

After about thirty minutes, my clothes are all hung up and I've moved on to unpacking my toiletries. I load up my arms with shampoo, soap, etc., and turn to take it all to the bathroom. I yelp, dropping all my products when I find Caleb leaning against my door frame. He scared the living crap out of me.

"How long have you been standing there?" My breathing is erratic and I need a moment to calm down.

He finds this funny, chuckling to himself. "Just came up to see if there's anything in here that needs hauled out."

"No," I huff while picking up all my stuff.

I try to walk past him, but his large frame blocks my door.

"Can you move?" I ask without making eye contact.

"You seem irritated."

Is he serious? "It's probably because some idiot hit my car, refused to take responsibility, and is now in my apartment."

"And your room."

My eyes snap to his. "I will never let you into my room."

He looks down at me through hooded eyes. "Is that a challenge, Kentucky?"

"Millie," I say through gritted teeth. "My name is Millie."

His smile widens and it pisses me off. I push past him, haphazardly tossing my stuff in the bathroom and heading downstairs to get away from him.

It's refreshing when I see our couches and chairs and not the crappy pieces that were left here. Not saying our furniture is brand-new or anything, but I'd rather have our own crappy furniture than someone else's. It's starting to feel like a home.

"It looks good," I say to no one in particular.

One of his friends looks me up and down. "Yeah, it does."

I arch a brow at him. He's almost as tall as Caleb with shaggy blonde hair and tanned skin. He looks like he left his surfboard at the beach to come here.

"Down boy," Bonnie tells him.

"Aw, come on Bon-Bon," a guy with a knuckle tattoo says.

Bonnie rolls her eyes and Caleb smacks the guy on the back of the head.

"That hurt?" I nod toward the tattoo.

He shakes his head. "Not at all. It's not the only one I have." He goes to take his shirt off but thinks twice about it when he sees Caleb. "It's a joke, man. Chill out."

Everyone breaks off into their own conversations when Caleb zeroes in on me.

"You never asked about my tattoos."

His arms are folded over his chest, displaying his half sleeve. Dammit, why is everything he does sexy?

Tearing my eyes away from his weirdly attractive arms, I shrug. "Didn't need to ask. I bet you cried the entire time."

His chuckle is dark. "I can assure you I did not cry. And how would you even know what it feels like?"

I lift my brow in answer.

"You have tattoos?" He sounds surprised. And he should be. I'm lying through my teeth.

I lift one shoulder. "Maybe you just can't see them."

Wow, that was way too flirty. I watch as his eyes slowly take me in, wondering where said tattoos could be hiding.

"Stop looking at me like that," I demand.

He bites the inside of his cheek to keep from laughing. "Like what?"

Why does he think this is so funny? It's infuriating.

"Stop bugging my roommate," Bonnie tells him.

"I was just telling her how I'm adding to my sleeve soon."

"Mom's going to kill you. You know she hates tattoos."

"Yeah, but she loves me," Caleb says with a shit-eating grin.

Zola looks back and forth between Caleb and Bonnie before adding, "You two look really similar."

"Don't say that," Bonnie groans. "I refuse to accept the fact that I look like this doofus."

"You're just jealous I got the pretty genes from mom," Caleb teases.

Bonnie rolls her eyes. "I knew I should've eaten you in the womb. Would've saved me so many headaches."

"You guys are twins?" I ask.

"Unfortunately," Bonnie says with a smile.

"Explains how close you are. I think my brother would pretend I didn't exist if I went to Carnegie Mellon with him," one of Caleb's friends chimes in.

"Winger U has it all. Hockey for him and it's close to home so I don't have to do my laundry," Bonnie adds.

Once Bonnie walks them all out, I take the opportunity to sneak back upstairs.

Later that night when my room is somewhat put together and I'm researching local auto body shops, Bonnie knocks on my open door.

"I heard about your car."

I sigh heavily, "Did your brother tell you?"

She tilts her head to the side. "Caleb? No, Zola told me. What does Caleb have to do with it?"

I shake my head. I don't want to stir the pot and make enemies with my roommate on day one.

"Nothing, never mind. I'm just looking for shops around that won't charge me an arm and a leg to fix a bumper. I can't exactly drive around with it hanging off."

I'm focusing on my web search when I notice Bonnie is still there.

"Sorry," I apologize for being rude, "I'm just super annoyed about the entire situation. It doesn't give me a right to be snarky at you."

She shrugs. "No need to apologize. I'd be pissed too. I just wanted to give you the number for a family friend who is really good with cars."

My fingers pause their typing. "A family friend?"

"Yeah. He does good work and his prices are reasonable. He doesn't charge all those random fees that end up being a couple hundred bucks."

My teeth dig into my lower lip, mentally going through the money in my bank account.

Seeming to know what I'm thinking, Bonnie says, "Raphael does payment plans. He's a pretty reasonable guy."

I open my mouth to reply when she walks up and hands me a piece of paper.

"In case you decide to call him."

As she walks out of my room, I pull apart the folded Post-it note and stare at the ten digits.

Chapter Four

Caleb

"Did you install a lock on your door?" Buzz asks me as he passes me in the hall. He's one of the basketball players that rooms a few doors down from me.

"You didn't?" I chuckle. "It may be my first year living here, but I've been to plenty of parties here. I know what happens when people go upstairs. Do you really want all that happening on your bed?"

He freezes in place, thinking over my words. "I'm going to head to Walmart before the party."

I slap him on the shoulder. "That's probably a good idea."

Dressed in jeans and a henley, I head downstairs. A bunch of guys are playing video games while a few continue moving stuff that would be hard to replace down to the basement. I collapse on the couch next to Zeke, another basketball player. He's a Junior like me and a pretty cool guy.

"What's the game?"

"Grand Theft Auto," Zeke says.

We both wince when he runs over someone.

"Brutal."

The first people through the door are none other than the sports groupies. Puck bunnies, ballgirls, jersey chasers. The names change, but the girls never do. Personally, I'm not big on puck bunnies. Have I messed around with a few of them before? Hell yeah. But like my dad always said, "Don't stick your dick in crazy." Considering Kentucky seems all kinds of crazy, I should probably stop thinking about what she would look like with my face between her thighs. I've always been a slow learner though.

Not long after, more students arrive and before I know it, the house is packed. I'm hanging out with a few of my teammates when I spot Bonnie heading my way.

"Bon-Bon!" I shout over the noise. As she makes her way through the crowd, the overprotective brother in me takes over and I pass her a sealed water bottle. She rolls her eyes but still takes it. Bonnie's not an idiot, but guys can still be assholes. I've told her before and I'll tell her again, if she wants to come to a party here, the only people she can accept drinks from are me or my teammates. I don't care if it sounds controlling. I'd rather be an overbearing jerk than deal with my sister getting put in a dangerous position because of something as stupid as a horny guy.

My expression changes to pure surprise when I see her roommates trailing behind her. Zola's eyes are glued to someone behind me, but Millie's baby blues are looking everywhere but me. She couldn't be more obvious if she tried.

Maybe I've been checked into the boards too many times, but her attitude is beyond sexy. Pair that with tits that are begging for my mouth and curves I can grab onto as I wrap her legs around me. Okay, I'm probably getting ahead of myself, but there is definitely an attraction there. Even if she denies it, I see how she looks at me.

"Don't drink from the keg," I tell Bonnie, leaning in close. "Code to my room is 1991 if you want to make yourself a drink."

She sighs as she rolls her eyes. "You trust me that little?"

I shake my head. "It's not you. It's the random assholes that are flooding my house right now. I'm serious, Bon-Bon. Don't—"

"Drink any open containers or accept drinks from strangers." She lowers her voice to mimic me. "Yeah, I get it."

My gaze darts to Millie who is trying to stifle a laugh.

Bonnie pushes me back as she and her roommates file past me. Millie's wearing some tight ass jeans that make her ass look fantastic.

I don't realize I'm biting my lip until Kai comes out and slaps me on the shoulder.

"What has you drooling like a dog?"

I tap my beer bottle to his and toss the rest back. "Where the hell did you come from?"

Kai's eyes keep drifting around the room. "You remember that girl I told you about? The one from this summer?"

I chuckle to myself. "Which one?"

"Funny, jackass." He deadpans. "The one I never got the name of. From that giant party in—"

"Oh, shit. I forgot about that. What about her?"

"I think I saw her here. I don't know. The person I saw was with some guy and she was not with some guy when we met."

"How do you know?"

His eyes darken and I actually think he might take a swing at me. "She would've told me. She didn't seem like that kind of girl. I'm gonna go find her."

After Kai disappears, I grab two bottles of beer and am on my way outside when I spot Bonnie. Zola and Millie aren't with her and she's talking to some guy I don't know. I watch him slide his hand around her waist and I try making my way over to them through the crowd. A hand wraps around my wrist, dragging me outside and away from Bonnie.

"What are you doing?" Millie smacks me on the shoulder before taking one of the beers.

"That wasn't for you." I go to take it back when she pops the top off using the rail on the deck and starts chugging. Fuck, that's hot.

"Bonnie is having fun. Stop playing the overprotective big brother for one night."

"I don't even know who that asshole is. What if he—"

She covers my mouth with her hand to silence me. "You mean what if Bonnie meets a cute guy and actually has fun? Everyone here knows she's your sister. No one is going to let anything happen to her. Just let her enjoy herself."

I grab her wrist, pulling her hand away from my mouth so she can see my scowl.

"Hey, Jasper!" I call over to one of the Sophomores on the hockey team.

"What's going on?" He turns his eyes on Millie and his smile suddenly appears. "My name's Jasper. And yours is..."

Millie opens her mouth, but I continue. "Not important. Can you tell some of the guys to keep an eye on Bonnie and the guy she's with?"

Millie's mouth drops open in horror. "Are you serious right now?"

Jasper nods and heads back into the party.

"You are an insane control freak," she says as she pulls her arm out of my grasp.

I roll my eyes at her dramatics. "No, I'm not. But I am protective over my sister and I don't give a shit what you think about that."

Millie's red painted lips press against the mouth of the beer and her throat works the liquid down. I force myself to look away before I start thinking about certain things. Things such as those lips wrapped around my dick. Things like her swallowing me down. Things like that red lipstick of hers all over my cock.

"You okay?" she asks, bringing me out of my fantasy.

I clear my throat, pop open the beer, and down the entire bottle.

"Easy, killer," she teases.

Some drunk girl bumps into Millie from behind, bringing us closer. The hand Millie isn't holding her beer with lands on my chest to steady her. She barely comes up to my chin, which I love because I can tower over her like the big, bad wolf.

"I hate parties," she mutters.

"Huh?"

"I didn't party in high school."

"Everyone goes to parties in high school."

Millie breathes out a laugh. "I have a feeling our high school experiences were very different."

"And why's that?" I ask, placing my hand on her waist. She doesn't move away like I thought she would.

"Just taking a wild guess here. You were a jock who spent his free time getting drunk and hooking up with girls. I, on the other hand, hated going out and usually spent weekends by myself at home."

Something weird pangs in my chest at the thought of Millie all alone on a Saturday night.

"It's a good thing you came out tonight."

For a brief moment, I forgot her hand was on my chest until she started moving her fingers back and forth. Her touch sears through my shirt and it has me feeling bold.

The corner of my lip tilts up. "Want to know what I'm thinking?"

She peers up through those thick dark lashes, looking so innocent. "That seems like a loaded question."

"Why do you say that?"

"Because I feel like the answer would be something—"

"Dirty? Wicked? Hot?"

My tongue darts out, licking my bottom lip and I take note that she's watching my movements very closely.

I think Millie's about to answer when Jace grabs my elbow. "Dude. Out front. Now."

Millie takes a few steps backward, whatever moment we were just having vanished into thin air. "I'm over this party anyway."

I groan as Jace and I push our way through the party. "Perfect fucking timing."

"Don't yell at me. Talk to Kai about it."

Some chick and a dude are having it out on the front lawn and dozens of students with red solo cups surround them. Jace brought me out here for this? Is he kidding? Kai is laser-focused on the couple with a look he usually saves for right before he breaks someone's teeth in a game. The dude having the fight takes a step toward the girl and looks like he actually might take a swing at her when Kai steps in.

"Is there a problem here?" Kai asks. Obviously, it's rhetorical but the idiot answers.

"Quinn's fine. We were just leaving."

Ah. So this is why Jace grabbed me. I look to my other teammates who are positioned in a circle formation around the scrum and we each start in. Me, Jace, and the other five guys settle in behind Kai with looks that tell this loser not to fuck with us. He's wearing khakis for fuck's sake.

Kai, the dude, and the chick go back and forth until Kai grabs the girl's hand and pulls her behind him. It's kind of funny that someone who is six inches shorter and 80 pounds lighter is going toe-to-toe with one of the top shit kickers on our team.

"Guys," Kai hollers and that's when each of us takes a step closer. We don't typically do shit like this, use our height and stature to intimidate people. But for guys like No-Name over here, it goes without question. The kid puts his hands up in defense, slowly backing away.

We all start to turn around when he yells from the sidewalk, "She was a prude anyway. Couldn't give good head to save her life."

Oh, he fucked up. He really fucked up. Kai starts laughing, a deep ominous laugh. The guys and I hang back as he strolls down to the sidewalk. Surprisingly, Kai doesn't hit him though. Kai does say something that must scare the shit out of him because he practically runs away.

I'm heading back to the party when I see Millie hanging out with a group of girls near the bushes. So she didn't leave. I debate about going over. Maybe to finish our conversation. But then she turns toward the road and I decide to let her be. For tonight.

First week of classes is the best. No one is ready to leave summer behind and we spend the entire time going over a one-page syllabus. The best are the professors who treat you like a best friend and just want to talk about summer break the entire class. Lucky for me, my first day is only filled with two easy classes in the morning which means I get a nap in before practice. Some of the rookies are still hungover which coach notices right away. Needless to say, the entire practice is a snippet of what being in hell feels like. I sleep like the dead once I get home.

On Thursday, I'm leaving one of my Gen Ed classes when I spot one of the guys from Ballentine.

"Hey, man." Rodriguez, our goalie, bumps his knuckles against mine. "That party was freaking crazy."

"Yeah. A great way to start out the year."

"Can't wait for the next. Oh, shit. I forgot my backpack." He spins around, rushing around the students.

I watch him run up the hallway as I walk backward. My laughter is interrupted when someone bumps into my back causing me to stumble and drop the notebook in my hand.

"Seriously?" The angry voice from behind is way too familiar. "Watch where you're going."

Spinning around and finding Millie on her knees in front of me is a sight I wasn't prepared for. Her books and papers spread out on the shiny linoleum floor between us has me dropping to the ground.

"I can do it myself," she grunts as she rips a paper from my hand.

"Just offering a helping hand, Kentucky."

At my voice, she freezes and it brings a wicked smile to my face.

"Of course, I had to bump into you," she mutters. I'm not sure if she meant for me to hear it or not, but either way, it makes me chuckle.

"If you're the one who bumped into me, shouldn't I be the one yelling at you to watch where you're going?"

I hand her some papers before picking up my notebook, rolling it up, and sticking it in my backpack. Her irritation is written all over her face. Does she not realize how much pleasure I get by messing with her?

"It's like you hitting my car all over again," I say, putting the final nail in the coffin.

Her eyes widen in fury and I think I see steam coming from her ears.

I watch as she clenches and unclenches her hands while taking deep breaths. Her phone rings and after glancing down at it, she silences it and slides it in her back pocket.

"You're annoying and now you've made me late."

I step to the side and gesture for her to walk past. Millie huffs and rolls her eyes before passing me.

I turn to watch her walk away when she looks over her shoulder and shouts over the noise of the students around us.

"Stop staring at my ass!"

Chapter Five

Millie

"Crap! Crap! Crap! Where is it?" I mumble, practically tearing apart my backpack.

"Huh?" Zola finally pulls one headphone out of her ear.

"My bio notebook. I put it in here after class." I keep digging through my bag when it dawns on me. "And then Caleb bumped into me and I spilled my books on the ground."

My heart plummets down to my ass when I pull out a tattered black notebook, opening it to find doodles of hockey sticks and squiggles I think are supposed to be writing.

"Caleb stole your notebook?"

I take a deep, calming breath. "He must've picked up mine and left me with this crappy excuse for a notebook."

I groan in frustration and then narrow my eyes at Zola when I hear her giggle.

"Sorry," she says with a smile, "but it's kind of funny. Out of everyone to steal your stuff."

My unamused look doesn't change and she stops talking.

"I'm just gonna..." Zola's sentence fades away as she puts her headphone back in and resumes her work.

I could just flip through the textbook, but I really need my notes to study. Why do teachers think it's a good idea to have quizzes during syllabus week when every single student's brain is still in summer break mode? Damn Caleb and his stupid notebook that is practically falling apart.

"I'll be back," I sigh.

I'm at Ballantine in no time, banging my fist against the front door. A guy with short red hair that desperately needs combed answers the door, swallowing the bite of food in his mouth. His eyes scan up and down my body before asking, "Is it my birthday?"

I purse my lips. "If you just implied I'm a stripper, your pick-up lines need some work."

He shrugs as I push past him, jogging up the stairs. I was up here the other night, but have no idea which room is Caleb's. Ballantine is huge and houses way too many guys. I don't have time to knock on each individual door, so I do the next best thing.

"Caleb!" I shout. "Caleb! I brought that cream for your rash. The doctor said to be careful because you're super contagious."

A few doors down on the left, Caleb's head pops out. His gaze is confused until he spots me. I storm toward him, pleasantly surprised that worked.

"What the hell are you doing here?"

I push past him without answering. "Where is it?"

"Sure, come in," he deadpans. "You know, I could've had a girl in here. Unless you like to watch. If that's your kink then—"

"Ha. Ha. You're such a comedian. Now, where is my notebook?"

I'm digging through clutter on his nightstands when I find a pile of tissues and gag.

"I need to wash my hands right now."

Caleb laughs to himself. "Wouldn't have thought you had such a dirty mind." I snarl and he continues. "Relax. I had a runny nose earlier."

I wipe my hands on my pants because even if that's true, his snotty tissues aren't any less disgusting than the ones he used to clean up his, well, whatever.

"I only have a little time today and I need my notebook. I had it when I left class and didn't at the library, so give it to me."

We stare each other down for a moment until he walks to his desk, opens a drawer, and pulls it out. I go to grab it when he lifts it above his head.

"Caleb," I grunt as I jump for it. Jackass keeps pulling it away from me and I hate him so much right now. "This isn't funny."

"Maybe not for you."

I give up jumping and decide on another tactic. I poke him hard in the stomach. Not expecting it, he keels over but is still tall enough that he holds my notebook out of reach.

"You are so annoying! What do I have to do so I can get my notebook and not have to see you again?"

His one eyebrow quirks up and I instantly regret my choice of words.

With an evil smirk, he says, "A kiss."

"Excuse me? I must be going deaf because I swore you just said to kiss you."

"I did."

I want to smack that stupid shit-eating grin off his face right now. "Ew."

He shrugs, turning away from me. "I guess you don't want your notebook back then."

"Seriously? You want me to prostitute myself for my own property? What is the matter with you?"

He starts laughing again and it's really pissing me off.

"It's just a kiss. One simple peck. You know what? Fine. Just take your notebook." He tosses it to me and I frantically try to grab it, dropping it on the ground. "It's weird. I usually get a feeling about people and never would've thought you were a prude."

"I'm a prude because I won't kiss a jerk who I have no desire to kiss?"

Caleb walks over to his closet, looking at me over his shoulder. "A prude and a liar."

I open my mouth to protest when he reaches behind him and pulls his shirt over his head, tossing it in the hamper. I freeze, looking like a gaping fish as his back muscles flex. That is so not fair. It should be illegal for such a jerk to have a face like that and muscles like those. Maybe I could just wander over there and touch his muscles for a second. I could pretend I tripped and fell and the only way to save myself from bashing my face open was to lick every divot and ripple of his abs.

I'm stuck in my own fantasy when I feel fingers graze my chin. I come back to reality, realizing my mouth is still open and Caleb is helping me shut it. His fingers linger on my chin, swiping over my bottom lip.

"So which is it?" He asks inches from my lips. "A prude or a liar?"

Suddenly I'm having trouble breathing. With him standing so close, kissing him doesn't seem like the worst idea anymore. The silence is heavy, our breathing the only sound in the room.

"Neither," I say before standing on my tip toes and pressing my lips to his. Caleb's body tenses like he didn't think I would actually do it, but after a moment he relaxes. His lips are soft against mine and shivers run down my spine as his hands grip my waist. It's like he needs to grab me to make sure this is real. I could easily take this one step further. I'd simply dart my tongue out for a taste and he'd take over. He seems like the domineering type of guy, but maybe that's a persona. Maybe he's really a giant cinnamon roll who likes to cuddle afterward. It's only when his fingers dig into my skin that I jump back. I reach up to touch my lips, wondering what the hell I just did. Caleb's lids are hooded, his look predatory as his chest heaves rapidly.

"I should, um..." I let my sentence fade away as I turn for the door quickly. Only five steps to his door and once I have it open, I'll run like the freaking devil is chasing me. Fours steps. Three steps. Two steps. One—

Caleb's hand wraps around my wrist, spinning me back around. His mouth slams against mine and I'm too stunned to move. He's kissing me. Caleb is kissing me. Again. He felt it too. When his tongue licks my bottom lip, the daze is broken and I drop my notebook to the ground, winding my arms around his neck. He towers over me and I open my mouth for him as my fingers play with the curls of hair at the nape of his neck. Our tongues meet, each fighting for dominance. He tastes like spearmint gum, making me melt even further into him. Grabbing my hips, he pulls me flush against his body. I gasp in surprise when I feel his erection press against my belly. I have no idea how it is possible, but I'm completely soaked and we've barely done anything.

The fact that he's just as turned on as me by simply kissing, makes this ten times hotter. His one hand snakes into my hair, tugging at the same time his teeth bite my lower lip. I moan at the combination of pain and pleasure. I'm not technically sure if this qualifies, but I've never had a man be rough with me. Treat me like I'm not some delicate doll. Then, his teeth and lips and tongue are on my neck, my jaw, my chest. I'm struggling to breathe as his mouth moves lower. How far am I going to let this go? There's no way I want to have sex with him. Right? I shriek in surprise as he lifts me up, my legs automatically going around him, and carries me to his bed. Caleb sits down as I straddle him, groaning at the feeling of him between my legs. His one hand grabs my ass, guiding me to grind against him. A feeling I haven't felt in a very long time stirs low in my belly. His other hand slides up my shirt, fingers slowly inching up my ribs when his bedroom door flies open.

"Hey, do you still have the—"

"Get the hell out!" Caleb screams as I bury my head in his shoulder.

The guy in the doorway stutters something before leaving the way he came.

Neither Caleb nor I move for what feels like forever. In reality, it's only seconds, but I think we're both wondering the same thing.

What the hell just happened?

"Um," I hold onto his shoulders and force myself to stand on shaky legs. "I, um…"

I don't know what I'm trying to say. My brain is currently in the buffering stage, so instead of talking I grab my notebook and run as fast as I can out the door and all the way back to the library.

Zola and I study for the next two hours in silence. Well, she studies. I re-read the same sentence over and over while analyzing what just happened with Caleb. I could've stopped it. I could've pushed him away and told him to leave me alone. But I didn't. I invited him in and pulled him closer. I wanted more. None of this makes sense. And why do I have the burning urge to do it again?

Looking in the mirror on the back of my door, Zola's adjusting her boobs to fit into her new top when Bonnie emerges from their room.

"You coming out with us tonight? Millie's going to be the DSF," Zola tells Bonnie.

Bonnie's brow furrows, coming further into my room. "What the hell is a DSF?"

"Designated Sober Friend," I inform her. "I'm not drinking so Zola can have a night to let loose and not have to worry."

"Maybe another night." Bonnie doesn't elaborate, disappearing down the steps as I finish applying the last of my mascara.

Zola's eyes narrow. "Are you and Bonnie good or is this rooming situation not working out for you?"

Zola and I really wanted to live together, but could only find three or four-bedroom places when we apartment hunted last year. Zola and Bonnie knew each other from class and Zola introduced us at the end of last semester. It wasn't exactly friendship at first sight. She won't admit it now, but Bonnie totally thought I was a bitch when she first met me. According to Zola, I tend to have RBF (resting bitch face) when I'm tired. It's not my fault Zola wanted me to meet Bonnie right after I pulled an all-nighter trying to pass one of my exams.

"What? Bonnie's nice and I like her. I just don't know how to act around her. Blame my horrendous socialization skills on my parents."

"And your RBF."

When I was younger, I never did figure out the whole friend thing. Having friends meant inviting them over to hang out and that meant explaining my family situation to them. It was just easier not doing it at all.

"I promise. I like Bonnie," I reassure her. "We'll find common ground. It'll just take some time."

"So," I spin in my chair to face Zola, "what are the rules?"

She rolls her eyes at me, so I continue, ticking off the rules on my fingers as I go. "No exes, no puking, and no running off."

I know she hears me, but she doesn't respond. "Zola! Repeat the rules."

She groans, throwing her head back dramatically. "Fine. No exes, no puking, and no running off."

I start giggling at her. "I'm serious. Tonight's supposed to be fun and chill."

"I know. I know. No drama," she promises.

I give her my most threatening warning glare which makes us both laugh. Zola has a very destructive history with her loser ex-boyfriend and every time she drinks or gets high, she always finds her way back to him. That's the real reason I'm staying sober. I want her to have a night where she doesn't have to worry about waking up in Blaze's bed because of her subconscious sabotaging her.

We grab an Uber to Pour Decisions, a bar off Main Street. The bouncer is sitting in a chair by the door, not even watching the people walking in, so we don't bother showing our fake IDs. Lucky for us, it's still early in the night and we snag two chairs at the bar. Zola orders her drink and I grab a water.

"Are you going to tell me why you've been so squirmy around Bonnie the last two days?"

I choke on my water. "I haven't been squirmy."

"You totally have been."

I shake my head, taking another big drink. She goes to lift her cup to her mouth when she pauses and slowly turns to me.

"Now that I think about it, you've been acting weird since you stopped by Caleb's. Holy shit! Oh my God! Did something happen?"

"What? Ew. No. Never." I divert my gaze, but I know I'm caught. I've always been a bad liar.

The club gets busier, people pressing into our backs as they try to get the bartender's attention. We take this as our cue to grab our drinks and head to the dance floor. I'm hoping the music will help her forget our current conversation, but the first word out of her mouth is Caleb's name.

"It was just a kiss," I tell her as we dance, but struggle with our shoes sticking to the ground. Gross.

"A kiss?" she shrieks. "You kissed Caleb and didn't tell me? Was it good or did he like suck your tonsils out?"

"Ew," we both giggle. "I don't want to talk about him. It wasn't a big deal. We kissed for a few seconds and were interrupted by one of his roommates."

"You were interrupted?" she shouts even louder. "That means you were really into it then. Oh my God! Don't tell me you got caught having sex with Bonnie's brother?"

"How did this go from me kissing Caleb to having sex with him?"

Someone bumps into me and I go flying into Zola, spilling her drink all over our shoes. I turn around to aim my glare at the person responsible but my eyes drift over their shoulder and land on the man of the hour. Of course, Caleb would be here. He's talking to a few of his buddies over near the bar and I bite my lip without realizing it. Stupid body getting all excited seeing him in his stupid tight shirt with his stupid big muscles. Okay, I need to cool down.

"I need to go to the bathroom," I yell over the music. Zola nods and starts following me when someone she knows intercepts us. They hug and Zola introduces me as my eyes dart around the bar, unable to locate Caleb.

"Hey," I look at Zola's friend, "I have to run to the bathroom. Can you hang with her for a moment?"

Zola nods enthusiastically and continues dancing as I dive between people. I finally make it to the small hallway where the bathrooms are when a hand pulls me into a nearby broom closet. I try to scream, but once the door is shut, my back is pressed against it, a hand placed tightly over my mouth.

"Hey, Kentucky. Come here often?"

Chapter Six

Caleb

I try controlling my laughter, but her angry eyes are too cute. She looks like what I picture a bunny would look like if it was mad.

"What the hell?" she pushes my chest and I pretend to fall back.

"Relax, it was a joke."

Rolling her eyes, she goes to turn around to open the door but I step into her space. I use my height to my advantage and have her craning her neck to look up at me. I don't even try to hide the fact that I can't tear my eyes away from her tits. Her top is tight and cut low, perfectly displaying her cleavage for me...and any other asshole with eyes.

"You wear that for me?"

Her lips twist in disgust. "I would never wear anything for you."

"Good. I think I'd like you better naked." I wink at her, pissing her off further.

Millie's face pinches into a scowl. "You really need to check your ego. I didn't even know you would be here. Actually, I'm starting to think it's time to call it a night."

She takes a step forward, her foot landing on mine, but I don't move.

"The night's just starting. Where are we going next?"

Millie shakes her head. "*We* are going nowhere. *I* am going to grab my friend and go somewhere that isn't infested with stupid jocks."

I clutch my heart, pretending that one hurt. It didn't.

"You're kind of a smart ass. I like it."

"Well, don't. Just leave me alone and pretend I don't exist. And I'll do the same to you."

"Now, where's the fun in that?"

Seeming to finally understand she's not going anywhere, she sighs heavily.

"Fine. What do you want?"

I look at her questioningly. "What do you mean?"

"What do I have to do for you to leave me alone?"

My eyebrow quirks and she smacks me in the chest. I chuckle at her reaction.

I deepen my voice, "You haven't been thinking about me?"

It's taking everything in me not to grab her and pull her to me. To lift her up, wrap her thighs around my waist, and feel her against me. I haven't stopped thinking about her lips since she ran out of my room like a bat out of hell. I could've killed Jace for barging in.

Her eyes dart around the room before she swallows. "No. Not at all."

"You would be a terrible poker player," I say inches from her mouth.

Her lips part and for the first time in a while, I have no idea what this girl wants. Typically, it's easy to figure out chicks. But Millie is different. I think she wants me to kiss her, but I also think she wants to put my head through the wall. It's weird. She's been a pain in my ass from the moment we literally ran into each other, but I can't stop thinking about her. Fuck, this is annoying.

Something changes in the air and Millie stands taller.

"I have wanted to tell you something though," she says.

I relax my body, curious to what she's going to say. Is it too presumptuous to think she's going to tell me she's always had a fantasy of screwing someone in a broom closet? The next thing I know, pain is shooting through my leg and I hunch over to grab it as Millie runs out the door. The spitfire kneed me in my freaking thigh of all places. I thank whoever is watching over me that she missed her target.

I stumble out after her, wanting to spank her for kneeing me, but also congratulate her for getting one over on me. This girl really is messing with my head. I push my way through the crowd, finding her running out the main door. I quickly follow after her. Lucky for me, her purple hair stands out in a crowd.

"What do you mean she's gone?" Millie is talking to some blonde who seems way too drunk to even be standing.

"It's fine," she slurs. Blondie places her hands on Millie's shoulders and I can feel the anger radiating off her. "Blaze is taking good care of her. Relax."

"Son of a..." Millie backs away, letting Blondie stumble, and grabs her phone out of her purse. When she looks up and sees me, she curses. "What did I do wrong? I was trying to let my friend have a carefree night and then you show up and Rita can't keep track of drunk Zola and now she's with him."

What the hell is going on? "Him? Who is him?"

"Her stupid townie boyfriend," Millie practically shouts in my face. "She met him last year and he sunk his nasty claws into her. I was supposed to watch her tonight and now she's with him. This is all my fault."

Millie looks up to the sky and growls like an animal. That was hot. I feel if I tell her that, she'll make sure she hits her target this time. I value my balls too much to open my mouth.

"Stupid Uber app," she mutters to herself.

"Why are you calling an Uber?" I ask.

Her evil glare lands on me. "Because I don't have a car. Remember?"

I did not know Millie had this much angst in her. Sexy and dangerous. I like it. I grab my keys out of my pocket and hold them up.

"I'll drive. Let's go."

I start walking to my car when she speaks up. "I'm not going anywhere with you."

Spinning around, Millie stands with her hip jutted out and her arms crossed. Such a little brat.

"Stop being stubborn and lets go. Like you said, you don't have a car."

Her heels click after me and once we reach my car, I open the passenger door for her.

Thinking I won, I smile victoriously until she shakes her head. "I don't think so. I've only been drinking water. Give me the keys."

I laugh when she holds her hand out.

"You're kidding, right? Last time you were behind the wheel of a car, you ran into me. Besides, I only had one beer tonight." She opens her mouth to tell me off when I continue. "And that was two hours ago before we even left for the bar. We can either stand here and argue some more, which don't get me wrong, it's kind of turning me on, or we can go find your friend. What's the decision?"

She lifts her hands like she wants to hit me, curls them into fists, and shakes them angrily.

"I hate you so much right now."

"Not super fond of you either," I tell her after shutting the door behind her.

"Where am I going?" I ask after I put my buckle on and start the car.

"I don't know the address, but I know how to get there. Just get to the light and turn right."

When we don't move, she looks at me and gestures to the road. "Why aren't we moving?"

"Put your seatbelt on."

"Are you serious right now? Zola could be in trouble and you're worried about my seat belt."

She wants to have this pissing match, fine by me. I turn the car off and cross my arms over my chest. She mutters something under her breath but finally clicks the belt across her chest.

"Was that so hard?" I ask her with a smile.

"Just drive."

Chapter Seven

Millie

I am going to kill Caleb. First, he distracted me when I told Zola I would help her tonight and now he's being unbelievably obnoxious as we find Blaze's house. It's been a while since I've been there and it's dark so we've gotten turned around a few times. Every time he huffs in irritation, it makes me want to reach over and punch him square in the balls. I can't believe I missed him earlier and kneed him in the thigh. Such a beautiful opportunity, wasted.

"Here," I point to the shady house in front of us. "Stop the damn car."

"I'm coming in with you," Caleb says and I shake my head.

"No, you'll just be in the way. Just pull over."

Caleb barely stops the car at the curb when I jump out. I'm going to rip Blaze apart. He and Zola never hurt each other physically, but they were so bad for each other. With drugs and booze added to the equation, their entire situation is just begging for the cops to be called.

I pound on the door so hard my fist aches.

"Zola! Are you in there?" When there's no answer, I bang louder. "Blaze! Open the damn—"

Blaze rips the door open, eyes crazed and bloodshot. His hand wraps around my wrist before I can say anything and he jerks me inside quickly, shutting the door behind us.

"What the fuck is your problem?" Blaze's question is aggressive, but he says it with a calm air about him. Shit, he's high as a kite. My eyes land on Zola in the living room, jumping and dancing around. To no music.

"What did you—"

I'm interrupted when the front door flies open and Caleb storms into the apartment. His eyes land on Blaze and in an instant he has him pinned against the wall, his forearm across Blaze's throat.

"Caleb, what are you doing?" I shout.

"Baby!" Zola calls to me. "You came to the party."

She skips over to me, giving me a hug and sloppy kiss on the cheek. I grab her face and stare into her eyes. Her pupils are the size of dinner plates and I want to kill Blaze even more.

"What did you give to her?" I yell at Blaze over my shoulder.

"I want to dance! Let's dance!" Zola drags me a few steps and continues jumping up and down.

"She asked you a question, asshole," Caleb spits at Blaze, pressing down on his windpipe.

"Caleb," I warn.

He relaxes his hold a little, only giving Blaze enough room to talk.

"Chill. Zolie likes to have fun. You're messing with the vibes going on—"

His next word is garbled as Caleb reapplies pressure to his throat.

"Dammit, Caleb!" I shout.

"What did you give her?" Caleb demands.

So much yelling happening and Zola is in her own universe. Part of me wishes I was on the ride with her because all I'm getting right now is a raging headache.

"It was a little bit of E. Zolie needed to relax—"

"We're leaving," I tell Zola and she nods along with me.

"Can we have a dance party in the car?"

I brush her hair out of her face. She's slick with sweat like she's been dancing for hours. "Of course, babe. Let's go."

I wrap my arm around Zola's waist, holding her close to me and guiding her out the door.

"Caleb, let's go," I holler over my shoulder.

"Woah. Do I know how to walk?" Zola looks me dead in the eyes and my headache starts turning into a migraine. I help her take turns lifting each leg when I hear Caleb.

"Leave Zola alone. And if you ever think about fucking touching my girl again, it will be the last thing you do."

His girl? Who the hell is his girl? He's definitely not talking about Zola, but that would mean he's talking about me. And that is completely out of the question.

Once Caleb catches up with us, he picks Zola up and carries her to the car. Caleb's knuckles are white as he grips the steering wheel on the drive home. I'm beyond mad at Blaze right now for being such an enabler, but I can't stop thinking about what Caleb said. How he called me his girl. Why did he do that? I'm not his girl. We shared one kiss. That's it.

The drive back to our apartment is silent except for the sounds of

Zola dancing in the backseat. Once again, to no music.

"What are you doing?" I ask Caleb when he parks and turns off the car.

"I'm helping," he grunts. That's all he says as he gets Zola out of the backseat and carries her inside. I lead him to her room and he sets her down gently.

"I got it from here," I tell him, guiding him out the door.

"Where's Bonnie?" Caleb asks, looking at Bonnie's empty side of the room.

"I don't know. She didn't want to come out with us tonight and right now, I really don't blame her."

After I take Zola's boots off, I remove her big hoop earrings and necklace. Next, I grab her trash can and place it next to her bed. She's out cold which makes turning her on her side a challenge. Once I have her positioned safely, I tuck her under her comforter and turn on the fan she sleeps with every night. When I turn around, I'm surprised to find Caleb in the doorway. A glass of water and a few tablets in his hand. I take them and set them on her nightstand. Pushing the hair out of Zola's face, I kiss her on the forehead and whisper how I'm going to kill Blaze.

I follow Caleb downstairs. Neither of us sit down, opting to stand in the entryway, not knowing what to say.

"Thank you," I mumble.

"What was that? I can't hear you."

I exhale sharply. "I said thank you."

He tries to repress a smile. "Not the best 'thank you' I've ever gotten, but I'll take it."

"You're right. It wasn't very nice of me. But I'm pretty pissed right now. My best friend is high off her ass because her stupid druggie ex-boyfriend, who she always goes back to when she's drunk, gave her something while I was supposed to be watching her tonight. I was maybe even going to help her find someone else whose name didn't sound like it was from some crappy '90s movie. I told her I would be there and I wasn't."

"Because of me?"

I clench my jaw as Caleb takes a step closer.

"I'll bite. I pulled you into that closet and kept you there. But Zola's a big girl. It was nice that you were trying to let her have unrestricted fun for a night, but her running off is not all on you. And I am not the reason Zola ran off. So now it's time to get off your high horse and thank me for driving you around."

"Are you fucking serious right now?"

He takes another step. "Tell me thank you for not only driving you to your destination but getting you two out of Blaze's house and helping you carry your comatose roommate to her bed. Even if you don't want to admit it, if I wasn't there to help with Blaze, you two would still be stuck. And who the fuck names their kid Blaze?"

I bite my cheek to keep from laughing at his last question.

"I think it's supposed to be a nickname. You know, because he's always high," I say and we both start laughing.

Once we both calm down, silence fills the air.

"Thank you, Caleb."

His eyebrows raise. "For?"

Smug bastard.

"For driving me to pick up Zola and for helping with Blaze and for carrying her and helping me put her to bed."

"See," Caleb takes the final step and stops in front of me. "Was that so hard?"

He tucks a loose strand of hair behind my ear, his hand sliding around and grabbing the back of my neck.

"I'm going to kiss you right now and you're not going to knee me in the balls."

I smile and laugh as his lips land on mine.

Chapter Eight

Caleb

The buzzing of my phone wakes me from a dead sleep. I squint through the darkness, the harsh light already hurting my head. Seeing Bonnie's name slide across the screen has me swiping to answer the call.

"Bon-Bon? You okay? Shit, what time is it?"

"What?" she shouts over the line. "Caleb! It's me. It's Bonnie."

I groan, scrubbing a hand down my face. She's totally shitfaced.

"Where are you?"

"I made friends in class. They're so nice." Her words are beginning to slur together.

"Just tell me the address. I'm on my way. And your ass better be there when I pull up."

"You're the bestest brother ever."

After three tries, Bonnie finally gives me an address of where to go and I hang up. I look across the room at Millie and am surprised she slept through that call. I wasn't exactly quiet. She's lying on her back, her one arm draped above her head. A spot of drool rolls down her chin and it takes everything I have not to bust out laughing right now. She looks so damn cute.

Millie was such a badass barging into that asshole's apartment to find her friend. It was hot as hell. And when that stupid fucker grabbed her, I could've killed him. I knew she wanted me to wait in the car, but the second I saw him wrap his grimy little fingers around her wrist, I couldn't just sit there anymore. I haven't seen him around before, but I'm not into the whole drug scene. Tried it a few times and it messed with my game too much.

I bet a few guys from the house could give me more information. If anything, I could dig up enough dirt on him and maybe help keep him away from Zola. I wish I could say I had the desire to do that because I'm a nice guy. Really it's because I know Millie is close with Zola and watching her take care of her friend was hard. The worst part is I could tell it wasn't the first time Millie has had to do it.

I know I shouldn't have kissed her. Millie was vulnerable and had a long night, but I couldn't help myself. Her lips were warm and she tasted like heaven. Every bone in my body was vibrating with the need to strip her bare when her tongue swiped along my lips and I let her in. Her taking the initiative was sexy. When the kiss seemed to be bordering on making out, I backed away. She was confused at first, but I think that was the moment exhaustion took over. We turned on the television and within five minutes, she was asleep on my shoulder. I slid out from under her and moved to the other couch to sleep. I wanted to be here in case something happened and she needed me, but I also thought her waking up on me would freak her out.

Brushing the hair out of her face, I place a soft kiss on her forehead before heading toward the door. I make sure to lock up behind me and double-check once I'm outside. In five minutes I'm at the address Bonnie sent me. She's outside, leaning on some dude and looking way too cozy. I pull up to the curb and jump out of my car without turning it off.

"Bonnie. What the hell?"

"Caleb!" she happily shouts. "You came."

I pinch the bridge of my nose and sigh. "Of course, I did. Who the hell is this guy?"

"Oh. This is…" Her brow furrows as she looks up at the guy. "Who are you?"

My glare turns murderous and No-Name shimmies away from

Bonnie.

"I was just watching out for her until you showed up."

I hold my hand out and without protest Bonnie stumbles over to me, tripping over nothing and falling against my chest. I catch her and help her to my car. After she's buckled in, I turn to look at the group she was with.

"Am I taking anyone else's drunk ass home?"

The blonde one giggles behind her hand. "Nope. Just her. We're staying here for the night. Unless..."

Her eyes take their time admiring every inch of me and I rush around the car and speed away.

"I had some drinks," Bonnie tells me after a few seconds of silence. Honestly, I thought she had passed out already.

"I can tell, Bon-Bon."

She gasps dramatically. "Oh, no. You're mad at me. Aren't you?"

I chuckle softly. "Not mad at you. I'm just tired. It was a long night. I'm glad you called me though."

"Long night? Why? What's the long night?"

I exhale heavily. There's no way I can tell Bonnie, especially drunk

Bonnie, that I helped rescue her roommate, made out with the other, and then was sleeping on *her* couch when she called me to come get her.

I'm saved from having to answer her as I pull into her parking lot.

"Can you walk?" I ask. She answers with a loud snore. Getting out of the car, I walk around and dig her apartment keys out of her purse. I unbuckle her and carry her to her bedroom. Déjà vu at its finest. On our way in, I did notice the couch empty. Millie must've woken up and gone up to her bed. After I tuck Bonnie in, I sneak out of the apartment. Again.

Chapter Nine

Millie

I'm cuddling on the couch watching TV when Zola stops in front of me, holding options.

"Popcorn or Buncha Crunch?"

"I'm still full from the giant lunch you made us."

"Okay," she sets the two bowls on the coffee table. "Well, do you need anything? Another pillow, more blankets—"

"Zola," I hold up my hands to stop her. "You don't need to do this."

"Yes, I do," she whines as she collapses next to me.

"You really don't. I was supposed to watch you last night and I got side-tracked."

"Yes, but I—"

"Stop. Stupid Blaze is a bad influence on you and we both know it. Last night was my idea so you don't need to keep apologizing. We're good."

"Promise?" Zola sticks out her pinky finger and I smile.

"Promise," I say, hooking mine around hers.

We're halfway through the final episode of *Love is Blind* when Zola announces, "I have to pee."

"So go pee," I tell her, attempting to push her off the couch.

"After we find out if they get married. I need to know."

"The pause button was invented for a reason." Grabbing the remote, I pause the show and physically push her off the couch. We both laugh as she dramatically tumbles to the floor.

I'm about to go get another drink when my phone starts buzzing. I groan when I see it's a text from an unknown number.

"Stupid scam text messages," I mutter.

"Bend your arm and take a picture of your elbow," Zola tells me as she stands up. At my confused expression, she shrugs. "It'll look like a buttcrack."

I laugh and toss a handful of popcorn at her retreating back.

Curiosity getting the better of me, I swipe across my phone screen.

Unknown: You miss me yet?

That's a weird message. Usually the scammers either ask to sell my house, which is odd since I don't own one, or tell me I won a raffle I never entered. Against my better judgment, I reply.

Millie: Am I supposed to know who this is?

Unknown: The guy recovering from being kneed in the thigh...

My mouth pops open. There's no way. How did he...

Millie: How did you get my number?

Caleb: You fell asleep early last night and you don't have a passcode on your phone

Millie: Changing that right now

Caleb: That's cute

Millie: What's cute?

Caleb: You acting like you aren't excited I texted you

Millie: Why the hell would I be excited?

Caleb: You seemed excited last night when you kissed me

Shit. I did kiss him. Again. I have no idea why. Well, no. That's a lie. I did it because I wanted to. Because he helped me out with Zola and how he acted toward Blaze. I was caught up in the moment. My teeth worry my lower lip while my fingers hover above my phone keyboard.

Caleb: It's okay to admit you liked it. I liked it.

"What's that face for?" Bonnie asks.

My head snaps up. "Where did you come from?"

She laughs, slipping off her shoes. "I just walked in the door. You seemed very entranced by your phone."

"Nope." I quickly click my phone off and shove it under my lap. "Nothing—"

"You had a weird look on your face."

"No. No weird look."

Bonnie walks up, grabbing some popcorn. She's skeptical but nods as she backs away.

"I'm going to shower, but want to do take-out for dinner?"

"Hell yes!" Zola shouts as she bounds down the stairs. "I'm craving Chinese."

"Orange chicken would totally hit the spot," I join in, hoping Bonnie forgets about our conversation.

My phone buzzes again as Bonnie is walking away and I don't miss her side glance. Zola grabs the remote and presses play while I discreetly slide my phone back out.

Caleb: You don't need to say it. The noises you made when my tongue was in your mouth gave you away

My eyes widen and I unintentionally gasp. I turn to see if Zola noticed, but her brows are pulled together, heavily focused on the show.

How the hell am I supposed to respond to something like that? I'm not even sure if I like Caleb as a person. I guess I don't have to like him in order to like how he makes me feel, but I've never been *that* girl.

Zola's shriek brings me out of my daze and I power off my phone. I can't think about Caleb right now.

"I can't believe she did that!" Zola's mouth hangs open in shock. "How can she leave him at the altar like that? She just told the entire room that her fiancé is bad in bed."

"Yeah, that's so horrible." I literally have no clue what she's talking about, but maybe if I play along she won't question it.

"And the worst thing is that guy is still in love with her." She shakes her head in disapproval. "Poor delusional lovesick puppy."

"Take mine," Bonnie says, waving her credit card at me.

I grab it and stuff it in my back pocket after sliding my feet into my shoes. "I'll keep the receipt and we can split it."

She shakes her head, "No need. I got this one."

"Thanks," Zola and I say in unison.

It's a ten-minute walk to the only Chinese restaurant in town and the weather is nice tonight, so I take my time enjoying the calm and quiet evening. The warm wind rustles the leaves that have fallen early.

It's still early so people are probably napping before they pregame for parties. After the last few days, I think I need a night at home with just my roommates. Specifically with no men. My phone buzzes, ruining my nice walk. I roll my eyes when the word "Dad" slides across the screen and press ignore. I've rejected how many of his phone calls lately, how does he not get the hint?

After I grab the two bags of takeout — holy crap, how much food did we order? — I'm heading back to my apartment when I see a familiar shadow turn the corner. Panic seizes me and all I think is that I need to hide. He hasn't seen me. I don't want him to. With only a few seconds before Caleb spots me, I rush to the giant green dumpster in the alley next to me and crouch behind it. I'm squatting because I refuse to sit on this gross ground near the rotting fruit that never made it into the trash and after only a few seconds, my legs start shaking. I close my eyes, listening for any footsteps, and pray that I'm not breathing too loud. After a few moments, I'm about to stand up when three hard knocks come from the other side of the dumpster.

Chapter Ten

Caleb

"Come out, come out, wherever you are."

I'm assuming Millie thinks she's clever, but hiding behind the dumpster? She's sandwiched between two buildings in a very dark alley. If she really wanted to get away from me, she should've tried harder. When she makes no noise, I kick the dumpster this time.

"Kentucky, you can either come out on your own or I can come back and get you," I threaten.

It works because within seconds, she's straightening up. Millie lifts her chin, trying to act tough, as if she wasn't just hiding like a child.

"Caleb. Hi. Funny running into you."

My shoulders shake with laughter. "That was the worst hiding spot you could've picked."

Her eyes narrow. "I didn't have much time to think about it."

"Well, your flight or fight response sucks."

Pursing her lips, she takes a step to walk past me and my hand instantly flies out, landing on her stomach. She jumps back like my touch shocked her.

"Where do you think you're going?"

She lifts the two bags in her hands. "Home. The food's getting cold."

Shoving my hands in my pockets, I don't move. I take my time trailing my eyes down her body. The messy bun in her hair, her giant sweatshirt hiding her delicious curves that I'm itching to touch, and then my gaze moves lower.

"Are you not wearing pants?"

She scoffs, shifting both bags to one hand then lifting the bottom of her sweatshirt to reveal tiny bike shorts. I grab the fabric and pull it back down, using the movement as an excuse to get closer. With each step, I'm carefully leading her away from the disgusting dumpster and further into the alley.

"I like the idea of you without pants on."

This time I get an eye roll. "I don't have time for you right now—"

"No?" With every step I take toward her, she takes one step back until her back is pressed against the brick wall. Her eyes dart around like she's looking for an escape and a smile spreads across my face knowing that I have her trapped under me. Some kind of...primal feeling sweeps through my body.

"Put the food down," I say low enough for only her to hear.

"What?" she asks, confused.

"Put the food down." I nod my head to the ground. "Right there."

Her brow furrows, but when she sees I'm being serious, she does it. Good girl.

"Why did I need to do that?"

I step closer. She tries to melt into the wall, but with each deep breath, her tits rub against me.

"You didn't. I just wanted to see if you would obey me."

She sighs and bends to retrieve the bags, but I press my hands against the wall on both sides of her face.

"I didn't tell you to pick them up."

"What the hell do you want, Caleb?"

I inhale deeply through my nose, loving the perfume she's wearing. Or the soap she uses. Shit, maybe this is just the way she smells. And if it is, she has to taste incredible.

Lowering my voice to a whisper, I ask, "Why were you hiding from me?"

Her eyes glance down to my lips and I smile victoriously.

"I - I wasn't," she stammers.

My tongue darts out to lick my lips, barely grazing hers. "My little liar."

Her body betrays her and leans forward into my lips as I pull away.

"You're an asshole, you know that?" She says through gritted teeth.

"Now, now. Name-calling isn't going to get you what you want."

Millie laughs humorlessly. "And what do I want?"

My left-hand leaves the wall, ghosting down her collarbone, in between her breasts. Her breath is shaky as my hand drifts lower and lower, stopping at the hem of her sweatshirt.

"An apology." Her eyes sharpen in surprise. "I distracted you when you promised to be watching out for your friend."

She waits a moment and says, "That's it? Have you ever actually apologized to someone before? You have to say the words—"

Not interested in being scolded, I find the waistband of her shorts and shove my hand down them. She gasps as I cup her.

"Fuck," I groan into her neck. "You're already soaked. Is this all for me?"

"Definitely not," she pants as I press the heel of my hand against her clit.

"I don't like liars," I tell her. "I do, however, like punishing liars."

I attempt to remove my hand when she grabs my wrist. "It's, it's for you. Okay? Just, please, don't stop."

She bites down on her lower lip and I don't think I've ever been this hard without a hand on my dick before.

"Move."

Her brow scrunches together. "What are you talking about?"

"Get yourself off. Use me, Kentucky."

Her breath catches in her throat and when she doesn't immediately move, I use my other hand to guide her hips.

"I've never, I can't—"

I can't bear to listen to her doubt herself, so I stop her talking by shoving my tongue down her throat. She moans into my mouth and continues to soak my hand. I haven't been this turned on in a while and I can't believe it's behind a fucking dumpster of all things. My teeth bite down on her lip and that's when she grabs onto my shirt, pulling me in. I'm not sure if she even realizes it, but I'm not moving her hips anymore. She's doing this all herself. Her eyes flutter shut as she moves and fucks herself using my hand. The sounds coming out of that mouth have me gritting my teeth so I don't blow my load.

Her knees shake under her and I need to see her come. I need to see her fall apart. Without warning, I shove two fingers into her and hook them to hit her G-spot. Her eyes fly open as she screams out my name. I wrap my free arm around her back, steadying her while she coats my hand. I kiss her as she rides out her orgasm, my tongue tangling with hers. Once I know she can stand on her own again, I pull my fingers out and watch her as I lick them clean. Her eyes widen in shock.

I lean in, whispering in her ear, "You taste delicious. Next time, it won't be just my fingers in your pussy."

I back away, picking up the bags and heading toward the sidewalk. When I turn around and she's still plastered to the wall, heavily panting, I ask, "Are you coming or not? The foods getting cold."

The walk back to her place is silent. Not a word or sound between the two of us. It makes me wonder what's going on in that head of hers. At one point, when she wasn't looking, I had to adjust myself because walking around with a hard-on fucking hurts. Once we're at her front door, we both just stand there. Me waiting for her to make eye contact and her looking at the ground like it's the most fascinating thing. She looks like she's still processing everything that just happened as she slowly grabs the bags, grazing my fingers with hers.

"Do you, I mean, I guess you can come in if you want. Your sister is in there, so…"

Damn, she's cute. She's so nervous right now even though I just fingered her in public. Well, she fingered herself using my hand, which is now in my top three favorite sexual experiences.

"I'm good. See you around."

I turn away and it takes every single fiber of my being not to turn around, throw her over my shoulder and fuck her into oblivion. Another day.

Right now, I have somewhere to be.

"What the hell are we doing here?" Jace asks. He's leaning against a street sign as I cross the road to get to him.

I gesture for him to follow me. "Just a quick errand. I can do it alone, but figured backup never hurts."

He stops walking. I don't. "Backup? The fuck, Booker?"

Originally I had plans to go grab some food with a few of the guys from Ballentine, but my run-in with Millie reminded me there was something I needed to do. Like I said, I can do it alone. However, I don't trust the person I'm going to see.

Strolling up the grassy hill without a care in the world, I knock three times on the wooden door. I scoff at the chipped white paint. This block of apartments is on the edge of town where most drug deals happen. I'd bet my left nut the landlord is probably some addict who saves the money he makes for other activities. When no one answers, I kick the door.

"Jesus, dude. What are you doing?" Jace whisper yells at me.

"Yeah?" Blaze asks through a yawn, opening the door and rubbing his eyes.

Once he blinks a few times and realizes who is at his doorstep, he tries to slam the door in my face. I was expecting that. I throw my shoulder into the door and stroll on in, kicking it shut behind me, leaving Jace outside. He doesn't need to be in here unless Blaze has some druggy friends lurking around.

"What the hell?" Blaze asks, voice shaky with nerves.

I smirk when I see the red mark around his neck. He deserved way worse.

I shove my hands in my pocket and walk around the living room. This place is a piece of shit. Instead of actual furniture, they have folding chairs around a wobbly picnic table. The carpet is peeling up, some spots looking like it's been burnt. Part of me thinks the walls are supposed to be white, not a brownish color.

"I don't want to be here long," I explain.

"Um, okay." I turn and find Blaze's eyes darting to the door.

"No need to run," I chuckle. "I'm just here to deliver a simple message."

His shoulders relax an inch. "A message?"

My face hardens as I stare him down. "You will stay away from Zola. You will never call, talk, or see her again. If I find out you contacted her in any way, let alone gave her any type of drug, I will come back."

He starts laughing, probably a nervous tick. "Come on, man. Zolie and I are cool."

I tried standing away from him because he smells like ass on a hot summer's day, but at his words, I step close enough to see the sweat forming at his hairline.

"Zola," I emphasize her name, "and you are not cool."

A single drop of sweat rolls down his temple and I turn for the door.

"I truly hope to never hear your stupid name again." I'm walking toward Jace when I spin back around with a wide smile. "Oh. One more thing. If you ever touch my girl again, I promise you a bruised neck will be the least of your problems."

I wake up early on Sunday to go for a five-mile run and then head to the gym after. This way I'll be too busy worrying about my stamina and not how Millie sounds when she comes. I'm in the middle of biceps curls when I drift back to last night. Her eyes shut tight, her face scrunching moments before she exploded. I've never been with someone who looks like her before. Her tits and ass are, hands down, the sexiest things about her.

She has curves, real curves like a real woman. Even the day she ran into me, once she stepped out of the car, all I could think about was getting her on her knees. I remember how Millie shied away when I touched her belly and that makes me want to hunt down any fucker who has made her feel anything but worshipped. The thought distracts me and I curse as I drop the dumbbell, barely missing my foot. Shit, what is happening to me?

Chapter Eleven

Millie

Getting dressed for work this morning is almost painful. It wouldn't be so bad if it weren't for the uniforms. Cherry On Top is this cute '50s-style ice cream shop on Main Street. Everything is vintage, from the music to the button-down, low-cut uniform we wear. I happen to be the only employee with a rather large chest, so pretty much every time I lean down to scoop up some ice cream, the girls are on full display. It's awful and I hate it, but the money is good and being able to pay my rent is even better.

Even though we don't open until mid-afternoon, we are scheduled early because we hand-make all the ice cream. Between that and inventory, it takes a while. It wouldn't be so bad if, once again, we didn't have to wear these stupid tight uniforms. I understand they're "vintage" and "classic" but they are beyond uncomfortable. I swear, the day I graduate and quit this job, I am burning this monstrosity.

After six hours of scooping ice cream, mixing milkshakes, and mopping the floor when kids drop their cones and the parents rush them out before cleaning up, I'm free. The apartment is empty when I get home, so after I shower and change into comfy clothes, I settle on the couch. I start scrolling through my phone, ignoring another call from my dad, and somehow find myself on Caleb's and my text thread. I shriek as I throw my phone across the room.

Okay, that was a pretty dramatic response. But how did that happen? I don't even remember opening my messages. Scrubbing my hands down my face, I groan loudly. I thought working would take my mind off what happened last night. That it would help distract me from the fact that Caleb got me off in an alley. The entire time, I wanted to push him away. I almost told him to stop countless times. I couldn't though. It felt too good. He felt too good.

I've never had a physical connection so powerful that I couldn't wait and I needed that person right then and there—and certainly never when 'then and there' was an alley behind a dumpster. Caleb kept moaning my name and making these sounds that had my knees weak. I swear, if he hadn't been holding me up, I would've actually collapsed on the ground when I came from just his fingers. I get that some women can orgasm at the drop of a hat, but I'm not like that. I've never been like that. I've actually had guys get so fed up with trying, that they just stopped. It's humiliating when your body isn't doing what it's supposed to do. And it's worse when the person you're with makes you feel like something is wrong with you.

Freshman year I met this guy who lived in my building. He seemed sweet and really nice. For our first date, he took me to the nicest restaurant in town. It was only Applebee's, but it's the thought that counts, right? I was pretty inexperienced involving sex and by that I mean I was completely inexperienced. It never seemed like an issue until we had been dating a few weeks and I slowly became more comfortable around him. I loosened up and one night, let him put his hand down my pants. Nothing happened. I mean, it felt nice, but not mind-blowing like people made it out to be. I made a few moans because that's what people on television shows did. I was just happy when it was all over. Apparently, he thought I really liked it because a few nights later when we were in his room, he laid me down on his bed and tried again. This time was a little more aggressive. And it hurt.

"Ow. Wait. No." I push on his chest to try and get some space between us.

"What's wrong?" he asks, panting hard.

"I don't, I don't think that's right," I mumble.

He sits back on his knees, looking down at me. "I've never had complaints before. That usually works."

I avoid his gaze when I tell him, "Well, it didn't feel good to me. It kind of hurt."

He inhales sharply, probably realizing he's not getting lucky tonight. "Um. Okay. We can stop then. Do you think it's you?"

"Huh?"

"Like something's wrong with your body? Maybe I'm not the problem."

I don't think he meant to be cruel. I don't think he meant to embarrass me and make me feel two feet tall. Laying on his smelly blue plaid comforter, fully clothed but my jeans unbuttoned, I felt completely naked. I couldn't think. It was like my brain was malfunctioning and didn't know how to respond.

Finally, after a solid two minutes of silence, I looked up and said, "I think we should break up."

Forcing myself to get off the couch, I pick my phone up and make the decision to turn it off for the night. Clearly, my subconscious wants me to talk to Caleb, but I am not ready for that.

Physiology is slowly becoming one of my favorite classes. Professor Weckman is one of the younger professors, which means he is more relaxed than most. It's only his second year of teaching at WU and from what I've heard, everyone loves him. I only have his class once a week which means I get to spend two and half hours listening to all my fellow students *ooh* and *ahh* over him. It's no secret that he's good-looking — tall, engaging smile, pretty eyes. Not exactly my type, but it's obvious a few students have a crush.

I picked a seat toward the back to try and blend in. I'm really interested in what we're studying but I also don't like to be the center of attention. I figured sitting further away would deter Professor Weckman from calling on me. I was wrong. He is the type of teacher who asks a question and doesn't wait for hands to go up. He calls on whoever he wants and apparently today that's me. Luckily, I'm able to give the correct answer, but I don't like everyone's eyes on me.

Once class is over, I'm on my way out the door when I hear a few girls talking.

"He looked at her the whole class. So unfair."

"I know, right?"

I feel their eyes glued to my back and it makes me think they're talking about me. Wait, are they talking about the Professor and me? God, I hope not. That actually kind of creeps me out. I mean, Professor Weckman is attractive, but he's my professor. Teacher and student relationships might be some people's thing, but it's not mine.

"You are never going to guess what these girls in class said today," I say as I close the front door behind me. I pause when my eyes land on Caleb. He's sitting on the couch, drinking a beer and smiling.

"Why are you here?" I blurt out before thinking. My rudeness doesn't discourage him. His gaze is molten hot and I'm shocked that I feel my panties dampening by one freaking look.

Bonnie walks out of the kitchen, carrying a bowl of fruit. "I thought I heard you come home. What were you saying?"

Bonnie pops a berry in her mouth, waiting patiently. My eyes dart between the two of them and I decide it's better to just forget it ever happened.

I shake my head. "Um, nothing. Just stupid stuff."

"I hate stupid stuff," Caleb adds.

Walking through the living room to the kitchen, I grab a snack bar and head upstairs. Considering all I see when I look at Caleb is him licking his fingers clean after they were inside me, I think it's best to stay away.

"You want to join us?" Bonnie asks.

"Maybe another time," I say quickly and run upstairs.

Once I'm upstairs, I grab my books out of my backpack and decide to try to get some homework done. It's only five minutes later when

I hear the rap of knuckles on my door that I realize I've been zoning out, thinking about Caleb downstairs. In my apartment. And the look he gave me when I walked through the door.

I clear my throat, sitting up straighter. "Come in."

My back is turned, but the second it opens, I know who it is. His scent invades my room and I inhale deeply.

"Why are you always here?"

I spin in my chair to find him leaning against the doorframe and looking sexy as hell. His hair has that messy look to it, making me want to run my fingers through it as I —

No! Bad Millie.

"Well, I like hanging out with my sister. And you're here. It's a bonus to come up and mess with you."

I fake laugh and spin back around to my homework. Part of me wonders if he actually does come around because he knows he'll see me, but then I shut that idea down fast. He said it's because he likes to mess with me. Not because he likes me. I hear his steps pad on the carpet. He's not walking closer though. I turn and see him looking around my room. The walls bare of pictures, the bed is messy, and the floor in front of the closet is covered with clothes I need to wash. Or are they clean?

"What are you working on?" he nods to my desk.

"Going over my notes. Why are you still up here? I thought you were hanging out with your sister?"

He shrugs. "I was until she ditched me for her new girl. It's a shame. I liked her old girlfriend way better."

"Girlfriend?" I ask. I know Bonnie just got out of a relationship, but I just assumed it was with a guy.

"Yeah. Wait, you know Bonnie's bi, right?"

"Yeah. Yeah. Totally. I mean yes. I knew."

He looks down at his feet and chuckles. "My little liar."

I roll my eyes and ignore him, trying to focus on my work.

"You really never noticed?"

I exhale sharply, slamming my pen on my desk. "I don't know what you're thinking, but I'm not judging her. Her sexual preference doesn't change how I see her. Actually, wait. That's a lie. That fact that she's able to pull both men and women makes me weirdly jealous of her."

Caleb laughs again. "Are you seriously trying to tell me you didn't know?"

I shrug my shoulders.

"What about the doormat for your place? The word 'Hello' is in rainbow colors."

"I just thought it was pretty."

"What about all the rainbow decorations in this place? The throw pillows and blankets?"

"It seemed like a cool design choice." When Caleb continues to stare at me with an amused expression, I say, "I get it, okay? I'm naive and ignorant and a total idiot. Now can you leave so I can get some work done?"

Part of me thinks he's gone because the room is silent for a few seconds before he clears his throat. "Why are you rewriting notes? That seems counterproductive."

I sigh heavily. "I scribble them down during class and rewrite them after so they're neat and easier to read. It helps me retain the information."

He nods his approval. "That's an interesting study technique."

I shrug. "Works for me. Plus, I really like this class. It has one of the new professors and he seems really cool."

He continues his perusal. "No pictures on the walls?"

"Huh?" I pretend to not hear him.

"Most girls have pictures up in their rooms of all their high school—"

"I don't," I interrupt. There is no way in hell I'm going to stand here and talk to Caleb about my social status, or lack thereof, in high school.

Before he opens his mouth to ask another prying question, I ask, "Don't you ever have practice? I thought you were supposed to be on the hockey team."

"I am," he tells me with a smile that makes me want to get him naked.

I clench my thighs, hoping he can't tell what's going on in my head. His eyes drift down my body and I'm terrified to know what he's thinking.

"The season's just starting. Practice on Tuesday and Wednesday. Thursday is usually a rest day but the coach typically tells us to get our asses in the gym. Fridays and Saturdays are reserved for games."

"That's only five days. What about Sunday and Monday?"

"Sundays are for recovery and homework. Monday is back in the gym. You don't get abs like these at home."

He lifts his shirt, revealing a six-pack. I roll my eyes, pretending I don't care but take a quick glance before he drops the fabric again.

"I hope you didn't do that thinking I would show you mine." It was meant as a joke but his eyes darken and I fear I'm heading into dangerous waters.

Thankfully he changes subjects. "I can say that I've never seen a jigsaw puzzle in a girl's room before."

"Mock if you will," I say, walking over to my small corner table. The puzzle I'm working on is 750 pieces and I just started it last night. It's a picture of the New York City skyline. Well, it will be. "I like puzzles. It helps me unwind. My brain kind of shuts off when I'm focused on piecing together things. It's why I chose my major." I look up at him, only now realizing how close we're standing.

"Which is?"

"Forensic science," I tell him with a smile on my face.

"That is a pretty big smile," he chuckles.

"Laugh all you want, but I love my major. I basically am learning how to put giant puzzles together for a living. It's awesome."

Caleb stares at me, probably thinking of all the ways he can make fun of me for being a total nerd. I don't care though. I spent four years of high school thinking I was the weird girl for taking part in activities that interested me. I'm in college now and if you don't like what I like, that's fine. I don't care. I am a tad nervous when he doesn't say anything immediately though.

"Can I help?"

My eyebrows shoot up. "What?"

"The puzzle. I've never done one. Can I help?"

I'm too stunned to speak and that's when he moves even closer.

"Close your mouth," he uses his fingers to shut my jaw, "and have a seat with me."

I have no idea what parallel universe I traveled to, but when Caleb pulls me down on his lap and starts helping me sort through pieces, I can't stop smiling.

"And you're not an idiot," he mumbles.

"What?"

"I said you're not an idiot. And I don't like you talking about yourself that way. Okay?"

"Okay," I say as my smile grows.

I just crossed the road that leads to campus when my phone vibrates in my pocket and I pull it out to make sure it's someone I want to talk to. It isn't. I click the side button to shut it off and look up moments before I bump into...someone who looks vaguely familiar.

"Hi?" I say, not sure if we actually do know each other or not.

He must get my confusion because the first words out of his mouth are, "I'm Reggie. From the move-in party."

I nod, laughing at myself. "Right. You were over with the baseball guys, right?"

"Shortstop. You're Millie, right?

"That's me. Sorry, I didn't mean to almost run you down."

He adjusts the strap of his backpack. "No worries. Everything okay?"

"Great," I say quickly. "I got distracted. I'm just on my way to class."

"What building?"

"Pikna Hall."

"I just remembered I need to talk to one of my professors in that building. Want to walk together?"

"Um," I pause, Caleb's lips fluttering through my brain. I have no idea why. Reggie just asked to walk with me to my building. It's hardly flirting. "Sure."

We've only walked a few steps when Reggie says, "I wanted to talk to you at the move-in party, but you vanished pretty quickly."

I don't know what to say to that so I just say, "Um, yeah, it got a little crazy with the fight on the front lawn."

"That was nothing—you should have seen the brawl at the party after the baseball team won the game against CSU last year," he laughs. "But I wanted to ask if there's any chance you're free later this week?"

I open my mouth to answer, unsure of what I'm going to say when Caleb appears in front of us. Where the hell did he come from?

Caleb nods at Reggie.

"Hey man," Reggie says.

"Hey." Caleb gestures between us. "How do you two know each other?"

I just stand there like the monkey in the middle.

"The move-in party," Reggie says.

Caleb nods slowly. Something about it feels ominous and creepy. "Didn't realize you two met. It was a pretty packed party."

"Yeah, it was."

My gaze goes back and forth between the guys, confused as to what is happening, but too nervous to say anything.

Reggie bumps my shoulder with his. "I'll catch you around, Mills."

"It's Millie," Caleb adds.

I politely smile goodbye to Reggie.

Caleb and I stand in silence. It's beyond awkward. I take the initiative to walk away first when his hand shoots out, landing on my stomach and stopping me in my tracks.

"What was that about?" he asks and I turn to look at him.

I'm struggling to comprehend what just happened. I think part of me is annoyed at Caleb for making things so uncomfortable when all Reggie and I were doing was talking.

I shrug. "Just talking."

His gaze narrows.

I sigh heavily. "You know, if you really wanted to show Reggie up, you could've just whipped your dick out and waved it around."

I try walking away when he jumps in front of me.

"Are you always thinking about my dick or just when you're talking to other guys?"

I stick my finger in my mouth and pretend to gag. "You are beyond annoying and now I'm going to be late to class."

"I'll walk you." It's a statement, not a question.

Anger courses through me. "First you get in a pissing contest with Reggie over us simply talking and now you're going to act like a jerk? I don't think so."

"Stop being a brat and let's go."

My eyebrows shoot up. "Excuse you?"

"I said 'You're being a brat.'" He enunciates each word like I truly didn't hear him.

"And I'm saying you can get bent."

"Millie—"

"I'm going to class before we make a scene because you're being a possessive jerk over nothing!"

"It's not nothing, I don't want you anywhere near Reggie, and I was walking in the same direction as you but whatever..."

Chapter Twelve

Caleb

Did I overreact when I saw Millie talking to one of the baseball assholes? Probably. Do I feel bad? Not one bit. Reggie's a tool and she doesn't need to waste her time talking to him. And I don't care how much she says they were "just talking," she's full of shit and she knows it. I watch as she stomps in the opposite direction of campus. I clench my fists, resisting the urge to throw her over my shoulder and smack her ass for being such a brat. If only that shit didn't turn me on. I adjust my straining cock as I turn and walk the other way.

I haven't been able to stop thinking about her and it's starting to piss me off. She's obnoxious and infuriating and beyond sexy. The logical thing would be to stay away from her and forget she exists, but no one ever accused me of being smart. Plus, she's roommates with Bonnie. I couldn't ignore her if I tried.

I breeze through my classes, looking forward to getting on the ice and working out my pent-up aggression. I'd prefer getting it out by bending Millie over, but that doesn't seem to be an option at the moment.

Practice starts out like typical. Pucks scatter the ice as we run drill after drill. It's mind-numbing and doing nothing to help. I need to hit something. When coach calls us all back to the bench, each of the guys takes turns herding all the pucks to the net. We surround the net as one of the freshmen gets down and puts every single puck away. The sharp sound of the whistle gets our attention and everyone instantly quiets down. Coach is a tough motherfucker. He played hockey in high school and was noticed by a scout but instead of college, he decided to join the army. Fast forward and he gets shot in the leg and medically discharged. He acts like he hates us all, but deep down we know he has a soft spot for his team. At least, we like to think that.

"First game is on Friday. I know practices just started up again, but I'm going to assume each and every one of you has been working out and practicing this summer. Not drinking or fucking around with drugs. Right?"

Some guys mutter under their breath.

"Right?" he shouts.

We all jump to attention and in unison, "Yes, sir."

Blatant lies and coach knows it.

"It's against the Sea Dogs and their goalie is rumored to be good. That means offense needs to pull whatever stick is shoved up their asses out now because what I just saw during drills makes me nervous."

I grit my teeth. I play right wing.

After his uplifting speech is over, coach rattles off players and separates us into two teams.

"First team to five gets to leave. The losers run suicides until I tell them to stop."

Our teammates selected for the opposing team, who without a doubt would take a bullet for us, have an evil grin on their faces. It's cute they think they're going to win.

Jace and I are on the same line. We kick ass together and we know it. I can almost guarantee that's why coach split us up. Jace skates by me, smacking my ass with his stick to get my attention.

"Loser washes winners jockstrap?" he jokes.

"I'd rather shotgun a piss warm Natty Light than go near anything that's been up close and personal with your dick."

"You should probably stay away from your sister then."

My smile falls and I turn on my skates, preparing to kill my best friend.

Kai grabs the back of my jersey, spinning me around to face him.

"All right, boys. Play nice. But seriously, you should stay away from Bonnie."

They both laugh like fucking hyenas.

I point to both of them. "I'll remember that."

Kai skates backward, hands in the air like he's surrendering. "Fucking kidding man."

My legs shake as I collapse in bed. Thirty minutes of suicides and I felt like I was dying. Coach laughed as the losers (me included) stumbled off the ice. He fucking laughed. Then he tore us apart in the locker room. As much as I hate his guts right now, he's right. It was pathetic how badly we lost. Long story short, he told us to get our shit together or not bother showing up to the game on Friday. Propping my left leg up, I grab the ice pack and secure it around my slightly swollen knee. Back in high school, I partially tore my MCL during a game. It never healed correctly and acts up every once in a while. If coach found out, he'd bench me for sure.

Grabbing my phone, I scroll through a few social media apps before getting bored. I'm not tired enough to go to bed and have zero desire to do any homework. Suddenly, my door is kicked open, and before I can ask what the hell is going on, a fucking jockstrap is tossed onto my lap.

"Pay up, loser," Jace shouts from the door.

"Mother-"

Jace and a few other guys are cackling in the hallway when I chuck the jockstrap away from me. I mime throwing up as I wipe my hand that touched the nasty material on my shorts.

"Relax." Jace walks in, picking up his jock. "Just a joke. This one's clean. Well, clean-ish."

"You better pray I can't find you when I'm done icing."

Backing away, he pretends to shake with fear. "I'm so scared."

When the door shuts, I laugh to myself, wondering why all my friends are dipshits.

Grabbing my phone again, I open my contacts and find her number. A smile tugs at the corner of my mouth as I begin typing.

Caleb: Your panties still in a wad over the base-

ball loser?

Kentucky: Why on Earth would I text you back when that's how you start the conversation?

I silently laugh at her response.

Caleb: You do realize, even though you are being a brat, you still responded

Kentucky: Stop calling me a brat!

Caleb: Stop being one.

When Millie doesn't instantly message me back, I wonder if I took it too far. I tend to do that. I set the phone on my chest, staring up at the small crack in the ceiling. To my surprise, my phone vibrates.

Kentucky: What do you want, Caleb?

Caleb: To know what you're wearing...

I smile, picturing her rolling her eyes. This time, there isn't a doubt in my mind she'll respond. She might act like there's nothing between us, but she's such a liar. My liar.

Kentucky: A moo moo. Super thick and long. I usually pair it with my chastity belt

Damn, she's funny.

Caleb: And later tonight?

Kentucky: Guess you'll never know

She makes messing with her so easy.

Caleb: I could find out...I do have a key to your apartment

Kentucky: How the fuck do you have a key to my apartment?!

Caleb: Bon-Bon gave me one in case of emergency

Kentucky: Being horny and lonely isn't an emergency. DO NOT USE THAT KEY!

Caleb: Bossy. I like it. Want to know what I'm wearing?

Kentucky: *rolling eyes emoji*

Caleb: Is that a yes?

Kentucky: Goodnight Caleb!

I don't want to be done talking to her. I like talking to her. I type the one thing I know will make her respond.

Caleb: If you go to bed now, you might miss my apology

Kentucky: ...

My fingers type and delete multiple times. I'm not really the type of person that ever has to apologize, so I'm not sure how to do this.

Kentucky: This is a really shitty apology in case you were wondering

Caleb: Fuck. Fine. I'm sorry.

"Fuck!" I yell to myself before dialing the phone.

"I don't know who taught you how to apologize, but—"

"Would you shut up for two seconds? Reggie is a douche and you don't need a guy like that sniffing around you. I didn't mean to be a total dick. Just accept my apology." When she doesn't respond, I mumble, "Please?"

"Wow. I don't think I've ever heard such a heartfelt—"

"Millie," I warn.

I can hear the smile in her voice. "I suppose you're forgiven. But I'm a big girl and can handle myself."

"I—"

"I'm not done," she interrupts me, and fuck, if it isn't the sexiest thing ever. "Reggie and I were talking and you felt threatened for some stupid reason. You and I are not dating and I don't know what is going on in your head, but suck it up and act like a man. Not some jealous teenage boy."

I lick my lips, needing to touch her. Lick her. Do something to her because holy shit was that the hottest scolding I've ever had. Without thinking, I grab myself through my sweats and am already hard.

I groan into the phone. "Fuck, Kentucky. No one talks to me like that."

"Have a good night, Caleb."

The phone clicks off and I waste no time. Grabbing the tissues and lotion off my nightstand, I picture Millie tearing me a new one.

Except this time, she isn't wearing a fucking moo-moo. I fall asleep with the biggest shit-eating grin on my face.

Chapter Thirteen

Millie

"Let's make you into a freaking unicorn!" Zola's holding multiple boxes of hair dyes with the biggest grin on her face. It's starting to freak me out.

"When you said you were going to Walmart and asked if I needed anything, I asked for one box of purple hair dye. Just one."

She nods. "I know."

I can't help my laughter as I stare at the kitchen table covered with grocery bags. "So instead of getting one box of purple, you got one box of each color they had?"

"Obvi you rock purple hair, but why not try something more adventurous?"

"Like rainbow?"

"Yes! Exactly!"

"Why don't we dye your hair rainbow and I'll—"

Zola's face turns stone-cold. "My mom would legit kill me."

"Did you hold up a beauty store?" Bonnie asks, walking into the kitchen and putting her dish in the sink.

"One box. I asked if she could pick me up one box since she was going to the store."

"But look at all these super fun colors." Zola starts pulling more boxes out of bags. "Come on. Let me give you pink and blue and purple and green hair."

Bonnie and I exchange a look. Can she understand my cry for help through just a look?

Laughing to herself, Bonnie walks over and grabs the purple box. "Come with me."

I breathe a sigh of relief and follow her upstairs when Zola yells after us, "Who knew my roommates are a bunch of fun-suckers!"

Bonnie and I are still giggling as we make it to my room.

Grabbing one of my bath towels, I wrap it around my shoulders and clamp it together using a claw clip. While I'm doing this, Bonnie grabs my desk chair and places it in front of my mirror that hangs on the back of my door.

"You sure you want to do this in your room?" she asks, snapping her latex gloves on.

I shrug. "There's not enough room in the bathroom for both of us and every time I do it myself, I end up missing sections or getting it all over my scalp."

She smiles as she squeezes the dye into the small mixing bowl. Her face is serious as she sections off my hair.

"You have really nice hair," she tells me.

"Thanks."

My phone buzzes in my pocket the second she swipes the brush down a piece of my hair.

"You can answer," she tells me. "I'll be careful."

Leaning to the side to grab my phone, I find myself smiling. Then I remember I'm mad at him and cut that shit out. Figuring it'd be a little awkward talking to Caleb while Bonnie is helping me, I decide I'll message him later and drop my phone on the ground.

Bonnie clears her throat behind me and I know she saw my screen. There's an uncomfortable moment of silence where it feels like all the oxygen in the room has been sucked out. Should I say something about it or change the subject?

"The weather's been really nice lately," I blurt out and instantly regret it. That was easily the lamest thing to say.

Bonnie chuckles. "It's okay. We can talk about the elephant in the room."

"I didn't know if you would want to talk about your brother or not."

"I mean, keep the dirty details to yourself, but you don't have to tiptoe around me. It's fine if you're dating my brother."

"Oh, we're not dating."

She pauses mid-stroke. "I'm confused."

"We're just, um, we're talking. Just friends."

My unsure eyes meet hers in the mirror. What *are* Caleb and I doing?

She nods like she understands where my head is at. "All I ask is that you don't become one of those puck bunnies. They are insufferable and I can't in good conscience continue to call you my friend if you become one."

My shoulders shake with laughter, but stop when her brush accidentally lands on the towel. "Sorry, no more laughing. But I promise that will not happen."

Coiling up a dyed part of my hair, she adds, "It kind of makes sense."

"What do you mean?"

"I don't know how to describe it. There is a weird energy when you two are around each other."

"Good energy?" I ask slowly.

"Very good energy."

"He's kind of annoying at the moment." The words just burst out of my mouth. Holy shit, I just told his sister that I think he's annoying. Is she the kind of sister who is going to punch me for saying that? Or maybe she thinks it's funny and can totally relate? Please be the latter.

"Just at the moment?" she jokes.

"Some guy from Balls Hall was talking to me and Caleb went all Alpha Male on us. I'm surprised he didn't piss on me to stake his claim."

Bonnie sighs. "His last girlfriend wasn't the best to him. They weren't serious or anything, but she was a shit. Just don't be too hard on him. He's a guy who plays hockey, so that leaves him with only, like, 40% of a functioning brain left."

This makes us both laugh.

Bonnie points her gloved purple finger at my reflection. "But don't let him off the hook too easy either. Make him sweat a little."

When more than half of my head is covered in purple dye, Bonnie says, "He was probably calling to invite you over for the game. The guys at Ballentine love to watch their sports."

"I thought he had practice tonight?" The question is out of my mouth before I can catch myself.

"They do," she tells me after a few moments of silence. "It ends before the game starts. Want to come with me?"

Without overthinking, I say, "Sure. Sounds fun."

Only a few seconds have gone by when Bonnie starts giggling to herself.

"What's so funny?" I ask.

"You two are just friends, huh? Is that why you didn't even ask what game we are going to watch before agreeing?"

We both make eye contact in the mirror before laughing.

After I wash and dry my new purple hair, Bonnie and I walk over to Ballentine. I follow her to the main TV room where at least a dozen very attractive men are scattered on the couch and floor.

"Kentucky?" Caleb asks when his eyes meet mine. I awkwardly wave when Bonnie grabs my hand and pulls me through the room. We settle on the couch, Caleb between us, with me stuck in the corner. Pulling my feet up under my butt, I try relaxing into the cushions.

"I didn't know you were coming over," Caleb turns to me.

I worry my lower lip, wondering if this wasn't my best idea. "Bonnie invited me. I hope that's okay?"

Caleb nudges my knee with his elbow. "You're always welcome here. I didn't know you watched hockey."

"I don't," I sigh. "Is that what this game is?"

Caleb's head falls with laughter. "Before I forget to tell you, your hair looks great."

"Just my hair?" I tease.

Another guy turns the volume up as the game starts. I watch the puck go back and forth and back and forth and I remember why I don't watch hockey. After a minute of not understanding what's happening, I pull my phone out. The second it starts ringing, I put it on Do Not Disturb. The room fills with cheering and booing and I'm completely lost, but it's better than hanging out at home alone.

"Oh, shit!" someone yells.

I glance up and there's a huge fight happening on TV. At least five guys are sprawled out on the ice. One with blood trickling down the side of his face.

"Crap," Bonnie groans as she looks at her phone. "I'll have to catch you guys later. Apparently there's an emergency with my group project. You coming?"

My eyes drift from hers to her brothers. I could go. I'm not watching the game. But a part of me doesn't want to. I think I want to stay and...hang out with Caleb.

She must understand my dilemma because she decides for me. With a laugh, she's up and gone before the fight is even over. The guys are yelling at the players, egging on the fight, as if they can hear them.

"My pap used to say if you yell loud enough, they can hear you through the TV," Caleb says.

I smile with a nod and divert my attention back to my phone.

Caleb's hand wraps around my ankle and lightly squeezes, getting my attention.

"You know, if you put your phone down for two seconds, I could teach you something about hockey. Make it more enjoyable for you."

It dawns on me how rude I've been.

With a smile, I tuck my phone away and say, "All right. Be my hockey guru. Teach me."

At my words, Caleb's eyes seem to darken. I lick my lips thinking I'd rather be doing something else right now. Caleb's eyes divert to my mouth and I think we're both wishing the same thing. At least we were until something big happens on the TV and the entire room breaks out in booing. Whatever trance Caleb and I were in, broken. And now I'm stuck watching hockey instead of watching Caleb take his clothes off. Boo.

Caleb grabs my legs, placing them across his lap. Within seconds he tightens his grip and shouts at the game.

"What just happened?"

"That was probably one of the biggest open ice hits I've ever seen," he says.

"It's like watching a car crash," someone adds.

"I thought you were allowed to hit in hockey?" I ask.

"You can," Caleb explains, "but there's a difference between clean and dirty hits."

I turn my attention back to the screen just as one player looks down at the puck and someone from the opposite team slams their shoulder into his head.

"Now that's a dirty hit," Jace adds with a laugh. I recognize him from the move-in party. I remember thinking it isn't fair how hot all hockey players are. His shaggy blonde hair mixed with ice-blue eyes would make any girl melt. It's kind of funny how different he looks now. At the party, he was dressed nicely and looked like every girl's dream. Now, in his living room wearing basketball shorts and a shirt with a hole in the armpit, he looks like any normal guy.

When the game continues on, the guys start yelling at the TV.

"No penalty?"

"What the fuck was that, ref?"

As the guys complain about the referee, I turn to Caleb. "Wait, if that was a bad hit then how come there's no penalty?"

"Because there are only two qualifications to being a ref." Jace holds two fingers up. "Blind and stupid."

Caleb sighs. "A lot goes on during the game they happen to miss."

"Come on! Shoot it!" Caleb shouts.

On the screen like ten players in green jerseys - ten seem like too many people, but I'm not actually counting - surround the other team's goalie. The ref blows the whistle, but they don't stop. This time, he blows the whistle louder until the team in red jerseys all but jump on top of the green team to get them to stop.

The guy on the floor in front of Caleb cups his hands around his mouth and yells, "Scrum!"

"Okay, are you guys just making up words to mess with me? What the hell is a scrum?"
"Just another word for a fight," Caleb says.

Well, that just sounds dumb. I don't feel bad for not knowing that.

"The Stars tried stabbing at the puck after the whistle blew so the Devils had to defend their goalie."

"They had to?" I ask which earns laughter from each guy.

"Yep," Caleb nods. "Unspoken rule of being on a team. When one person is under attack, you all are."

"I never really got into sports in high school," I tell Caleb as his fingers brush up and down my leg. "I didn't get the hype. They always seemed kind of boring."

Grasping his chest in mock outrage, I roll my eyes at his dramatics.

"It's easier to understand if you go to an actual game. Watching it on TV is cool and all, but there's nothing like the thrill and excitement of being in the arena with the players and fans going fucking insane."

I shrug. "It seems pretty violent."

"My first NHL game, one of the players took a puck to the nose.

Blood everywhere. It was awesome."

"That's barbaric!"

He shakes his head like it was no big deal. "He was fine. He skated back out with a cage a few minutes later and finished the game."

"A cage? Am I supposed to know what that is?"

Caleb laughs and I smack his shoulder. "It's for his face. Some guys just wear a visor, but others that want to protect the money maker wear cages."

"Still seems unnecessarily brutal to me."

"Because you've never been to a game."

Stealing Caleb's drink, I take a sip when the referee blows his whistle yet again.

"How do they even get to play? The refs blow the whistle every five seconds."

When Caleb doesn't answer, I turn and find him staring at me with a smile on his face. "What?"

"Nothing," he shakes his head. "It's cute that you're trying to understand. I like it. Did you know that hockey refs used to use cowbells instead of whistles?"

"What? That sounds fake," I say through a laugh.

"For real. But fans would bring their own cowbells to intentionally mess with plays, so they switched to whistles. Plastic, not metal because the metal would get too cold."

"Well, you know what they say," I tell him and he looks at me curiously. "Everything's better with a little cowbell."

We're laughing when his hand rests on my knee. "Seriously though, you should come tomorrow. I think you'd like it."

I purse my lips. "I don't know that I actually would."

He lowers his voice, "Shall I use my powers of persuasion?"

I giggle in response but stop when he pushes my legs off him and stands.

When he offers me his hand, my brows pull together. "The game isn't over?"

He waves that away. "Come with me. There's no way the Stars are coming back anyway."

Hand in hand, Caleb guides me up the stairs and we stop in front of a door with a keypad. My shoulders shake in laughter as he presses the buttons.

"Paranoid much?"

Looking over his shoulder, one brow raises. "You've been to a party here. I don't want any of that in my bedroom."

"Fair."

His room is what I imagine a hockey arena to be like. Random hockey pucks are scattered around the room, a jersey hangs on his wall next to a signed picture of what I assume is a famous hockey player. A weirdly small hockey net sits in the bottom of his closet next to a pile of dirty clothes.

"You're a pretty crappy shot."

"Huh?"

"I assume you've been shooting your dirty clothes into that net instead of putting them in the perfectly good hamper right next to it?"

Caleb chuckles at me. "It's a knee-hockey net."

"You're looking at me like you think I know what that is."

Walking over to his closet, he picks up the pile of laundry and dumps it into the hamper. "It's the same as regular hockey, but you—"

"Play on your knees? That seems uncomfortable."

"It's fun as hell. I could show you sometime."

I nod, not having any desire to do that and continue my look around his room.

Caleb points to a whiteboard hanging above his bed and I walk over to join him.

"This may seem stupid to you, but this is why I do it. The thrill of getting to see those numbers increase. To see how good I am. It's a fucking trip."

Dark smudges surround the numbers. He must update this after every game. That's kind of cool.

"Tell you what," he says, walking behind me and pulling my hair over my shoulder, exposing my neck to him. "If you come to the game tomorrow and end up hating it, I'll be your personal slave for a day."

"Oh. I like how that sounds," I say as Caleb's hands settle on my waist, his lips on my neck.

"But, if you end up loving it—"

"Unlikely."

I feel his smile against my skin. "If you end up loving it, you'll have to admit that you were wrong and I was right."

"What?"

"What do you think?" he asks, his fingers grazing the sliver of skin between my shirt and jeans. My skin lights up with every touch while a burning sensation develops low in my belly.

"Um," I stutter through a shaky breath, struggling to focus on his words with his skin on mine.

"I know you don't understand hockey, but it's only because you've never had someone to teach you. Let me teach you."

His lips barely touch my neck while his fingers undo the button and zipper on my pants.

"Tell me to stop," he whispers in my ear, "and this all stops. I don't want to push you."

I turn my head just enough that our lips are lined up. "Did you hear me say stop?"

Before he can say another word, I lean forward and capture his lips with mine. I try to take control, but the second his hand snakes down into my panties, I'm a puddle. He shoves two fingers into me, pressing his palm against that tiny bundle of nerves that seem to control my entire body. I gasp into his mouth when his other hand slides up my shirt and under my bra. The sensation of him pulling and tugging on my nipple mixed with his fingers feverishly entering me makes my knees weak. For a moment I think I'm about to fall, about to crumble into a total mess. That's when Caleb's hand drops to my waist and holds on tight while my legs completely forget how to work as I practically combust just from his hands on me.

"I've got you, Kentucky."

Chapter Fourteen

Caleb

When I'm on the ice, I try to forget about the stands. Forget about all the people here. Whether they're cheering or booing, I hate distractions. Tonight is different though. I'm practically vibrating when I skate out with my team. I have no idea why, but the only thing that has changed recently is Millie and the many orgasms I've been giving her. Maybe she's like a good luck charm? I'm in a deep stretch when I find myself scanning the stands. I tell myself that I'm just surveying the crowd, but I know what I'm really doing. I'm looking to see if Millie is here. If she actually came and is willing to hold up her end of the deal. A stupid grin takes over my face when I find her sitting between Bonnie and Zola. She's looking right at me and wearing the team's colors. Who knew Millie had school spirit?

Skating out to my position, I send a wink in Millie's direction. I wonder what she'll do when she loses the bet. If I'm lucky, she'll get on her knees and tell me how right I am. Realistically, she'll probably roll her eyes while having to admit she was wrong. Either way works for me.

"She yours?" The wing across from me asks, nodding toward Millie.

"You should keep your eyes on the puck."

I've never been one for chit-chat before.

"Nah," he chuckles, "I'd rather watch your bitch. She'll look real good underneath me tonight."

"Keep chirping," I tell him through gritted teeth. "You won't be talking soon."

The puck drops and Beaver immediately takes possession. I drop back, waiting for the perfect opportunity. I'm out of position, but I don't give a shit. Coach screams at me from the bench, telling me to get back in the game, but I ignore him. The second the guy who talked about Millie has the puck, I speed toward him. A huge smile spreads across my face as I slam him face-first into the board.

Using my elbow, I place it behind his neck to hold him there as I say, "Guys with pencil dicks don't really do it for her. But don't worry, I'm sure you'll find someone willing to touch you one day. Maybe even pull your hair for you while they're at it."

I'm ripped away by a ref and instantly put my hands in the air, showing that I wasn't doing anything.

Line change is quick, but we don't miss a beat. Davis picks the pocket of a Squid, sending the puck flying down the ice. Cardone reaches out to stop it, dragging the puck forward and flicking it to the goal in a sweet wrist shot. He lights the lamp and the bench goes nuts, jumping up and down and banging on the board in celebration. Cardone is skating down, bumping our fists when the ref skates out to the middle of the ice. The crowd quiets down just to start screaming again. This time they're booing instead of cheering. According to the ref, Cardone was offsides and the goal doesn't count.

"Shit," coach mutters behind us.

Cardone's entire being shrinks. You could tell he was on cloud fucking nine only to be dragged back down to Earth.

"No worries," Kai shouts over the noise. "You'll get 'em next time."

Cardone nods in acknowledgment, skating over the seat at the end of the bench.

"Shitty call," Jace mumbles as we hop the boards.

"Say it a little louder next time," I groan. The ref is eyeing up Jace like he already can't stand him and the last thing we need is a bullshit call against us. I thought referees were supposed to be unbiased.

The Squids have the puck before I even register where it is. What the hell is going on? We were told the Squids weren't up to par. Where the fuck did they get these rookies?

Everyone is stuck against the board, jabbing for the puck when it snakes out in between someone's legs. Stealing the puck, I deke the lone defenseman and go for the breakaway. Wanting to mess with him a little, I go backhand, forehand, and the second before he squats down, I go five-hole. Dropping down to one knee, I skate a few feet pumping my fist back and forth and screaming along with the crowd. Looking into the crowd, Millie is jumping up and down and cheering with the rest of the rink. Yeah, I easily won the bet.

Next shift, the puck flies around the board and I speed up to get to it first, not paying attention to my surroundings. One of their biggest guys slams into me, my shoulder knocking into the boards and shaking the plexiglass.

"Asshole," I groan. It takes me a second to regain my footing. Fuck, that hurt.

"You good?" Jace asks as he skates by. I nod, stretching my shoulder out and getting back in the game.

My eyes bounce back and forth. Cyprus's goalie skates up to meet the puck then passes it to their center who quickly moves it up the ice while we change on the fly, leaving the middle of the ice wide fucking open.

"Get back!" Jace yells from beside me. I grip my stick, wishing it was our line out there. Miller rushes down just as a snapshot zips right past Rodriguez's stick.

"Fuck," Kai shouts, throwing his water bottle down on the ground.

Coach taps Kai's helmet with his clipboard and Kai immediately picks the bottle back up. Coach is all for us taking our rage out on the ice, within reason. But he has zero tolerance for us losing our cool on the bench. My first year on the team, one of the Juniors missed a premium shot and broke his stick in frustration. Coach benched him the next game. Amongst all his speeches, he tells us repeatedly that we represent him when we're out on the ice and he will not have anyone on his team throwing hissy fits like a toddler.

On the ice, Beaver sends the puck down to me. It gets stuck against the board between my skate and a Squid's. I lean down and nudge him with my shoulder, stealing the puck and passing it to my left. The Squid falls back, trying to draw a penalty like some rookie.

"You forget your speedo, bud?" I chirp as I skate on by. Fucking divers.

Glancing up at the clock, we're tied and only have two minutes left to win this. The crowd is going insane, but I'm a little embarrassed. We should be demolishing the Squids, not struggling to beat them. Coach is going to destroy us at practice on Monday.

Kai's line skates out, getting in position in the face-off circle. Within ten seconds, the ref blows the whistle, drops the puck and Kai slaps the shit out of it. The puck moves in slow motion through the air. The entire place is silent, the air buzzing with energy as the puck flies straight past the goalie's helmet.

"Fuck yeah!" Beaver yells.

We all jump up as Kai turns to the stands and salutes them. One minute and forty seconds later the horn sounds.

The locker room is a mix of different feelings. Some guys are partying up and celebrating the win. Others, like me, are wondering how we were inches away from losing. Cyprus's team doesn't have the best record and that's where we messed up. We assumed that they wouldn't be good this year. We assumed they wouldn't have fucking rookies who could skate circles around us. It was humiliating. Yes, we won, but only by one goal. We should've destroyed those guys.

"You good?" Jace asks while I'm shoving all my hockey shit back into my bag.

"Yeah, man. That was too close to call."

He runs a hand through his damp hair. "Way too close."

"Practice is going to be brutal on Monday."

Jace slaps me on the shoulder in agreement. "Get ready for more suicides."

I groan, needing the weekend to mentally prepare.

"But look at it this way," Jace continues, "the after-party is the perfect excuse to celebrate the W and get lost in some chicks."

"Chicks? With an S? Who the hell do you think you are? James Bond?" Jace thinks he's the fucking playboy of Winger U.

He's right though. It's time to celebrate our win and deal with the repercussions after the weekend. And it's time for me to hear Millie grovel. Hoisting my bag over my shoulder, I grab my stick and head out of the locker room and to the lobby. I bite the inside of my cheek to hide my smile when I see her leaning against the wall, arms crossed over her chest and staring me down.

"You came," I say. I drop my stuff on the floor with a loud thunk and approach her, only stopping when our toes touch.

"Bonnie and Zola were coming and I had nothing else going on."

What a little liar. "Sure, you didn't."

Whatever is happening between us right now is weird. It's weird because it's not weird. We're in a silent stand-off and I'm the most at ease I've been all night.

My hand darts out, grabbing the hem of her shirt. "I didn't know you were one for school spirit."

Her shoulders shake with silent laughter. "Oh, for sure. I'm going to bring my poms-poms to the next game."

I lick my lips, instantly imagining her in a short cheerleading skirt.

Her hand comes lightning fast, smacking me in the shoulder. "Perv."

We both laugh, but I can't help when I wince. That piece of shit threw his entire weight into me when he checked me earlier.

Her brows crease in worry. "Oh, shit. I'm sorry. Are you okay?"

Not wanting her to see any weakness, I tease, "A kiss would make it better."

She rolls her eyes and tries to push me away. "I think you're just fine."

I grab onto her hand, holding it against my chest. "Are you coming to the after-party?"

She shrugs. "I don't know. I'm kind of tired."

My eyebrows shoot up in surprise.

Millie starts laughing at herself and it's so freaking adorable. What the hell? When did I start thinking of girls' laughter as adorable?

"I know how lame that sounds. It seems like all my professors decided to forgo the easy transition from summer and just toss us into the deep end."

"You don't have to explain. I just like messing with you."

Still holding her hand, I bring it down between us, rubbing circles over her skin.

"So, are you going to say it now or later?"

"Say what?" Her words are shaking and she clears her throat, repeating the words.

"The reason you stayed after the game. If you're not going to the after-party, it must be because you wanted to give me my prize."

She heavily exhales. "Well, um. God dammit. Fine. It was all right. You won, which is good."

I chuckle at her. "Yes, winning is good."

"There you have it then."

Millie tries to pull her hand away, but I tighten my grip. "So, what I'm hearing, and correct me if I'm wrong, is that you enjoyed the game. And that means I was right."

Her face falls flat and she hangs her head in exhaustion.

"I suppose so," she says, flipping her purple locks out of her face.

"If I was right, then what does that make you?"

"Seriously?" she scoffs. "I have to say the whole thing?"

I shrug my shoulders. "I mean, that was the deal."

Millie takes a calming breath before meeting my eyes. "Fine. I was wrong and you were right. There. Are you happy now?"

I lean down, my lips ghosting hers as I whisper, "Fucking ecstatic."

Chapter Fifteen

Millie

I really am tired and wanted to go home and get in bed. But then stupid Caleb had to smile his stupid smile at me. Anyway, that's how I ended up at Ballentine instead of my room. The second we step into the house, Caleb is ushered away by a group of girls and that's fine by me. He's not my boyfriend and I'm not his girlfriend. I quickly find Bonnie in the crowd and she tells me Zola already disappeared with one of the basketball players.

I grab a water from the refrigerator and am people-watching with Bonnie when Reggie appears.

"Hey, I know you," I joke.

"Millie. It's good to see you again."

Bonnie's eyes instantly light up.

"Bonnie, Reggie. Reggie, Bonnie."

They clink glasses and suddenly I feel invisible. Maybe I should disappear and let Bonnie have some alone time. I quickly scan the crowd for Caleb, not wanting him to interfere with his sister.

Bonnie grabs my elbow, leaning into my ear. "I really have to pee. Don't let Reggie leave."

I laugh but agree to hold him hostage.

Reggie nods in the direction Bonnie went. "So, how do you know Bonnie?"

"She's my roommate."

His gaze is fixed on her and I get the feeling he totally checked out her ass as she walked away.

After a few moments, I nudge his shoulder with mine. "You know you're staring at Caleb's sister's ass?"

Reggie chokes on his drink and I give him a sad smile as I hand him a napkin I found on the counter.

"Thanks. Um, how are classes going?" The music turns up, forcing him to lean closer so I can hear him.

"Surprisingly intense. I remember the first month of school being so relaxed last year."

"Getting older sucks," he teases and I laugh in agreement.

I'm about to take a drink of my water when an arm is thrown around my shoulders. I clench my jaw, not even having to look to know who it is.

"Reggie," Caleb yells. "What's going on?"

Reggie's smile turns hard. "Just coming to celebrate the win. Congrats, man."

"Thanks. Man."

I turn to look at Caleb, debating on if I should punch him in the face now or later.

"I'll catch you around, Millie," Reggie says before darting away.

"Bye, Reg," Caleb holds his cup up to his retreating form.

I shake his arm off me. "What was that? Are you already drunk?"

Caleb shakes his head. "So weird that he keeps just showing up around you."

"Yeah, so crazy that someone who plays sports comes to a party at the sports house. God, jealous much?"

Caleb humorlessly laughs as he takes a step closer to me, pushing a lock of hair behind my ear. "I should've known you were lying when you said you two were just talking. My little liar."

I smack his hand away. I wasn't flirting with Reggie in the least bit, but Caleb's attitude is irritating. "You act like you haven't been mobbed by girls tonight."

"Aww. Jealous much?"

"Not in the least bit," I say through gritted teeth.

"Liar."

"You're really starting to piss me off."

"And I'm not even finished," he mumbles into my ear before clearing his throat.

"Hey!" he shouts and the music screeches to a stop. "Listen up!"

What in the fuck is he doing?

"This," Caleb gestures to me and the people surrounding me instantly back away, "is Millie Bardot. She's mine. Off limits to everyone. If you don't like that, come say it to my fucking face."

My mouth drops open in horror. There is no way that actually just happened!

"Are you fucking kidding me?" I scream at Caleb. My words are swallowed by the music being turned back up to deafening levels. I place both my hands on Caleb's chest and try pushing him away, but instead he uses his strength to pull me closer.

"Test me again," he warns. "I told you, I love punishing liars."

I didn't stay at the party much longer. After his stupid announcement, Caleb hung around me, infuriating me with his stupid caveman behavior. I wish I could just walk away and forget about him. But he's been stuck in my head since move-in day and I don't think that's going to change any time soon. I hate that he acts like an alpha-hole, but I think I also kind of like it. Don't get me wrong, I am not property and will not ever allow someone to treat me as such. The way Caleb acts is almost more protective and something about it weirdly turns me on while pissing me off at the same time. I have no idea what the fuck is going on in my head anymore.

Saturday morning, I do a happy dance when I get a call saying that my car is done. Not that I drive a lot, but I've missed my crappy little car. It's a twenty-minute walk to Raphael's and lucky for me, the rain decided to hold off. Right after the accident, I wasn't planning on fixing my bumper for a while. I wanted to save my money, but when I talked to Raphael and he was super understanding of my financial status, it made me realize this was the best deal I was going to get. And like I said, I miss my car.

My sneakers crunch on the gravel as I cross the parking lot. Raphael's shop is a brick building about a mile from my apartment complex. It's a small place and if I didn't have the address, I definitely would've walked right past it. The door chimes echo through the shop as I push open the door.

"Be out in a second," a voice yells from behind the counter.

"Take your time," I say, looking at framed pictures of cars on the wall.

While I'm waiting, I grab my phone and start scrolling through social media. Nothing new or exciting is posted, but one picture does grab my attention. Someone from one of my classes posted a picture of her and some guy making out. That isn't what I'm looking at though. In the background is Caleb and me. He's pushing my hair behind my ear and I recognize this is right before he told the whole party I'm his. The asshole. I use my thumb and forefinger to zoom in on him and maybe I was too mad to see it last night, but his eyes are intense as he stares down at me. All hot and primal.

"Can I help you?"

I almost drop my phone and swallow through the cotton in my mouth. Holy shit, how did just looking at a picture of Caleb turn me on? I quickly close out the app and put away my phone.

"Hi. I got a call my car was ready. I'm Millie Bardot."

He nods, picking up a binder from the desk. He grabs my keys and slides them toward me.

"All right. You ready to see her?"

"Uh, her?" I question.

He chuckles. "The car."

"Oh. Right. Yes."

I follow Raphael through a pair of double doors and smile when I see my car in one piece.

"It looks perfect. Thank you."

His smile is unsure, like he thinks I'm joking. "Right. Since it took me a little longer to fix than planned, I'm not charging you full price—"

"I can totally pay the full price. I have a job in town and work most weekends and pick up shifts here and there."

He waves his hand like it's no big deal. "Don't worry about it. It was an easy fix."

Call me curious, but I've never been to an auto-body shop where they willingly give you discounts. Typically, I get up-charged like crazy.

"Um, okay. How much is the total?" I open my purse and pull out the wad of cash I grabbed from the ATM on my way here. "I have $75 with me—"

"Great," he says and I hesitantly hand him the money.

"I can give you more after my next pay period."

He nods. "That's awesome."

He's silent for a few moments which leads me to think he's done talking about payment. Which is kind of odd.

"Um, how much is the total again?"

Raphael scrubs a hand over his buzz cut. "With the discount, I got to figure out the numbers, but I'll give you a call when I do."

I look to my car, then the keys in my hand, then Raphael. "Just like that?"
"Just like that."

"Well, yeah, okay," I stutter, not sure what is happening. Is Raphael really just this nice of a person? "Thank you so much."

"No problem," he says with a smile.

After Raphael heads back through the doors, I get into my car and decide to shake off whatever weirdness that was. He helped me out and gave me a huge discount. I just need to be thankful and move on. I freeze when I go to set my purse on the passenger seat. The floors are clean. And the seats. And the cup holders. There's no dust on the dashboard either. Did Raphael detail my car too?

Chapter Sixteen

Caleb

Caleb: How many times do I have to apologize?

Kentucky: I'm not sure. How many times do you plan on being an alpha-hole?

Caleb: What the fuck is that?

Kentucky: An alpha-hole? It's someone who is an asshole and at the same time thinks they're an alpha. I.E. An alpha-hole

Caleb: Kentucky, don't make me beg

Kentucky: Actually, I would love to see that...

Caleb: I still have that key to your apartment ;)

My phone starts ringing in my hand.

"Give that key back," Millie softly demands.

"Bon-Bon gave it to me. If she wants it back, she can be the one to take it back."

"Ugh," Millie groans. "You're so annoying."

"Reggie is a douche," I say, wanting to get this part of the conversation over with.

"Caleb—"

"Just hear me out." I wait a few seconds and when she doesn't say anything, I continue. "I'm not a huge fan of Reggie. You know that. And yes I may have had a celebratory shot before I found you at the party. It's no excuse for how I acted like a tool. So I am sorry about that."

"And?"

I pinch my brows in confusion. Pulling the phone away from my ear, I look down at it and wonder if this is a trap. "And what?"

"And you fucking claimed me in front of everyone at that party! That was ridiculous and stupid and—"

"I'm not apologizing for that," I tell her. No need for her to waste her words. They won't change my mind. Was it an asshole move? Definitely. Do I regret it? Hell no. Whatever Millie and I have going on is new. I have no clue what it is or what to call it, but all I know is I don't want any guy sniffing around her. And announcing it at the party seemed like a good idea at the time.

She sighs heavily, "You're exhausting and I have to get ready for work."

"Where do you work?"

"Huh?" She shouts into the phone. "I can't hear you. I think the apartment is going through a tunnel."

"Such a lame excuse," I tease.

Millie huffs. "Fine. I don't feel like talking to you anymore and need to finish getting ready."

She doesn't even say goodbye before she ends the call. That was not at all how I imagined that conversation going.

Once I willed myself out of bed, some of the guys from Ballentine and I spent the rest of the morning working out at the football stadium. During one of our breaks, my mom called, asking the typical questions.

"How is Bonnie? Are you keeping an eye on your sister? When are you going to bring home a nice girl for your father and me to meet? How's school going?"

She thinks she slides the question about a girlfriend in there so casually. I love my mother, but she's not as sly as she thinks she is.

The guys and I are on our way back through town when someone suggests stopping for milkshakes. My eyes almost pop out of my head when we walk into Cherry On Top and the waitress happens to be Millie, and her tits happen to be straining the top of her uniform. She's helping another customer, but when her eyes land on me, she looks like a deer in headlights. I wiggle my fingers in a wave.

Zeke bumps my shoulder from behind. "That your girl?"

"Fuck yeah, it is." I lower my voice so it won't carry, "And if any of you even think about looking below her chin, I'll snap your knees in two."

They all laugh, but I'm dead serious. Her tits are practically out for everyone to see. I wonder if I could get her to wear that uniform when we're alone.

"How can I help you?" she asks as we move up in line.

"I didn't know you worked here."

With her customer-is-always-right smile in place, she says, "I didn't tell you? So crazy. I just love it when people I know come in and get to see me in this uniform."

"Four chocolate milkshakes," Zeke tells her.

She nods, grabbing the ice cream scoop and that's when my face instantly falls. When she bends over to scoop the ice cream, it's a straight shot down her shirt. I turn around and am pleased to see the guys looking everywhere but.

Leaving my friends at the register, I follow Millie down to where she's blending our drinks. "You still mad at me?"

She points to her ear, miming that she can't hear me over the loud noise. I wait until she stops, but once I open my mouth, she restarts the blender. I wait, tongue in cheek, until she's done. I don't miss the small lift to the corner of her mouth though.

I clear my throat. "I said, are you still mad at me?"

"You still a dick?"

"I was buzzed and I was stupid. I'm sorry."

She's shaking the blender to mix all the ice cream up but pauses at my apology.

"Having to apologize seems to be a weird habit of yours," she says as she turns off the blender and grabs four cups next to it.

"I can do better," I assure her. Her lips are pursed and I'm nervous she won't actually forgive me. "I made a mistake. I can do better."

She props her hand on her hip and narrows her eyes. "I can talk to whoever I want."

I nod. "I know. I'll stop being a...what did you call me?"

Her lips transform into a smile. "An alpha-hole."

"Yeah. That."

She rolls her eyes then passes me our drinks. The guys come over and retrieve theirs.

"Have a great day," she adds, but I grab her hand before she can head back to the register.

She glances down at my hand then back up to me with a smile. A real smile that makes my heart explode in my chest knowing I didn't totally fuck this up.

"I'll see you around, Kentucky."

I watch her walk over and help the group of guys that just came in.

"Can I try the caramel creme?" one asks as I'm about to turn around.

She nods, pained smile still in place as she bends down and scoops some on a tasting spoon.

Another guy chuckles while asking, "Let me try that chocolate fudge."

With another smile and nod, she repeats the process.

I tighten my grip on my milkshake, knowing what these fuckers are doing. Knowing that every time she has to bend down, her tits are on the verge of falling out.

"Don't do something stupid," Zeke warns.

"You know I only do stupid things after I've thoroughly thought about them."

A third guy from the group pops up with a tasting request when I walk around them and behind the counter.

"What are you—"

Grabbing the back of her neck, I bring her lips to mine. My tongue forces its way into her mouth, claiming her. I want all these assholes to know that she's mine and they can go back to circle jerking it with each other. She moans into my mouth and I make sure to clamp my teeth on her bottom lip as I pull away.

"I'll see you later, babe," I tell her, brushing my thumb over her lower lip. As I'm walking away, I stare down all the stupid fuckers that think they can treat women that way.

"Um, I'll just take some vanilla in a cup," the third guy finally says.

When we get back to the house, I find Kai in the viewing room. There's a giant TV screen in front of a boardroom table. The rich donors who will do anything to relive their glory years love seeing their money put to good use. Not that I'm complaining. The set-up is sweet. Kai's hunched over, elbows on knees with his eyes glued to the screen. It's a video of our last game. I knock on the table to let him know I'm in the room, but he doesn't even flinch. He only speaks up when I move closer and can see the game clearer.

"Sloppy passes. Our line changes were a mess. How the hell did we win?" Kai grabs the remote, turning the game off. "It's humiliating. It should never have been such a close game. Coach is going to have our asses tomorrow. What the hell happened out there?"

I shrug, not too worried about it. But I'm not the captain.

"We had an off game. It happens."

"It shouldn't," he groans, rubbing a hand down his face.

I check my watch, seeing it's after lunch already. "How long have you been sitting here?"

He shakes his head like he's trying to wake himself up or something. "I don't know. Maybe a few hours?"

"Hours?" I sigh loudly. "You need to leave this room. Get some food and some sleep."

"I guess. But Coach—"

"Will be more pissed if you suck ass at practice tomorrow because you spent all day in here instead of resting on your one freaking day off."

Nodding, Kai stands up and raises his hands over his head in a stretch.

"Maybe add showering to your list too," I add as I'm walking out of the room. "It stinks in here and I think it's because of you."

After I grab myself some real food and a shower, I change into some joggers and one of my Winger U shirts. My homework sits in the same place it's been since Friday and every time I walk past my desk, I feel like it's mocking me. I've been putting it off all weekend and now it's time to pay up.

I take my sixth calming breath in the last minute as I re-read the same damn sentence again. A few of the baseball guys are playing some game in the hallway making it hard to focus. Studying has always been my weak point, but it seems damn near impossible in this house. Looking around my room, I find my headphones under a dirty shirt. I put them on to try and tune out the noise outside, but it's hopeless. With a frustrated groan, I sweep my books off my desk, sending my notes flying.

"Well, fuck. That was dramatic," I mumble as I bend down to fix the mess I just made.

There's no way I'll pass my classes if I can't retain any of the information. Stomping around my room, I load up my backpack and do something I've never done before.

Chapter Seventeen

Millie

My vision begins blurring the words in front of my face, melting everything into one giant blob. I've been staring at my textbook for the last hour and am losing steam fast. Maybe it's because the Pepsi and cookie I consumed from the library cafe are the only things I've eaten since I got off work. Even then I just grabbed a quick sandwich from the gas station. Opening my phone, my eyes widen in shock that it's already five. I ignore the notifications and pack up my stuff.

I'm walking out of the library when I recognize a big brute sitting a few tables away from the door. My initial instinct is to rush home and avoid the sexy hockey player I somehow keep kissing. In fact, I almost do that but his furrowed brows and annoyed expression have me curious. Stepping out of the middle of the walkway, I take a moment to watch him. Not in a creepy way, but I haven't had the chance to see him like this, where he's in his own world.

Caleb runs his long fingers through his messy hair before picking his pencil up. He taps the eraser against his forehead over and over. Him doing that brings my attention to his face. How his nose has a slight bump to it which I'm betting he got from some hockey fight. His clean-shaven face is still sexy, but I think I like his scruff more. Damn, he really did hit the gene lotto when he was born. Caleb rolls his neck from side to side trying to relieve tension. What's got him so stressed?

Marching up to his table, I plop down in the seat opposite him.

"What are you doing?"

His face relaxes when he looks up to see me and, for some reason, it makes me smile.

"Trying to get through these notes, but I'd much rather be talking to you."

I roll my eyes. "So cheesy. What are you reading about?"

He inhales deeply through his nose. "You know, I'm not really sure. It isn't quite holding my attention."

"Is that why you've been on the same page for the last five minutes?"

Caleb's eyebrows rise in surprise. "Are you stalking me?"

"No, I was..."

My words fade away as I realize I kind of was. I stood across the room and stared at him for so long, I noticed the freaking page he was on.

"I know you like to, but you don't have to lie to me. You can just say you missed me."

"In your dreams," I tease.

Caleb's eyes lock on mine and the world goes quiet. No murmurs from students studying, no incessant beeping from people walking through the metal detectors at the entrance. Just silence.

Needing to interrupt whatever weird thing is happening right now, I clear my throat.

"Why don't you read to me? I'd love to hear what kind of stuff Caleb Booker deigns important enough to actually study."

I chuckle lightly, but stop when he looks away. His bold demeanor is gone and I'm surprised to see Caleb look almost shy. But why? I was just making a little joke. I thought that's what we were doing. A little playful banter. He starts shuffling his papers and trying to stuff everything back into his bag.

"Caleb?" I ask and when he doesn't stop, I place my hand on his arm. "It was a joke. Did I say something wrong?"

"I can't read, okay?" he snaps.

My mouth pops open. Not because of what he said, but because of his reaction. He's never raised his voice at me before.

"I'm just going to—" I push my chair back, but Caleb grabs my hand before I can stand.

"Fuck. Sorry, Kentucky. I didn't mean to shout at you. Don't leave."

His hand is warm in mine and his soft eyes have me nodding my head, agreeing to stay. Neither of us talks, but it's not comfortable like it was a moment ago. I feel the weight of his confession on my chest.

Caleb groans, running his hands through his hair. "That's not right. That's not what I meant. I can read. I just…"

"You just…" I gently prompt.

He scrubs a hand down his face with a groan. "It's not a joke, so don't laugh, but I have a learning disability."

I tilt my head, confused. "Why would I laugh at that?"

His shoulders visibly relax. "It's called dyslexia. It's just all these fucking letters. They mix themselves up and then I get confused and forget what I read and the whole process starts over. It's bullshit."

"You have dyslexia?"

He scoffs. "Just a fancy word for stupid."

Standing up just enough to reach him, I flick him in the center of his forehead.

He jerks back in surprise. "Did you just flick me?"

"Yes, and I'll do it again if I ever hear you call yourself stupid ever again. You are not stupid. Having a learning disability doesn't make you stupid. Frankly, you're stupid for thinking you're stupid."

It's only a few seconds before Caleb busts out laughing.

"What is so funny?"

Caleb leans back in his chair, widening his stance, and sighs. "That was not the reaction I thought I was going to get."

"What are you trying to say? That you thought I would agree and say that you're just another dumb jock?" He shrugs in agreement. "I'm going to flick you again, stupid-head."

This makes him laugh even more. I turn away from him, wanting to be annoyed but a smile tugs at my lips.

"Your high school teachers didn't help you with any of this? They didn't teach you different ways to read, develop—"

"No," he interrupts. "No one gave a shit. My parents tried to get me help, but the school didn't care. They cared more about me working on my slapshot."

"I'm so sorry. That's awful."

He doesn't say anything and I can sense how uncomfortable he is right now. Tense shoulders, clenched jaw, white knuckles because he won't relax his fists. Reaching out, I place my hand on top of his and ask, "Is there anything that helps you focus?"

He exhales heavily. "Well most textbooks come with audio but this one doesn't. I have to take notes and when I'm trying to read and then write, everything gets all mixed up. Typing on my laptop or iPad usually helps. It's weird, I don't understand why."

I nod as I listen to him when an idea pops into my brain. "What if I was your audiobook?"

His face scrunches. "Huh?"

"Grab your stuff and come with me," I tell him as I stand up.

With a low and husky voice that does something to me, he says, "Demanding. That's kind of sexy."

I glare at him when he places his hands up in front of him. "Don't flick me again."

Shaking my head, I head to the staircase. I don't bother turning around to see if he's following me. It may sound weird, but I can feel his presence. Once we make it to the first floor, I turn the corner and smile when I find a room open. The bottom floor of the library has five mini-rooms, a.k.a. quiet rooms, to help people study. Each room has one table with a few chairs and a window to see into the library. I open the door and gesture for him to enter.

"If you want to fool around, we should probably head up to the fourth floor. Unless you like people watching then—"

I smack him lightly in the chest. "Sit down and shut up."

"Next are you going to tell me you brought some rope and a blindfold?" he teases.

I exhale sharply. "No, but you're making me wish I brought a gag."

"Oh, kinky."

"Get your laptop out and get ready." I take the textbook he was reading and open it up. "What page are you on?"

"What is happening?"

"You're not listening. I said get out your laptop."

"Or what? You going to spank me for being a bad boy?"

I sigh and roll my eyes. He just laughs.

"Seriously, Kentucky. What's going on?"

"You said there isn't an audiobook for this text, so I'm going to read it to you while you take notes."

Caleb's frozen for a moment before shaking his head. "That's not going to work. I typically have to rewind multiple times and—"

"Then I'll reread the passage multiple times."

"That'll take forever."

I shrug. "I've got time. Now, open your laptop and stop talking back. Oh and tell me what page I need to start on."

Caleb's tongue darts out, running over his bottom lip as his eyes drift down to my cleavage.

I shake my head and laugh. "Uh-uh. Either eyes up here," I point to my face, "or on your laptop."

"Sir, yes, sir." Caleb mock salutes me and it makes me want to flick him again.

He wasn't kidding. I reread the first page at least three times for him. Each time slower than the last. I have no problem helping him out. I'm actually really proud of him for accepting my help. The whole situation just makes me sad. I can't believe Caleb's high school didn't help him in any way. No kid should just be left to fend for themselves. On another note, I'm pissed. His stupid school and stupid teacher made him feel like he was the stupid one? If I could go back, I would rip them to shreds. Okay, not really. I'd probably just yell a lot, but it's a nice fantasy to have.

I'm waiting for him to finish typing and can't help but think how cute he is. His brow scrunched as he hunches over his laptop.

"Can, um, can you read that last part again?"

"Sure."

I'm about to start reading when he sighs, leaning back in his chair and running his hands down his face.

"Do you need a break?" I ask. I don't want to offend him in any way, but I also want him to know I'm a safe space. I would never judge him. Especially not about something like having a learning disability.

He doesn't answer, and I can't help myself from talking. "I was helping Zola study one time and during our research, we found out that about 15% of the US population has a learning disability. That's like 10 million adults and children."

Pinching the bridge of his nose, he exhales sharply. "I mean this in the nicest way, but why the fuck are you telling me this?"

"Because you're not alone. There are lots of people out there who are just like you."

"Yeah. Okay," he says dismissively.

I should stop. He probably needs a mental break, but I can't. I just need him to know one more thing.

I rush my words out quickly, hoping he doesn't get even more irritated. "I just want you to know that I'm here for you and I can help whenever you need it. I'll never judge you or look at you differently. Unless you call yourself stupid again then I'll have to—"

Caleb's chair falls to the ground as he launches himself at me. His lips slam against mine. Fisting my hair, he tugs my head back and deepens the kiss. I moan into his mouth the second his tongue touches mine. When he pulls back, Caleb rests his forehead against mine.

We're both struggling to catch our breath when he whispers, "You really are perfect."

Chapter Eighteen

Millie

I hate the expression "When it rains, it pours." I mean, it can always get worse. I guarantee there are people out there who have had a shittier day than me. The homeless trying to avoid the rain, someone struggling to buy groceries for their family...

Reminding myself someone has it worse doesn't stop me from wanting to stand in the middle of the street and scream obscenities until my voice gives out. And since I don't want the cops called on me, I opt to use my fake ID at one of the bars on Main Street.

"What'll you have?" the bartender asks as I get comfy on the bar stool.

I could just get a beer. Something simple with not a lot of alcohol. I hate the taste of wine, so that's out. Maybe a mixed drink with lots of ice to water it down.

I close my eyes and take a calming breath. My mind races with the events of today. A surprise pop quiz at 8 a.m. that I obviously didn't study for and most likely bombed. Another call from Dad that I accidentally answered. A text from my mom basically begging me to get back in touch with him. And to top everything off, I have no fucking clue what is happening with me and Caleb. Are we friends? Do I like him? Does he have strong feelings for me? Maybe this is just a hookup and I'm over-thinking it?

I groan, open my eyes, and say, "Shot of tequila and whatever's on tap."

He's only gone for a few moments, but when he comes back he eyes me with suspicion.

"What?"

"Did the bouncer check your ID?"

Shit. I'm guessing he doesn't know the bouncer is around the corner chain-smoking with some girl instead of sitting at his post.

"Want to see it?" I pull it out of my wallet, trying to keep a neutral expression, and hold it up between my forefinger and middle finger. "I'm pretty sure I could drink you under the table."

What a bald-faced lie. The bartender is a brick wall. He could probably bench-press me while tossing back shot after shot.

My attitude must work because he just chuckles.

"All right, killer. Just take it easy."

The bartender sets down my drinks next to a bottle of salt and a lime wedge. I stare at the shot glass, the memory of that awful phone call coming back to me.

I'm getting ready to head out the door when my phone goes off, but I can't find it. The ringer continues to yell at me until I discover it under a pile of notebooks. Not wanting to miss the call, I quickly answer before it goes to voicemail.

"Hello?"

There's a heavy silence, like the other person is holding their breath. Then they release it in a long sigh.

"Kiddo. Hey. You answered."

I freeze in place, my face falling and my entire body urging me to toss my phone out the window. Or drop it on the ground and step on it until it shatters into hundreds of pieces. Anything so I don't have to endure this phone call. I open my mouth to say something, but I can't.

He clears his throat, "I didn't think you would answer. You know your voicemail is full?"

He says it like a joke. Like I'm not purposely avoiding him and his calls.

Finally, my brain catches up and I mutter, "Don't call me again."

My finger hits the end button before he can get out another word. I turn off my phone, put it in my back pocket, and decide I need a fucking drink.

Forgoing the salt, I hold his stare and toss back the tequila. I grit my teeth to avoid showing how rough that went down. The second he turns his back, I grab the lime and suck the juice then grab my beer and chug.

When half the bottle is gone, I feel a sense of calm take over. Okay, that's probably the buzz, but either way, it was much needed. The daughter of an alcoholic going to a bar to unwind. I'm the definition of a cliché. I twirl a lock of my hair as I scan the rest of the bar. It's a smaller place with a giant wooden bar to one side of the room and a few tables to the other. At the opposite end is a pool table and a darts set up. I've never played darts, but I bet I'm good at it. Grabbing my bottle by the neck, I head over to the target hanging on the wall and one by one pluck each dart out.

Cocking my arm back, I throw the first one.

"Shit," I mutter. Tequila definitely gives me a false sense of confidence. I totally suck at this. How the hell did my dart land halfway up the wall? I set my beer down on the floor next to me, now determined to get my next dart on the board. This really can't be that hard. I'm probably overthinking it. My next throw is too far left and

I audibly gasp even though no one is around. Thank God no one is around.

"Come on," I whine to myself. I just need one to hit the board. Just one.

Winding up, I set my sight on the bullseye. I can do this. The dart zooms through the air. I throw my hands up in victory! I did it! Well, sort of. I'm doing a little celebration dance when the sound of someone laughing behind me has me turning around. Only to find one of my problems staring back at me.

"There's no dart on the board," Caleb tells me after he swallows.

"Maybe not." I stand to my full height, determined not to show him any weakness. "But I tapped the board before it fell so I get at least a point for that. Right?"

He snorts. "No. You definitely don't."

My smile falls and I stick my tongue out at him.

I track down my rogue darts, aware of Caleb's eyes on me the entire time. I will get one to stick on the board. I am a strong independent woman and I can fucking do this.

"You drunk?" he asks. No judgment in his voice, just curiosity.

"No. I've had this beer and one shot."

His brows raise as he nods. "Nothing goes together like booze and sharp objects."

"I've had a shit day, okay?" I snap.

He doesn't say anything or do anything. He just stands there, staring at me.

"I'm sorry," I sigh. "It's just been a long day and shit just keeps piling up and I needed a break. I get that it's mid-afternoon and I shouldn't be drinking, but I really don't need a lecture."

Caleb holds up his bottle and shakes it, the liquid sloshing around inside.

"I could help you."

I chuckle. "Help me what?"

"Relax. Or at least teach you how to play darts because you clearly suck."

I gasp. "I do not suck. Those were just my practice throws."

"Sure they were," Caleb mumbles into his bottle before finishing it off. I do the same and we set our bottles on a table behind him.

I know what he's doing. He's goading me. And damn him, it's working. There's nothing I love more than a challenge.

Stopping in front of him, I lick a lonely drop of liquid from the corner of my lips. His eyes follow the movement, making me smile.

"What do you want if you win?"

His stupid smirk is out and I love it. Caleb shoves his hands in his pockets, taking a step closer to me.

"You come back to my place?"

I roll my eyes. So predictable.

"And what do I get when I win?"

He shakes his head, probably knowing I'm full of shit but unwilling to admit it. "You get to come back to my place."

I laugh out loud, tossing my head back. "I'm sensing a theme."

"Fine," he groans, "I'll come back to your place."

I smack his chest, pushing him away. Of course, he doesn't move.

"You're ridiculous," I say, still giggling.

"And you're perfect."

My laughing ceases. The look in his eyes has changed from light and funny to dark and dangerous.

"I - I'll go first."

I widen my stance and focus on the bullseye, but freeze when Caleb is at my back.

"What are you doing?"

His hand wraps around my arm, pulling it back. "Your first two throws were too forceful. Your last, not enough. You need to find the sweet spot."

His words are low and send shivers down my spine.

Relaxing my body, I let him take over. He guides my toss and my mouth drops open when my dart not only hits the board but sticks and doesn't fall to the ground.

"I did it!" I shout, jumping up and down and not caring for one second how ridiculous I look.

"Woah," Caleb steps back and places his hands up in front of his face. "You still have two very sharp darts in your hands. Remember the rule from kindergarten about not running with scissors? Well, this is kind of the same."

I look at the darts, almost forgetting they were there. "Oh, right. Sorry."

The game doesn't last too long. Maybe ten minutes. The first nine minutes were fun because I kept messing with Caleb on every turn. Threatening to flash him or tickle him during his turn. This is his final turn and if I did the math right, I'm pretty sure I won. Unless he gets a bulls-eye, he's done for. His dart lands on the green part which means I won. I start jumping up and down, loudly singing "We are the Champions."

"What the hell are you doing?" he laughs.

"Celebrating my win," I say with a giant smile.

His face scrunches. "But you didn't. You know you lost, right?"

I stop jumping. What did he say?

"What do you mean? I, I won. I got like 57 points."

Caleb's face is frozen in a confused state. Cocked head, brows pulled together in a frown and narrowed eyes.

"I don't know how to play darts, do I?"

Finally, he laughs. Like doubled over belly-laughing at me.

"It really isn't that funny," I mumble.

When he stands, he wipes a pretend teardrop away. "No, Kentucky. You really don't. But your confidence is sexy as hell."

Sighing, I grab my beer bottle and frown when I see it's empty.

"Your place or mine?"

"Seriously?" I whine.

"A deal's a deal."

I groan dramatically. "My beer's empty anyway. Let's go."

My entire body stiffens when Caleb places his hand on my lower back. It takes me a moment to remember how to walk as he guides me out the front door.

"Are you really that drunk off one beer?"

Obviously not. The game sobered me up, but I don't say that. Instead, I say, "If I'm willingly going home with you, I think I might be."

He chuckles and once we're outside, he pulls me closer to him.

Don't ask me how. Don't ask me why. But somehow I went from throwing myself the most pathetic pity party to playing video games with Caleb on his couch. This is a weird night.

When I told Caleb I'd never played Super Mario Kart, he said that was unacceptable and needed to change immediately. He gave me a quick tutorial on which buttons to press and when, but really I'm just pressing random things. I swear my little character hates me because it doesn't want to do what I tell it to do.

"Why aren't you going left?" I mutter in frustration.

Caleb laughs and I turn to him, frowning. "It's because you're looking at the wrong screen."

"What?" I shout and then realize he's right. I toss my head back and groan when I see that my character crashed into the median.

He's still laughing when I abandon my controller and grab for his.

"What do you think you're doing?"

This time I'm laughing as I push one of his hands off. Registering that he's not going to give his controller up, I start pressing random buttons to mess him up.

"You little—"

Caleb tosses his controller beside him and then tackles me to the couch. His fingers tickle along my ribs and I try rolling away but it's useless. I'm laughing so hard that tears streak down the side of my face.

"Not so funny now, is it?" he teases with a wide grin.

"I surrender! Uncle! Uncle!"

"What? I can't hear you?"

"I'm sorry!" I giggle.

What once was a funny moment turns serious the second his fingers stop moving. He slides his hands up my ribs, resting just below my breasts.

"You're a little cheat," he whispers against my lips.

"I'm sorry. Is there anything I can do to make it up to you?"

My hands are on his biceps, I move them up to the back of his neck and pull him down to me. I think he's surprised I made the first move because he doesn't kiss me back immediately. Only when my tongue enters his mouth does his grip on me tighten. I moan into his mouth as he takes over. His tongue swipes across mine as he settles in between my thighs. I wrap my legs around his hips and gasp when I feel him. He's hard and pressing against my most sensitive area. Caleb's hands slide down, finding the hem of my shirt and sneak underneath. The moment he pulls down my bra cup, I roll my hips up and against him.

"Millie," he groans. I do it again to hear him make that same noise. "Fuck. Kentucky, are you wet right now?"

I open my mouth to answer, but nothing comes out when his fingers tug on my nipple. I arch into his hand, needing him to do that again.

"I asked you a question," he whispers in my ear before biting down on my lobe.

"If you're so curious, find out for yourself."

Caleb's hand slides out from under my shirt and lands on the button of my jeans. Our breaths intertwine and I'm about to kiss him again when the front door opens and a hoard of guys shuffle in.

"Booker, what are you—"

"Check out Booker, upgrading from his blow-up doll!" someone shouts.

Suddenly the room is filled with slow clapping.

"What the fuck?" Caleb shouts, tilting his body to the left to block their view. "Guys, get out!"

Whistles accompany the clapping and I quickly fix my bra then cover my face. I know I'll laugh about this in the future because it is quite comical, but right now my face is fifty shades of red and I just thank God they came in when they did and not when Caleb's hand was down my pants.

Caleb flips them off and shouts, "Out!"

After a few more laughs, the voices drift away and Caleb's forehead falls against mine. "They are the fucking worst."

Chapter Nineteen

Caleb

I'm on my way back from class when my phone buzzes and I answer without looking to see who it is.

"I haven't heard from you all day and I was starting to get lonely," I tease Millie.

My smile falls away when my mother clears her throat. "Lonely? Oh, are you seeing someone?"

There's hope in her voice and I quickly clear my throat. "Hi, Mom. I, um, no. No, it's just a joke. The guys and I like to mess with each other."

Millie and I are hanging out more and more lately, but I'm not going to tell my mom that. If I do, the second she hangs up the phone, she'll start daydreaming about weddings.

"Sure, sweetie." She knows I'm full of shit. How do mothers always know? "Anywho, I just got out of Pilates and realized I haven't heard from you in a while."

Looking both ways, I run across the street when it's clear. "Yeah, I'm sorry about that. Classes and hockey have been crazy lately."

"Just classes and hockey? Nothing else?"

"Bonnie's doing great," I say, attempting to change the subject.

Mom laughs at me, knowing exactly what I'm doing. "I know. She called me the other day."

"I will call more, I promise," I say with a smile.

"All right. All right. Well, tell me about school."

I spend the rest of my walk from campus to Ballentine giving Mom a play-by-play. Minus all the Millie stuff. It's weird though because I have this itching desire to tell Mom about her. After we hang up, I jump in my car and make another call.

"You're done with classes for the day, right?" I ask when she answers the phone.

Millie giggles, "Yes, creep. Why are you asking?"

"I want to do something."

"And what exactly is that something?" Millie asks.

I chuckle low in my chest. "Come outside and find out."

I hang up the phone before she can respond. It only takes a few minutes for her to open her front door and find me sitting in my car in the parking lot. She shakes her head before disappearing back inside. I frown, wondering what the hell she's doing when she reappears and heads straight for me.

Millie crouches next to my rolled down window. "What are you doing here?"

"I told you. I want to do something." I reach up, grabbing the ends of her purple hair. "Your hair is wet."

"Brains and beauty. I must have hit the lottery with you." After a moment, she continues, "I just got out of the shower when you called me."

My eyes trail down her body, picturing her in the shower.

She scoffs, "Where are we going?"

I gesture with my head to the passenger seat. "Get in and find out."

"I don't follow orders."

My smile doubles in size. "But we both know you like to."

I lick the corner of my lip and watch her eyes zero in on it. Finally, she groans and joins me in the car.

The drive is only a few minutes and we have to park on the street and walk from there.

"You still haven't told me where we're going," Millie complains.

"I know." I don't elaborate because I know how pissed it's making her. She groans loudly and that's when I notice she's stopped in the middle of the sidewalk.

"Tell me or I'm not coming."

Looking around to make sure no one is close by, I stalk toward her and stop inches away.

I lower my voice so even if someone does walk by, only she will be able to hear. "We both know you like it when you aren't in control. So instead of being a brat, be a good girl and maybe I'll reward you later."

A quick glance down shows me she adjusted her stance, no doubt because those few words have her instantly wet. Turning back around, it takes no time for her to give in and follow me.

The door chimes as we enter Cactus's House of Pain. The scent of cleaning products surrounds us as we make our way through the lobby of the tattoo parlor.

"I thought Bonnie said your mom would have a stroke if you got any more tattoos?"

I roll up my sleeve, pretending to examine my half-sleeve when really I'm just showing off my arm. Yes, I realize it's a douchey thing to do. But as she bites down on her lower lip, I struggle to hide my grin.

"I think that has passed. Plus, I'm going for a full sleeve."

"So, why am I here?"

"Moral support?"

Her eyes travel around the room. "What if I want to get one?"

With her looking the opposite way, I take the opportunity to adjust myself because that is one of the sexiest things she's ever said.

"What would you get?" I ask. The evil side of my brain knows exactly what I would want her to have. A red outline of my hand on her perfect ass. Fuck, this is not the place to be thinking about spanking her. I close my eyes and think about things I know won't make me hard: watching baseball, taking out the trash, skating drills.

She shrugs with the cutest smile. "I don't know. I've never really thought about it before."

"You could always get a tramp stamp," I tease.

She pretends to laugh. "And what would my tramp stamp be?"

I approach her slowly. Her breaths turn shaky and I have to think about watching baseball again. "Just a few words. Property of Caleb

Booker."

Millie bursts out laughing and pushes me away. I let her, falling back with a stupid ass smile on my face.

"Wait, didn't you say you had one?"

"Um, no."

"Yes, you did. When we met. You said—"

She giggles. "I said maybe. I was just screwing with you because you were annoying me."

"My little liar," I murmur. I'm about to pull her to me when we're interrupted.

Cactus, the guy who has done the majority of my arm, comes out and greets us. When his eyes linger on Millie a little too long, I step in front of her, blocking his view. Don't get me wrong, Cactus is a great guy, but Millie is mine. This is just my friendly way of informing him. He nods a few times before taking us back to his room.

Millie pulls up a chair next to where I'm sitting, my left arm propped up. Cactus continues getting his station ready and then gets cozy on his stability ball.

"Ready?" He asks, adjusting the lamplight on his forehead.

"Let's do it," I tell him. The familiar hum of the tattoo gun fills the air and I take a deep breath at the first scratch. After a few seconds, the sharp pain fades away and it feels almost therapeutic. That's probably not a normal thought.

"Does it hurt?" Millie asks, watching the needle penetrate my skin.

I shake my head. "Not at all, Kentucky."

"Now who's the liar?"

"You're right. It's super painful. You should probably hold my hand for support."

She rolls her eyes, something she loves to do around me, but takes my right hand in hers. Her skin is soft and without thinking, I pull her hand up to my mouth and kiss her palm.

"Thank you for coming with me."

She smiles so hard her eyes crinkle in the corners. "Curiosity got the best of me."

Conversation fades away as I close my eyes and listen to the heavy metal music blasting through the room. Cactus is laser-focused, frequently taking small breaks to make sure the pain isn't too bad. The needle scrapes against my skin, but I don't feel any pain. All I feel is Millie's hand in mine. The sweep of her thumb over my knuckles.

Millie's eyes are zeroed on my arm when I ask, "How's it looking?"

"Really hot," she says. She's clearly zoning out because when she realizes what she says she starts back-pedaling. "That's not, that's not what I meant—"

"I'm going to smoke. Take ten," Cactus tells me and I nod in understanding. Once Cactus is out of the room, I turn to Millie. Her cheeks are the color of a tomato.

"You think my tattoos are hot?" I finally ask.

Her lips slowly part and the air in the room shifts in an instant. Without speaking, Millie stands up and rounds my chair. Taking a closer look at my new ink.

"It's bleeding." She sounds surprised.

"That'll stop soon."

Her fingers hover over it and I watch her chest slowly rise as she tries to control her breathing. Because of where she's standing, she's at the perfect height for my fingers to reach out and graze the skin right above her jeans.

"How wet are you right now?"

"What?" Millie glances around the empty room. "No. No, we're in public."

She licks her delicious lips and I slide my fingers into the top of her jeans, yanking her closer. Grabbing her with my other hand, I guide her so she's straddling me. Her hands rest on my shoulders and if I look down, I'll get a face full of her tits. Digging my fingers into her hips, I yank her down against my cock that's threatening to break free. She gasps, moving her hips on her own accord and I chuckle.

"You little liar. I can feel how soaked you are through your jeans."

"I was, um, getting ready when you called and, um..."

"And what?" I whisper into her mouth.

"I couldn't find any underwear."

My eyes almost pop out of my head. Did I hear her correctly?

"Are you telling me you're dry humping me with your bare pussy?"

I shift my hips up and get rewarded with those sexy little gasps.

"Caleb," she pants.

I grip her ass, grinding her on me. If there wasn't the possibility of Cactus walking back in any second, she would be naked with my cock inside her before her next breath.

"Baby. Baby, you need to stop." I try pausing her movements, but she isn't letting me.

"I can't. It feels too good."

I groan as she quickens her pace. "I'm so close, Caleb."

Fuck me.

Grabbing her shirt and bra, I rip it down quickly and pull her hard nipple into my mouth. She tries to speak, but I bite down. My teeth clamp down while my tongue swirls around her as I increase my hip movements. Millie buries her face into my neck, her teeth sinking into my skin as her orgasm tears through her. Her body spasms as she comes down and I help her fix her top before she climbs off me. Millie practically falls back into her seat next to me. My eyes fall to the crotch of my pants where there's a very noticeable dark spot. I smile to myself, wanting to be that asshole who gives himself a pat on the back.

Millie sees my grin and smacks my arm. "Shut up."

I'm still laughing when Cactus comes back in.

He heads straight for his seat, ready to get back to work. Before the needle touches my skin, he lowers his voice and says, "You're gonna have to leave one hell of a tip if you're gonna do freaky shit in here."

Chapter Twenty

Millie

"Hey," I approach Caleb who is tossing a football around with some guys on the lawn in front of Ballentine. Once I was done with classes for the day and dropped off my books, I somehow found myself drifting over to his place.

"What are you doing here?" he asks, walking over to meet me on the sidewalk.

I shrug. "Bonnie and Zola are busy and I guess we're friends or something now."

He chuckles, completely forgetting his friends and focusing only on me.

"I wanted to do something fun today."

"And I'm your last resort?"

"If you don't want to come, just say so." I go to turn and walk away when he grabs my hand to stop me.

"I didn't say that."

Still holding my hand, Caleb walks me to his car. He opens the passenger door for me and once we're both buckled, I give him directions to the only Escape Room in town.

"How was your class?" he asks as we merge into traffic.

I let out a deep breath, not really sure how to answer. "Um, I don't know."

He glances over with pinched brows. "What does that mean?"

"It means I don't know." I scrub my hand down my face and sigh. "I think I saw something super weird, but I'm probably just reading too much into things. I tend to do that."

"No, really?" he mocks.

I roll my eyes as he chuckles.

"What do you think you saw?"

"Take this left. I was one of the last people in class and was packing up my books when I noticed another student was down at Professor Weckman's desk with him. They were standing super close to each other. Like uncomfortably close. And I think I saw him grab her hand. I don't know. It seemed intimate. Like I said, it's probably nothing."

"Weckman? He's new, right?"

"New-ish. Make the right at the next light."

"Let me guess. He's young and hot?"

I grimace. "I would not call a professor hot. But he's not bad looking."

Caleb shrugs one shoulder. "Some people get off on the professor and student thing."

I stick my finger in my mouth and gag.

Caleb smirks. "Not your cup of tea?"

"God, no. A professor doing anything sexual with a student just seems unethical and wrong."

"Right. I forgot you get wet thinking about sexy hockey players with the last name Booker."

I shake my head and laugh at his lame joke as he rests his hand on my thigh.

"See that blue sign?" I tell him, "The parking lot is right behind it."

"The hell is an escape room?" he asks as he helps me out of the car.

"Basically we are trapped in a room and have to find clues in order to get out."

His face scrunches. "Is that legal?"

"Shut up and come on," I say, grabbing his hand and dragging him behind me.

We're ushered into a room that looks like an apartment. The living room is cozy with one couch opposite the television, a coffee table with a checkers game set up on it, and a bean bag chair off to the side. Around the corner is a small kitchen with a table barely big enough for four people to eat at. The walls are covered with artwork, take-out menus, and random pictures. Just from a quick scan of the room, I already see three different types of locks.

Caleb stares down the door like the employee will come back in to save him.

"What are we supposed to do?" He scratches his head as he looks around.

I look up to see the 60-minute timer has already started.

"Anything in here can be a clue, so walk around the room and see if you can find a key or a lock or something that seems out of place."

He nods, stuffing his hands in his pocket. I start walking around the room, opening up cabinets and checking behind books.

"You do this for fun?" he asks, peeking into the refrigerator.

"I told you, I like puzzles. If you don't want to help, you don't have to."

"I didn't say that." When I look over my shoulder at him, he winks. Why is he so good at that?

I frown at a stack of menus on the kitchen table that look weird. I'm reading through the contents when I feel Caleb against my back. Even though there's more than enough room, he's bumping into me as he tries to walk around the table.

"Excuse me," he teases. Another bump. "That was an accident."

"I'm sure it was." I try to elbow him, but he jumps away with a laugh.

A few minutes later when I'm eyeing the thermostat, he does it again.

"Stop it," I laugh, turning around to face him.

"Stop what?" he asks, the face of innocence. "I'm just trying to look for hidden clues to help us get out of here."

"Oh, really?"

"Yeah."

I try to walk past him when he stops me with a hand on my belly.

"You know, I can't find any clues. Maybe there aren't any. Hm, I wonder what else we could do to pass the time."

"You're an idiot."

"And you're sexy."

He nips at my lips, just enough to see if I'm into it.

"There are cameras in here," I warn him.

He steps closer to me, pressing his semi into my stomach. "Then let's put on a show."

Fisting my hair, he tugs my head back before claiming my mouth. My tongue finds his as I melt into him. My hands instantly wrap around his neck, pulling him closer to me. This is wrong. This is inappropriate. This is...so good. His hands travel up my ribs, his thumbs splaying just under my breast. Shivers run through my body as he deepens the kiss.

"Excuse me?" I hear over the intercom, but I don't fully process it. All I can focus on is Caleb grabbing my ass and hoisting me onto the counter next to us. Pushing my legs open, he steps between my thighs and gives me a knowing smile. He knows what he does to my body whether we're in public or private.

"Hello? You can't do that here!" The same voice again.

"We're going to get in trouble," I pant as he peppers my neck with kisses.

"Do you want to stop?" His teeth clamp onto my ear lobe as I press my hips into his. Damn this man. Caleb snakes his hand between us when the door to the room flies open, smacking into the wall. I jump back, startled at the noise.

"Out!" the employee yells, pointing toward the exit.

I'm mortified. Embarrassed beyond belief. But Caleb doesn't give two shits.

"Gladly," he says, bending down, tossing me over his shoulder, and hauling me out of the building.

We're both still laughing as Caleb practically pushes me into his room.

"I've never been kicked out of an Escape Room before."

Caleb grabs my face, bringing it to his but stopping a breath from my lips. "Take off your top."

I dart my tongue out, licking his bottom lip before pushing him away. Grabbing the hem of my shirt, I pretend to lift it before pulling it down again. Caleb makes a growling noise that has me practically dripping.

"I said," he approaches me, grabbing my shirt, "take your top off."

"And what do I get if I do?" I ask with a cheeky grin.

With a wicked smile, Caleb helps me take my shirt off then starts on my pants.

"I want to see you," he whispers, guiding my pants and panties down my legs. I take turns lifting each foot to help him. Running his hands up my body, I quiver at his touch.

"You smell so fucking good," he tells me as he unclasps my bra.

Taking a step back, Caleb takes in my naked body. He's almost drooling like a dog and that's when I register he's still fully clothed.

I gesture to his clothes. "Don't think I'm going to be the only one naked here."

I giggle at how fast he strips down and tackles me to the bed.

I moan as his lips find my jaw, my neck, my chest. Watching me through hooded eyes, he takes my hardened nipple into his mouth, sucking and biting. My hips lift to find some friction when he releases one and goes to the other. My head falls back against the pillow, needing him. Needing more.

"Caleb," I breathe.

My hand tangles in his hair as his kisses move south. He makes it to my belly button when I stop him.

"You, you don't have to do that."

His brows pull together. "Don't have to do what?"

"Go down. I know a lot of guys think it's gross and I don't expect you to. It's okay."

Caleb's entire body freezes before he sits back on his knees, staring down at me.

"What?" I ask.

"I'm trying to understand what you just said. Are you a virgin?"

I shake my head. "No. I've had sex with two guys, but they never got me there. Honestly, I've only ever made myself come. Before you came along."

"As much as my ego likes that, I don't know what kind of boys you've been with in the past, but this man needs you to spread your thighs while he eats this beautiful pussy like it's his last fucking meal."

His words electrify every nerve in my body and before I can make a sound, he literally dives between my legs.

"Holy—" I gasp as his tongue licks a path up my center. My eyes flutter shut and I can feel his smile against my skin.

"Want me to stop?"

"Shut up and do that again," I beg.

He chuckles, sinking his teeth into the inside of my thigh. Grabbing locks of his hair, I guide his mouth back to where it should be. Caleb flicks my clit with his tongue and my body spasms. Gripping his hair, I tug hard, making him moan into me.

"This is, this is too much," I pant.

Instead of slowing down, which I thought he might do, he wraps his hands under my hips, propping me up and putting me on full display. Caleb quickens his licks and strokes and I'm so utterly close. Two thick fingers are thrust into me and I completely shatter. Stars fill my vision and I'm actually dizzy as my orgasm rockets through me. Caleb's lips trail kisses along my inner thighs as I try to catch my breath.

"I think I'm dead. I think I've died and gone to heaven."
He chuckles against my skin. "It's a great way to go."

Lifting my head from the pillow, I stare down at him. "It's never been that intense before. Is it always supposed to be like that?"

Crawling up my body, Caleb's lips hover over mine. "Just wait until I have my cock buried inside you."

Grabbing his face, I bring his mouth to mine. I've never had someone talk to me like he does. I love the filthy words he says to me while he does filthy things to me. Pushing his shoulders back, I roll us over so I'm straddling him. His hands knead my ass as I rock my hips back and forth. His erection is right there. So fucking close.

"You are so unbelievably sexy," he murmurs.

My phone begins vibrating on the floor. I chose to ignore it, most likely knowing who it is, and continue kissing this sexy-as-sin man.

"Do you need to answer that?" he asks.

I shake my head, nuzzling into his neck. "God, no. What I need is your—"

I grunt in frustration when my phone starts vibrating again. Without thinking, I jump off Caleb and power my phone down.

Resettling myself on his lap, I say, "Sorry about that. Where were we?"

I'm about to kiss him again when he pulls back. "Who was that?"

"No one. It was nothing."

"Doesn't seem like nothing. Your attitude changed pretty quickly."

Without thinking, I mutter, "Jesus, I don't want to talk about it. Can you just have sex with me already?"

Closing my eyes, I sigh heavily. That is not at all what I meant to say.

Caleb's face falls, his hands still not touching my naked body. "As tempting as that is..."

Rolling my eyes, I hop off him and get dressed. These stupid phone calls have to ruin everything. Neither of us says a thing and I leave before I say something else I'm going to regret.

I have no idea what the hell is wrong with me. I completely exploded on Caleb for no reason other than him simply asking what was wrong. The entire night probably would've turned out differently if I just opened up and talked to him, but it's such a long story. Frankly, I don't even care to talk about it. I want to forget that my dad even exists and move on with my life. Maybe I should change my number again? No, that never works. Mom will just give it to him. Again. I get that she and my dad had this incredible love once upon a time, but that doesn't excuse his shitty parenting. I love my mom and she deserves the best, but I hate how she stands up for him. In reality, he's nothing more than a glorified sperm donor. From what she's said, he only acted like my dad for the first two years of my life. I'm just over the whole situation. And now he's messing with Caleb's and my relationship. Well, it's not a relationship exactly. I'm really not sure what it is, but either way, my dad is finding a way to interfere.

I haven't apologized to Caleb even though I know I should. I've spent all morning thinking about it, but every time I go to text him, I can't find the right words. I mean, what do I say? Sorry for being such a bitch? Sorry for having major daddy issues? I mentally roll my eyes at my own thoughts.

"Something to add, Ms. Bardot?" my professor asks.

Oh my God, I actually rolled my eyes and the professor saw. Crap.

"No. Everything's great."

I smile to diffuse the tension, but she still gives me the stink eye. This time I make sure she isn't looking when I roll my eyes.

"All right, we only have about twenty minutes left, so let's—"

The door is swung open loud enough it crashes into the wall and everyone's head turns to see who it is. My eyes widen in horror as Caleb, Jace, and some other guy I recognize from the hockey team come running in. Caleb darts behind the professor's desk and crouches down to hide. Jace goes in between the filing cabinet and the wall. The other guy runs to the back and hides behind some students.

"What is going on?" the professor practically shouts.

Caleb holds his finger to his mouth. "Shh. It's called hide and seek. Not hide and tell everyone where you are."

"Well, this is—"

Everyone starts laughing at the guys. Some of the girls start whispering when they recognize who these idiots are. I stare at Caleb with a look that says *What in the hell are you doing?* He just smiles and winks at me like the jackass he is. Buzz comes barreling in the classroom and all eyes instantly go to him. Buzz sees Caleb first and goes for him, but Caleb jumps up, and to my horror, runs toward me.

He jumps behind me, placing his hands on my shoulders as Buzz approaches.

"Oh my God, are you actually using me as a shield?" I shriek.

Buzz and Caleb are in a stand-off, all the noise from the room instantly gone, before Buzz goes for it. Caleb jumps away, weaving in between desks and running back out the door. Buzz dives after him, bumping my desk and a few others in the process.

The professor's face is buried in her hands and she's shaking her head, probably wondering how many years until she retires. Jace and the other guy run out quickly and that's when the class erupts with full-blown laughter.

"I give up," the professor announces. "Just everyone, leave."

What in the hell just happened?

Chapter Twenty-One

Caleb

I'm leaning against the light pole across the street from Mangan Hall, waiting for Millie. There's no way her professor was able to get the class calmed down. When my girl stomps down the steps, looking left and right, I know my plan worked. Her eyes narrow once she finds me. I should probably be scared for my life, but I'm too proud of myself to be worried.

"You moron," she shouts as she smacks my shoulder.

Once I start laughing, she can't contain hers either. "You gotta admit, it was funny."

"Professor Kelly is probably going to blame this entire thing on me. Why did you have to hide behind me of all people?"

I shrug. "Didn't know anyone else in the class. But my plan worked. You got let out early."

"You're so stupid," she teases. I think.

"You're probably right."

Wrapping my fingers around the strap of her backpack, I pull her closer to me.

"There was a reason for that epic game of hide and seek."

"Oh, really?"

I brush a lock of hair behind her ear and scowl when the wind blows it back.

"You showed me something you like to do and I want to do the same."

"I'm not having a threesome with you," she deadpans.

"Dammit," I stomp my foot. "Now I have to think of something else."

Millie goes to push me away, but I grab her hand and interlace our fingers.

"Even though that sounds like an amazing idea, that's not what I was thinking."

She heavily sighs, knowing exactly what I'm thinking. "Caleb, I don't skate."

"I know. That's why I had to make this a surprise."

"I don't like surprises, either."

My smile is wide. "I know that too."

Millie drags her feet the entire way to Winger Sports Complex, but I don't let up. She's not getting out of this.

"You didn't even participate in the escape room. I shouldn't be forced to go skating when you couldn't even help me solve a few puzzles."

My hold on her hand is tight. "I don't think that argument would hold up in court."

Quickly looking around the arena to make sure coach isn't here, we duck into the hockey locker room. I find Millie a pair of skates and help her strap hers on after I do mine. I'm tying her laces when I glance up and find her biting her lip.

"What?"

She leans back on her hands. "You look good on your knees."

With a playful growl, I bite her knee and she giggles. Fuck, I love that sound.

Placing both my hands out, she grabs onto them and I pull her up. She wobbles for a moment, her grip almost cutting off the circulation to my hands.

"Damn, Kentucky. I won't let you fall."

Her smile is shaky and unsure. "You sure about that?"

"Trust me."

Being the asshole I am, I jump on the ice and show off my skating skills while she waits. I make sure to wink at her as I skate backward. Millie stands with her arms crossed, unamused and annoyed. Speeding up, I skid to a stop at the door, spraying her with a dusting of ice.

"I'm leaving," she says.

"I was just messing around," I laugh, grabbing her wrist and guiding her onto the ice. Her skates immediately go in opposite directions and I catch her under her arms before she falls.

"I can't do this. I don't know how. Just let me go."

"Hey," I whisper, getting her attention. "Just look at me. I'm not going to let you fall."

Millie and I both nod. I let her take a minute to get used to the slippery surface before moving my skates. Her body starts shaking and I tighten my hold.

"You won't let me fall?" she asks, forehead creased in worry.

"Not unless you piss me off," I tease.

Her body visibly relaxes and I guide her to the side rail. She holds tightly onto my hand while the other one is practically glued to the wall.

Her breathing becomes more steady the further we go. We're slower than a fucking turtle with bad knees, but she's doing it. I knew she could.

Wanting to help her relax, I joke, "I could probably find one of those skating trainer things they use for kids. You know, the kind made out of PVC pipe."

I laugh at her murderous glare. "If I wasn't terrified of falling right now, you would be so dead."

I keep my attention to her feet, making sure she doesn't trip over herself. Once we're further from where we came on the ice, I lengthen our strides slowly. I want her to be comfortable and enjoy herself.

"Want to tell me why you stormed off the other night?"

Her body stiffens and I almost regret bringing it up. Almost.

"Not particularly."

"Because whoever kept calling you put you in a pretty pissy mood."

"I wasn't in a pissy mood," she snaps.

"You were. Just like you are now."

"Then stop bringing it up," she says through gritted teeth. Pulling away from me, she grabs onto the side with both hands and stops.

I laugh humorlessly. "You can get as mad as you want, but I'm just trying to figure you out." When she doesn't answer, I add, "And unless you plan on crawling back off the ice, we're pretty far away from the door, so you need me to get back."

She heavily sighs and I think she's going to tell me to go fuck myself, but then she starts talking.

"It was my dad. He keeps calling and I don't want to talk to him."

"Your dad?"

She nods, swallowing thickly. "He left when I was young. I guess my mom and him had this, like, epic love affair. But then they got pregnant with me. He stuck around for a couple years but then he disappeared. We were a single income house and my mom..."

She lets her sentence trail off. I reach out, placing my hand over hers. Letting her know I'm here for her.

"She worked a lot and dated a lot."

My stomach sinks at her words. "Did—"

Millie doesn't let me finish. "Oh, God. No. They just were around all the time and most of them were creepy. I usually hid in my room when she had people over. Anyway, I basically raised myself. When I got to high school, I found out the real reason Dad left. Apparently, his love of booze was stronger than the love he had for us."

"Oh, baby."

"He calls every so often. Says he's sober and wants to make amends. If I'm remembering correctly, this is the third time he's 'gotten sober' in the past year."

She says "gotten sober" like it's the biggest joke in the world.

"You don't think he's actually sober?"

She doesn't even hesitate. "Fuck no. The last time he said he was, I took him to get breakfast, obviously I paid, and his mug was filled with more Jack than coffee. I know he's just looking for more money. He's never wanted a family. And I'm old enough to realize that I don't need or want him around ever again. So, he can call and call until his shitty phone battery dies, but I don't want to hear whatever he has to say this time."

"That's awful. I'm sorry." My voice is soft as I inch closer.

"Don't pity me," she scowls. "I don't need it or want it."

"It's not pity. I don't feel sorry for you. You're a big girl and can handle yourself. I hate that you had to go through something like that. There's a big difference between pity and empathy."

Millie's eye falls to the ice, her teeth nibbling on her lower lip.

"I am sorry for upsetting you the other night, but I won't apologize for wanting to get to know you."

I think growing up with a twin sister affected me more than I realized. Bonnie was screwed over by so many losers that she threatened me with castration if I ever acted like one of them. This ended up making me more sympathetic toward women. At least, I think so.

Hearing Millie talk about her family physically hurts me. I have a mom and dad who love each other, a sister whom I get along with, and a few animals at home. I know how lucky I am. My parents always encouraged my love of hockey by buying me the best pads or getting up at 5 a.m. and driving me to practice. I was taken care of and shown love every day of my life. Millie opening up about her shitty parents makes me want to change my major and become a science nerd so I can develop a time machine, go back in time and take her away from those awful people. Give her the life she deserved. The life she deserves.

Millie groans in frustration, looking back at me. "Dammit!"

"What now?"

"Stop being nice. Be a jerk so I don't feel like a total asshole for storming out."

I shrug. "I mean, if the shoes fits."

Millie takes me by surprise, shoving her elbow into my ribs, but loses her balance. Quickly, I wrap my arms around her waist, trying to catch her, but fail epically. Millie falls on top of me, us both a laughing mess. Water soaks through my jeans and as uncomfortable as it is, I don't care. Because Millie's mouth is inches from mine and I'm about to kiss her.

"Hey! You can't be on the ice! What are you doing?" Someone shouts at us and I curse, registering how screwed I'll be if coach finds out.

Millie's eyes widen in horror as I help her up.

"I thought you said we could be here."

"In theory."

Holding on tight to her, I skate us quickly off the ice and rush us back to the locker room. She hobbles the entire way, not familiar with how to walk in skates.

"I'm going to freaking kill you," she mutters under her breath.

There's a wet floor sign down the hall and I quickly grab it, placing it in front of the locker room door.

"There," I say, shutting the door behind us. "No one should come in and he's most likely almost done."

Millie's head falls to my chest, her shoulders shaking with laughter. "I can't believe I didn't fall and break my neck back there."

"You and me both," I chuckle.

Guiding her to the bench, I take off her skates before my own. She rubs her feet and I hope she isn't too sore. We weren't out there that long.

The silence envelops us. Millie gets to her feet, walking around and looking at the mostly bare lockers.

"How long do you think we're trapped?" she asks.

"Can't be too long." I stand, watching her take it all in.

"Hm. I wonder how we could pass the time," she says with a sly smile.

I don't move. I hold my ground as she walks up to me. I tower over her and I love it. Her hand slides up my chest, but I stay still. Standing on her tiptoes, she hooks an arm around my neck and pulls my mouth down to hers.

Her lips are warm and I love the little noises she makes when I kiss her. I'm not even sure she knows she's doing it. I grab her waist, pulling her against me. She gasps when I press my dick into her. I'm at half-mast and we've barely touched. My hand moves to the front of her jeans when she pushes me away. Her pink lips are swollen and sexy as fuck.

"I was just thinking," she pants, "you guys walk around in here naked. Don't you?"

My brows pull together. "Sometimes. Why?"

Her smile is devious as she continues to back away. "Just realizing this room has probably seen a bunch of dicks."

My jaw clenches. "Are you saying you're thinking about other guys' dicks while I'm kissing you?"

Millie shrugs, a wicked look in her eyes.

I take the two steps to her, my tongue licking my bottom lip. Her eyes are locked on my mouth as I run my hand down her neck, collarbone and land on her shoulder. "You can be a real brat sometimes, can't you?"

She bats those lashes at me, pretending she's innocent. Applying slight pressure with my hand, Millie sinks to her knees willingly. Shit, the sight alone has me about to blow.

"Take it out," I softly demand. With deft fingers, she undoes my belt and button then lowers the zipper. She's practically salivating as I pull down my briefs.

"Now use that smart mouth of yours on my cock."

I don't have to tell her twice. My entire body twitches when her lips wrap around the tip, sucking and teasing me. Her tongue darts out for a lick before quickly retreating.

I growl, pushing the hair back from her face and grabbing her chin.

"Stop messing with me and suck it."

In one quick motion, she pulls me to the back of her throat and I'm forced to grab onto the wall behind her to keep from falling over.

"Good girl," I groan and she hums in response. I feel the vibrations throughout my entire body. Her hot mouth bobs up and down, her tongue swirling around me. Each time I hit the back of her throat, her tongue licks the base of my cock. Fuck, I'm too close. I don't want to cross any hard lines she has.

"Millie, baby, I'm, you need to stop if—"

Digging her nails into the back of my thighs, she takes me deeper. Looking down at her, I'm mesmerized. I push her hair back so I can see my cock disappear down her throat. She's so eager to please. Every muscle in my body stiffens and with my next breath, I'm exploding in her mouth. She swallows me down, moaning in the process. Holy mother-fucking shit. That was incredible.

I'm still trying to remember how to breathe when she quips, "Took you long enough."

She's giggling, thinking she's so funny. My girl is perfect.

Wrapping my fist in her hair, I tilt her head back. "I don't think you're done yet. Clean up the mess you made."

Her hand slides up, under my shirt and against my abs as she licks my dick clean.

Chapter Twenty-Two

Caleb

After making sure the coast is clear, Millie and I rush back to my place. I'm not going to lie, I'm still feeling a little hazy from the best blowjob ever. Stripping off my hoodie, I plop down on my bed and watch her peruse my room. It's interesting to see what stuff she stops to look at. A trophy from my high school hockey team. Random notebooks – some used some not. She picks up a dirty shirt, pointedly looking at me. I shrug, not really caring that my room is a mess. This is me. If she likes it, great. If not, I really don't care. Okay, that's not totally true. I'm starting to realize I care a lot about what Millie Bardot thinks. Particularly what she thinks about me.

"What's your major?" she asks while flipping through a random magazine she found on my dresser.

"Sports Medicine."

"Why Sports Medicine?"

"In case I can't get into the NHL, I still want to be involved in the sport. Hockey is my life."

She nods slowly, dropping the magazine in search of something more interesting. She stops when she finds a picture of me and Bonnie.

And so the inquisition starts.

"What's your favorite color?"

I chuckle under my breath. "Blue."

"Favorite ice cream?"

"Mint Chocolate Chip."

"Who the hell likes Mint Chocolate Chip? You might as well save the money and eat toothpaste directly from the tube."

I can't help laughing.

"Do my rapid-fire questions bother you?"

I shake my head. "Not in the slightest. I'm an open book, baby."

"All right."

I can see the wheels turning in her head.

"How many people have you had sex with?"

My brow shoots up. "Wow. From ice cream to sex. I like it."

"That's not an answer."

Scrubbing a hand down my face, I sigh. "Actual sex? Four or five."

"If you could only eat one meal for the rest of your life, what would it be?"

I answer without hesitation. "You."

She chuckles. "Favorite position?"

I'm liking the sexual version of Twenty Questions, but I can't resist messing with her. "Right wing."

She fake laughs as she makes her way over to me. Pushing herself between my legs, her fingers tangle themselves in the hair at my nape. She's waiting for a real answer.

"Cowgirl. I enjoy the view." I can't help staring. I mean, her tits are right in front of my face. It would almost be an insult not to look.

Millie sighs dramatically. "Shame. That's my least favorite."

"Well, what's your favorite?"

She tugs on my hair, forcing me to look up at her. "Doggy."

My eyebrows shoot up, surprised at her answer.

Running my hands up her thighs, I grab her hips and pull her closer. She gets the hint and straddles me.

"I like how it feels," she mumbles, her lips inches from mine.

Fuck. Me too. Millie's tongue darts out, licking her lips and it's taking every single part of me not to pounce on her right now.

"We don't have to do this if you don't want to," I tell her.

She nods, pulling her lower lip between her teeth. "I know. I want this. I want you."

"You do?"

Leaning back, Millie strips off her shirt, her bra not far behind. Her tits are absolutely perfect. Round and big with the most perfect nipples my mouth needs to be on. I've always been a boob man. It's my thing. But I've never been with someone this busty. And fuck, I've been missing out. I grab one, kneading it while my mouth finds the other. She arches into me as my tongue flicks against the bud. Just like in the locker room, I want to know her limits. I want to push her just enough. Looking up at her, Millie's eyes are shut and mouth parted. Gently biting one and pinching the other, I watch her entire demeanor change. So I do it again, but harder.

"Caleb," she moans.

Her hips start moving, rocking against my swollen dick. I don't give a shit that I came not that long ago. I'm ready for as many rounds as Millie wants to go.

"You're so hard," she pants.

Grabbing her hand, I guide it between us and have her palm me.

"You're perfect," I say into her skin.

Millie places both her hands on my shoulders, pushing me back onto the bed. Crawling up me, she all but shoves her tits in my face. I groan as my mouth seeks out her nipples. Fuck, she tastes amazing. All the while she's rubbing her sweet pussy over my dick. I want all these clothes off immediately, but watching her take charge like this is incredible. Such a fucking turn on. She shivers as I run my hand down her bare back. Millie gasps when my hand collides with her ass cheek.

"I need you naked," I breathe.

"Only if you do that again," she teases.

It's not sexy or sensual, but we both jump off the bed and tear the remainder of our clothing off. Not able to wait another second, I tangle my fingers in her hair and bring her mouth to mine. Her tongue swipes against mine and I jerk in surprise when her fist wraps around my dick. Millie strokes me as I shove my hand between her thighs. She's soaked.

Millie leans her head back, moaning when I shove my finger inside her and take the opportunity to bite her lower lip. My girl likes it a bit rough. She's so tight, I'm afraid I'm too big for her. Wanting to get her ready, I shove another finger and her entire body stiffens. Releasing my dick, she wraps her arms around my shoulders, her legs shaking with need.

"Caleb," she begs.

"Tell me what you want."

"I want you to make me come with your fingers."

"I can do that."

"Then I want to watch you lick me off them," she pants.

I groan, reminding myself she needs to come at least twice before I even think about getting inside her. As a gentleman should.

My lips trail kisses across her cheek, to her jaw then her neck. My fingers move at a glacial pace, stretching her out for me. She's raised on her toes, nails digging into my shoulders as I lick a path up her neck and stop at her ear.

"Will you scream for me?" I whisper. "Let everyone in this house know whose dick you're riding. Who you belong to."

Millie nods frantically as I pick up my pace. Curling my two fingers,

I use my thumb to press down hard on her clit.

"Yes, yes, yes," she pants as her pussy strangles my fingers.

"I told you to scream," I order, my other hand slapping her ass.

"Caleb!" she shouts. "Caleb, holy hell!"

I ride her orgasm with her, watching the way she relaxes in my arms.

"That was…"

"It's not over yet," I tease.

Picking her up, I toss her on the bed, loving how her tits bounce when she hits the mattress. I can't help it, my mouth instantly finds her nipples. Giving each the attention they deserve, all while my fingers tease her clit.

"Do you think you're ready for me, baby?" I ask.

Reaching my hand up, I brush the hair out of her face as she nods.

"I want to see you the moment my cock enters you. The moment you realize there is no other guy that will make you feel this amazing."

Quickly, I grab a condom out of my nightstand drawer and am surprised when Millie rips it from my hand. Using her teeth, she tears open the foil before rolling it down my dick.

"How do you do that?"

"Do what?"

"Keep getting sexier by the second."

Her smile is infectious and we both laugh.

I'm lined up with her, the smallest movement would have me inside her, but I pause to look up at her.

"Are you absolutely sure? We don't have to do this if you don't want to."

Her legs are wrapped around my waist and she presses her heels into my ass, forcing me forward and into her.

"Fuuuuuuuck," we both mumble. She's warm and tight and every single wet dream I've ever had.

"Are you okay?" I ask, struggling to stay still. Not to be arrogant, but I know I'm on the bigger side. As much as I need to move this very second, I don't want to hurt her.

"Stop asking me questions and fuck me like you've been dreaming about since we met."

This fucking woman.

Millie whimpers when I pull back, sad at the loss until I slam back into her. Every inch of her swallows my dick. I think I now know what heaven is. Not wanting this ever to end, I take my time. Slowly pulling out only to pound back into her. Her hand encircles my wrist and I'm confused for only a moment. I force myself not to come instantly when she moves my hand to her throat.

"You look incredible," I tell her. Sweat beads down my forehead as I apply the slightest of pressure to the base of her neck. "Submitting to me like the good girl you are. You fucking earned every inch of this."

Placing the majority of my weight on the hand still on the bed, I increase my speed. Millie hikes her one leg up higher, helping me go deeper.

"Do that again. Don't stop. Please, Caleb." Her voice shakes with each request.

I oblige willingly. Her face pinches together the same time her fists twist in the sheets under us. She's clamping down on my dick and I'm seconds from exploding in her. I need her to come first. I need to see her fall apart under me.

"You're mine," I whisper at the same time she completely shatters. Her screams fill my ears and I follow her within seconds. My arm shakes from the weight of holding me up as I fill the condom. I said that I wanted to watch Millie realize no other guy would ever make her feel the way I make her feel. But I think I had it backward. Millie has officially ruined me for any other woman out there.

Chapter Twenty-Three

Millie

I got an e-mail this morning that my class ended up getting canceled - I have no idea why, but who am I to complain? - so I used the time to grab coffee with Bonnie. Recently we've been hanging out more and I'm finding out how much we have in common. For example, she likes sharing embarrassing stories of Caleb when he was young and I love hearing them.

I'm walking past the bell tower, but switch directions when I see a brooding Caleb hanging out on the steps surrounding it.

"You have a minute?" I ask Caleb, sitting down next to him.

"For you? Always."

"So cheesy," I mutter as I grab the package out of my bag. I freeze, debating if this is a bad idea or not.

Caleb nudges my shoulder with his. "What's that?"

"It's a present. For you."

My heart is about to fly out of my chest and I quickly toss the gift to his lap. I nervously laugh as I avoid his stare. I'm still not sure what kind of relationship we have, but I'm not sure if gift-giving is taboo or not.

"You got me a present?" His voice is full of curiosity and I chance a glance at him.

One corner of his mouth lifts while he turns the plain white package over in his hands.

"What's in it?"

"Have you ever received a gift before? You have to open it to find out what it is."

He nods like I just explained the most complicated thing to him. His fingers carefully slide under the flap, tearing open the packaging. His brow furrows in confusion as he holds the flimsy plastic in his hands. He holds up the different strips, each with a transparent window.

"Um, thanks?"

This time my laugh is more relaxed. "It's for reading."

His expression remains the same, so I continue.

"It's a reading guide strip. You lay it over the text and the transparent window helps section out sentences to make reading easier. Less confusing. I read about different products online and this one had great reviews."

My words begin to falter when he still doesn't say anything.

"Oh shit. Did I overstep? I was trying to help, but...It's okay. I can easily return—"

Caleb grabs the back of my neck, pulling me to his lips. I'm too stunned to move and that's when he starts laughing.

"Kiss me back," he mumbles.

"You're not mad? You like it?"

His lips ghost against the corner of my mouth, my cheek, my ear. "No one has ever gotten me something so sweet. Thank you, Kentucky."

Before he pulls away, I quickly brush my lips against his.

"I can even show you how to use it."

"Now you're just trying to get me hard," he teases. "What are you up to the rest of today?"

Caleb's hand rests on my knee, his thumb rubbing circles on my jeans.

I shrug. "Not much. My class got canceled and I was just getting coffee with Bonnie before I found you."

"So you've been walking around with my present all day in hopes of seeing me?"

I shake my head and groan. He may be a little bit right, but I will never tell him that.

"I'm about to head over to the training gym. Want to come?"

Caleb packs up his stuff and stands up, holding his hand out for me.

"What would I do with you at the training gym?"

"Why don't you come and find out?" Caleb wiggles his fingers and I reach out, letting him pull me up.

He holds the door for me as we enter the campus' Sports Complex. This building is ungodly huge. On the way over, he told me he just needed to grab something from his locker and would give me a tour if I behaved. I hate that his words sent tingles throughout my entire body.

"Everyone decent?" Caleb hollers into a room before grabbing my hand and dragging me in.

There are only a few guys milling around as my eyes sweep the room. Tables with padding on them, the kind you see at some doctors' offices, line one side of the room. The other has a few giant steel tubs, cabinets lining the walls, and some chairs.

"This is the recovery room," Caleb tells me.

"And what are those?" I ask, pointing to the giant tubs.

He chuckles to himself. "Those are for ice baths."

I stare at him. What did he just say? "What did you just say?"

"An ice bath. It's a bath—"

"With ice. Yeah, I get that. Why would anyone ever do something so sadistic?"

Caleb shakes his head, still laughing.

"Stop laughing," I demand.

"It's helpful after a game. Reduces inflammation and relaxes muscles."

"That sounds like some made-up bullshit."

At my words, an evil look crosses his face.

"You should try it."

My head jerks back. "Why on Earth would I ever do that?"

Caleb takes a deep breath. "You're right. You wouldn't be able to beat my time anyway."

The jerk has the nerve to start walking away when I step in front of him.

"Mind games? I feel like that's below you."

He steps closer, hovering over me. "We both know it's not."

Caleb and I are in a stand-off. After a few moments, I feel the eyes of the other guys in the room on us. We probably look ridiculous; Caleb's hands shoved in his pockets while he wears his smug grin and towers over me. Me looking up at him with my arms crossed and what I hope is determination in my eyes. He can't actually be serious. There's no way. Getting in a tub full of cold water and buckets of ice sounds like the slowest and most painful way to die. Okay, maybe not die. But this doesn't sound fun. Damn my competitive nature.

"Fuck it." I toss my hands in the air. "Do you have clothes for me to wear?"

His eyebrows shoot up. "Um, clothes?"

I gesture to my sweater and jeans. "I'm not jumping in wearing these and there's no way in hell I'm getting naked."

"Want my shirt? You could go in wearing that and whatever you have on under those jeans?" Caleb grabs the hem of his shirt, but I shake my head.

"And give you a free show? I don't think so."

Caleb's tongue swipes over his bottom lip. He's now realizing how serious I am. "You won't beat my time. Probably isn't even worth it to try."

I clutch my chest, pretending to laugh. "Just watch me."

Caleb finds me some clothes from the lost and found to wear. They smell musty and gross and just as I'm about to refuse, I remember his taunt. I will not let Caleb Booker beat me. Well, I at least won't go down without a fight. After the tub is filled, I stand and watch as bin after bin of ice is dumped in. The water splashes and I jump back. This is a really bad decision.

"Backing out already?" Caleb's at my back, doing his best to intimidate me. Little does he know, I'm too stubborn to back down now.

I straighten my spine and pray my nerves aren't showing. "Never. I was just thinking about what your face will look like when I destroy whatever time you hold. But you couldn't have given me clothes from your locker? I smell like a wet sock."

Caleb chuckles. "If you wore the clothes that have been stuck next to my hockey pads for weeks, I can guarantee you would smell worse."

I grimace as he pulls out his phone and clicks the timer app.

"You're not timing me," I tell him.

He tilts his head to the side. "And why not?"

"Because I don't trust you not to mess with the numbers. Obviously."

I swear Caleb rolls his eyes at me as he turns away.

"Jace, get over here."

Jace walks over and puts him in a headlock. They wrestle for a minute before Caleb jabs him in the ribs and he backs off laughing. Once Caleb explains what we're doing, Jace gives me an unsure look.

"You sure you want to do this? Ice baths are no joke."

I sigh heavily. I hate being doubted. "I can do it."

Jace nods, avoiding my gaze and focusing on his phone.

Caleb gestures to the tub. "After you, Kentucky."

My eyes widen as I stare at the ice cubes bobbing up and down in the water. "Me?"

"Yeah. You're going first."

"Um..."

"She's not going to do it," Jace mutters. "Stop messing with her."

I look at Caleb even though my next words are directed at Jace. "I don't know who this Jace guy is, but I hope you'll inform him that if he ever wants children in the future, he should watch how he talks about me."

Caleb's shoulders shake with laughter as I turn and face the tub.

"Is the timer ready?" I ask, hating they can hear the shake in my voice.

"Yep," Jace answers.

"Start it," I tell him, and then, before I can change my mind, step into the water.

The second my big toe touches the water, my entire body turns into an ice block. I try turning off my brain as I place both feet in the tub. I think I'm in shock or dying or something like that. I'm still standing after ten seconds and I honestly don't think I can sit down.

"Holy mother of—"

I don't get to finish my sentence as water splashes out onto the floor and arms wrap around me from behind. Caleb brings me down in the water with him and I realize I lied before. Now I am dying.

"Caleb! What the fuck?"

I'm sitting between his legs and he holds tight, pressing my back against his chest.

"Grab my arms," he orders. "Use me as your anchor, Kentucky."

My hands are violently shaking when he repeats himself. This time, I find his forearms and hold on for dear life.

"Think of something warm," he says into my ear.

"What? Are you kidding me right now?"

His voice remains calm as he continues, whispering in my ear, "You're on a beach. It's hot as sin and you have on the tiniest little bathing suit. Baby, you look perfect, and a bead of sweat trails down between your perfect tits. All you can think is you're so hot, you think you might die if you don't get in the water."

My breathing is erratic as I dig my nails into his skin.

"Say it," he demands. "I want to hear you say it."

"Ten seconds," Jace shouts.

"I'm on a beach. It's- it's warm."

"Time!" Jace yells and Caleb removes his arms, grabbing me and hoisting me out of the water. My entire body shakes and I'm nervous my knees are about to give out.

Caleb grabs a towel and wraps it around me before getting one for himself.

Pulling me in, he says, "You did it. You won."

"What? How?"

Jace grabs another towel and Caleb takes it from him, wrapping it around me.

"You beat Caleb's time," Jace says, turning the phone to show me.

I shake my head and not because I'm cold. "No. No, I didn't. He, he was in the water with me."

"Not for the first ten seconds," Caleb adds.

I can't feel any part of my body, so I'm not entirely sure my face shows the level of shock I feel.

Caleb pulls me close again, resting his forehead against mine. "You beat my time. You did it, baby. I'm so fucking proud of you."

Later that evening, after a very hot shower, Caleb and I are cuddling in his bed watching something on his TV. Honestly, I'm not paying attention. This might sound dramatic, but I feel completely drained after the ice bath.

"You cold?" he asks as I lay on his chest.

I nod and he grabs a blanket and tosses it over us. I'm already wearing his sweatshirt and sweatpants with thick socks, but the chill still lingers.

Soft lips graze my forehead. "You killed it today."

"I thought I was going to die," I admit, burying my face in his chest.

"Nah. I wouldn't let that happen. I'd be too bored without you around."

I pull back my arm to smack him in the chest, but he catches it and brings it to his mouth. His kisses against my knuckles are warm and have me relaxing further into him.

Chapter Twenty-Four

Caleb

Earlier today, I told Millie I was picking her up. I didn't tell her why or where we were going, but I knew her curiosity would get the best of her. Now we're in my car, driving to said surprise, and I'm so pumped for tonight, I'm shaking. With one hand on the wheel and the other resting on her thigh, I don't even try to hide my smile. This feels good. Whatever we're doing, this feels right.

"Seriously, where are we going?" she asks for the umpteenth time.

I shake my head. "It's called a surprise for a reason."

She groans. "I'm still recovering from the frostbite from my last surprise."

"This surprise won't be as cold," I say through a laugh. When she narrows her eyes, I add, "Promise."

"Won't be *as* cold?" She looks down at her jeans and thin long-sleeve shirt. "You didn't say we were going somewhere cold. I would've dressed warmer."

I take my eyes off the road for a millisecond to glance at her. "You're dressed perfectly. And you look beautiful. I don't remember if I told you that already and if I didn't, I apologize."

She bites her lip to keep from smiling.

"I guess you look good too," she teases.

Her face pinches in confusion as I pull into a parking garage. I'm out of the car and opening her door before she can question me again. I don't meet her eyes because I know not knowing what's happening is killing her. Instead, I walk to the trunk of my car and open it.

"I have something for you," I tell her and hand her the folded up fabric.

Her forehead creases. "Your hockey jersey?"

"Put it on," I gently demand. I bite my lip and groan when she does exactly that. "Good girl."

She rolls her eyes at me, but I see the smile she's trying to hide. "So why am I wearing this?"

Taking the hat off my head, I throw on my other jersey. Millie grabs the hat before I can put it back on and places it on her head. Damn, she looks good.

I pretend to look behind me before saying, "We've got time for a quickie."

She laughs, smacking me in the arm. "Come on! I'm dying. Just tell me."

Intertwining our fingers together, I lead her out of the garage. Her head spins in different directions as she puts the pieces together. Our jerseys, downtown, thousands of Penguins fans wearing black and gold proudly.

"We're going to a hockey game?"

"Not just any hockey game. Your very first NHL game."

The crowd is insane. It's been a while since I've been to a Penguins game and it feels good to be back. Even better that Millie's with me. After waiting in line for drinks and popcorn, we're finally sitting down as both teams skate around the ice, warming up for the game. I look over at Millie when some of the players are stretching and she looks like she's in her own fantasy world. Placing my fingers under her chin, I turn her face to me.

"How come you don't look at me like that?" I tease.

She giggles and leans over to kiss my cheek. "Little do you know, my favorite part about coming to your games are the stretches before."

"Really?"

"Yeah. Jace has a great ass."

Tongue in cheek, I wrap my arm around her waist and attack her ribs. She shrieks as my fingers find her ticklish spots.

"I was joking," she squeals. She's breathless from laughing, but I don't let up.

"Are you sure about that?" I smile.

"Yes," she pants, "you have a way better ass."

Laughing, I pull her into me and kiss her lips. "Damn right, I do."

From the get-go, the Penguins dominate. Their passes are crisp and stick handling is on point. By the end of the first, we have 16 shots on goal with only 4 shots on our goalie. We also are leading 1-0. In the second, a fight breaks out between a few players and when the crowd stands up to cheer on our guys, Millie joins.

"Fight! Fight! Fight!" chants throughout the arena.

Blood droplets cover the ice as two more guys join in.

"Get him!" Millie shouts. She jumps up and down and hollers with the crowd. When the guy next to her turns and holds his hand up, she high-fives it with hers. The girl I like is having fun watching my favorite sport; this is like a wet dream or something. When she sees me staring at her, she turns to me with a worried expression. Without thinking, I grab her by the neck and slam my lips against hers. My tongue sneaks into her mouth as she gasps. I don't care if this isn't appropriate for a family-friendly place. I'm so fucking turned on right now.

"You are fucking incredible," I breathe. Her cheeks flush and when she turns back to the game, I'm pretty sure her hand skims against my erection on purpose.

The third period is intense. After the Oilers tie the game with two minutes left, everyone is on their feet. With thirty-two seconds left, one of our defensemen takes ownership of the puck. The slapshot soars between players and up past the goalie's shoulder. Millie is holding the last bit of popcorn when the siren goes off. She jumps up and down, popcorn going everywhere as she winds her arms around my neck.

"We won," she screams.

I chuckle at how cute she is and join in with the applause.

I thought Millie was hot before I brought her to the game, but watching my girl scream and shout at the players was downright incredible.

Wrapping my arm around her shoulder, I pull her into me. "I think I'm confused. Was this a good surprise or bad one?"

Millie turns her body toward me, running her hand under my jersey and along my skin as she kisses me. Like the horny fucker it is, my dick twitches to attention and I have to pull back. I'm not opposed to the idea of sex in a public place, but maybe not where 20,000 Pittsburgh fans would be watching us.

"I'm glad you liked it, Kentucky. Let's get out of here."

Taking her hand in mine, I guide her up the stairs and we join the mass of people making their way for the exit. Millie grabs onto the back of my jersey, staying as close to me as possible. We're about to round the corner to the exit when some guy bumps into Millie, sending her to the ground. Luckily, she catches herself before her face smacks off the floor.

"You okay?" I ask, dusting some dirt off her arm.

"Yeah. I'm fine."

Hearing her say she's okay, I turn to the guy that bumped into her. Naturally, he's wearing the other team's jersey.

"What the hell?"

He's burly and smells of stale beer. I could easily take him.

"She was in the way. You guys need to walk faster."

"You need to apologize," I order.

He laughs this off, trying to walk around us. I step into his path as Millie grabs my arm.

"Caleb, it's fine. Let's just go."

"Yeah. Caleb," the guy spits. "Just go."

I shake my head, laughing humorlessly. "I don't think so. You either apologize for knocking my girl to the ground or your team won't be the only one suffering a beat down tonight."

He stares me down as if I'm going to back off. This guy couldn't scare a fucking mouse. To show how serious I am, I take a step closer to him with the biggest smile on my face.

"Come on, big man," I taunt. "Your decision."

He looks behind him at the traffic jam he created and huffs. "Sorry. Whatever. Just move."

"Since you asked so politely," I add, tossing my arm around Millie and making sure she makes it out of the building without any more stumbles.

Millie's quiet the entire walk to the parking garage, but the second we reach the car, she shrugs off my arm and turns on me.

"What the hell was that?"

"What are you talking about?"

"I can handle myself, Caleb," she snaps. Millie walks around me, opening the passenger door but she's not getting away that easily. I shut the door and when she turns to yell at me again, I place my hands on either side of the car, caging her in.

"He was a jerk and I wasn't stepping down. He could've hurt you and I don't like when people hurt what's mine," I practically growl.

Her features soften slightly when she starts giggling. "Yours?"

Fuck. This was not how I wanted to do this.

"Yes," I sigh. "I can't do this shit, Kentucky."

Her brow furrows in confusion. "What shit?"

"Whatever this is. I need you to be mine. All mine."

Millie's mouth pops open in surprise. "What do you mean? Like your girlfriend?"

A chuckle escapes me as I cup her face, my thumb running over her lower lip. "Exactly like that."

A slow smile spreads across my face and I can't wait any longer. I grab the nape of her neck and pull her mouth to mine. She sighs, wrapping her arms around my waist and stepping closer. Sliding my hand up into her hair, I tighten my grasp, and Millie moans as my tongue meets hers. What was supposed to be an innocent kiss turns hot and heavy real fast when she grabs me through my jeans. Without thinking any further, I reach behind her, open the passenger side door, and jump in. Millie bites her lip in excitement and tries to straddle me, but I stop her.

"I thought..."

Her words fade off when I pull the lever on the side of the seat and it shoots back, giving us more room.

"Get over here."

Millie and I laugh as she struggles to get her leg over my lap.

"Ow, shit," she mutters.

"Are you okay?"

"Yeah, I just hit my knee on the gear shift."

"Here." I slide slightly closer to the door and instantly regret it.

"Oh my God!" Millie gasps, realizing in trying to get comfortable her knee slipped and landed on my hard-on. I clench my jaw, not wanting to show how much pain I'm in. Fuck! It feels like she just snapped it in half. My head falls back, hitting the headrest as I try not to cry. Holy shit! That hurts more than I thought it would.

Millie is frozen on top of me, hands covering her mouth in shock. "Are you..."

She moves her hand to touch my shoulder as I struggle to breathe.

"I'm okay," I grunt, willing the urge to vomit to go away.

"I'm so sorry. I didn't mean to. Can I do anything? Do you want me to get off?"

I tighten my grip on her thighs. I don't want her to move an inch until I have this horrendous feeling under control.

"Don't move," I pant. "Just give me a second."

She nods. I can't tell, but I think there are tears in her eyes.

"Kentucky, I'm fine. I just hope you like me for more than my dick because I think you broke it."

Chapter Twenty-Five

Millie

"I really am sorry," I tell Caleb again as we walk into his bedroom. Well, I walked. He kind of limped up the steps. I thought about offering my help, but I figured I bruised his ego enough for one night.

The ride back to campus was quiet except for the music. I felt awful when my knee slipped, but with every single turn we took, he groaned more and more. I can't believe I've only had a boyfriend for a few hours and I already broke him.

"Millie. I'm fine. Really."

"Are you sure I didn't actually break it? I could take you to the doctor—"

Caleb chuckles, "Hell no. Once the need to vomit went away, it wasn't too bad."

I glance down at his crotch then quickly back up to his face.

"How's it feeling now?"

He shrugs. "Better."

I want to fix what I did. Make him feel better. Biting my lower lip, I take a few steps closer to him. "Would it help if I gave it a kiss?"

His eyes practically pop out of his face like a cartoon character as I get on my knees.

"Um," he stammers, "it's definitely worth a try."

Quickly, I undo his button and zipper then pull his jeans and boxers down. I look up with a wicked smile as I grab his hand and guide it to my hair. He knows what I'm trying to do and instantly tightens his grip. I want to make him feel good and I know being in control does that.

Carefully, I wrap one hand around the base and lightly kiss the crown. I feel his body shiver under me as he sighs.

"How's that feel?" I ask innocently.

"Heavenly," he groans, guiding my head back down.

I let him control me as I wrap my lips fully around his hard-on. I'm still nervous about the damage I did to it, so I lessen my movements and slow my pace. I run my free hand up his thigh and around to his perfect ass. I swear, it's not fair he has a nicer ass than me. My tongue swirls around him as I move my head. When Caleb's hips jerk forward unexpectedly, my nails dig into his ass.

"Fuck," he grunts. "Sorry. You just feel so good. I love your mouth."

I moan around his cock, feeling myself getting wetter by the second.

I start moving my head faster when Caleb says, "I love your mouth, but I love your pussy more."

Before I can blink, Caleb has me up and straddling his lap on his bed. When did he take his shirt off? I lift my arms in the air and he rips my shirt off then quickly undoes my bra.

"That's better," he mumbles before his mouth finds my nipple. I arch my back into him, inhaling sharply when his teeth bite down.

"Caleb," I pant.

"My dirty girl likes that, doesn't she?"

Caleb's mouth moves to my other breast as his fingers slip into my leggings. My hips move on their own, dying for friction.

"Caleb, please," I beg.

"What do you want, Kentucky?"

"Touch me."

I yelp as Caleb flips us over so my back is on the bed and he's between my thighs. Lifting my hips, I let Caleb strip me. He licks his lower lip as his gaze slowly takes in my naked body.

"Where should I touch you?" His fingers land on my collarbone. "Here?" They move to my shoulder. "Maybe here?" Down to my belly button. "What about here?"

I narrow my eyes and he just chuckles.

"I know," he continues, sliding down my body and grabbing the back of both my thighs. "How about here?"

I gasp when his mouth lands on my clit and his fingers stroke me.

"Yes. Oh my God, yes. There."

He laughs and the vibrations tickle. His tongue licks slowly and it's so painful, it almost hurts. I squirm, trying to get him where I want and he places a hand on my belly to stop me.

"Give me your hand," he orders.

I do and he drags it down to where his is.

"I want you to play with yourself while I eat this delicious pussy."

His words only make things hotter and I obviously have no choice but to do as he says.

I've always had trouble with pleasuring myself. I don't know if it's because I'm too in my head or because I know what's coming next, but it rarely makes me orgasm. The second my middle finger brushes my clit, I already know this time is different. I'm beyond sensitive and my body jerks as I rub circles while Caleb's tongue does truly evil things. The low stirring in my belly is there and it's getting bigger by the second. Caleb's hand snakes up my body, pinching and rolling my nipple between his fingers. My body is almost in overload. There's too much happening and I can feel myself about to combust any second. I look down at Caleb when he moves his mouth and starts sucking on the finger I was using to get myself off. In that moment, I know I'm done for. Stars blur my vision as I explode, Caleb's hand covering my mouth so the entire house doesn't hear my screams. He kisses my inner thigh before crawling back up my body.

"I think I'm dead," I tease.

Caleb laughs as he kisses my jaw, my neck, my collarbone. His lips feel incredible and I want them on every square inch of my body. He sits up, reaching for his nightstand drawer and fishing out a condom. He rips the foil packet open with his teeth and why is that so damn sexy?

"Are you sure this won't hurt you?" I ask, genuinely nervous about breaking a part of him I'm very fond of.

His smile widens and he leans down, brushing his lips against mine.

"I promise."

With his answer putting me at ease, I reach down as I lift my hips, and guide him inside me.

"Fuuuuck," he moans.

I start moving my hips when he grabs one of my ankles and puts it on his shoulder. When he does the same to my other ankle, my brows shoot up into my hairline, never having done something like this. The first thrust has me seeing God or whoever is up there. Holy hell! How have I never heard of this position before? Every thrust of Caleb's hips has him hitting that perfect spot.

"Holy...this...Caleb!" I say, struggling to form a sentence.

He smiles, tossing his head back as he picks up speed. That stirring in my belly is back and bigger than before. I'm barely given a warning before I'm squeezing down on him and falling to pieces.

Caleb's brain is working way faster than mine right now because I barely process when he flips me over onto all fours. I look over my shoulder to see Caleb lining himself up with me and bite my lip in anticipation. Thank God he isn't done yet, because I need more of him. His hand slides up my spine, leaving goosebumps all over me. Caleb fists my hair, tugging my head back the same time he smacks my ass. The sensation is surprising and exhilarating.

"Do that again," I tell him.

"Do what? This?" He smacks me a little harder and I swear I'm so close to coming again.

Caleb fists his dick, rubbing it over my center.

"Caleb," I shout.

"Yes, Kentucky?" he asks through a laugh.

"Either stop teasing me or I'm going to find someone else to—"

My words are cut off by a sharp slap on my ass. Instantly, his hand massages where he just hit.

"Now, now," he tuts, "that's not any way to speak to your boyfriend, is it?"

I can't help my smile at remembering that he's my boyfriend and I'm his girlfriend. I'm having sex with my boyfriend and his incredibly talented dick. I am so lucky.

I lean back at the same time Caleb pushes forward and my eyes roll back into my head.

"Yes!"

"Do you think anyone else could make you feel this way?" he asks with another powerful thrust that has the headboard colliding with the wall.

"No," I pant. "Never."

Leaning down, Caleb whispers in my ear, "Say that again with your hands on the headboard."

Doing as he says, the change in position has me squirming against him. All at once, Caleb's hand is in my hair, his dick pounding into me while he smacks my ass again. My muscles shake and I'm struggling to hold myself up as I come apart at the seams. I have never orgasmed this many times before. Caleb has to be a wizard or some shit.

"Look at you," Caleb says, still riding out my orgasm with me. "You take my cock so well. Such a good girl."

It's only moments later that Caleb finds his own release.

Caleb and I are walking into Winger Sports Complex, heading toward the rink for his game. We're here ridiculously early because the team is supposed to arrive for games hours in advance.

"Good luck, boyfriend," I tell him. I pull away from our intertwined hands when he tightens his grip, dragging me to him and brushing his lips over mine.

"Thanks, girlfriend."

"We're disgusting and obnoxious," I tease.

"Don't act like you don't love every second of it."

"Are you going to win?" I ask as I run my hands down his chest. He's wearing a suit and looks way too good.

"You gonna give me a present if I do?" His hands wrap around my lower back, slowly sliding down to my ass.

I shake my head. "That's too easy."

He grips my ass hard, making me giggle. "What do I have to do then?"

"That depends. What do you want?"

He swallows thickly and I think I'm going to like whatever he says. "You. Naked. Underneath me." Letting go of me, he runs his fingers over his tie and holds it up. "With this covering your eyes."

My eyebrows shoot up to my hairline in surprise. His eyes darken as he runs his thumb over my bottom lip.

"You'd look so fucking good like that."

Electricity lights up every inch of me. I gasp and he smiles, knowing exactly what he does to my body.

"That's," I force myself to swallow the sand in my mouth. "That's a pretty big reward."

He nods, agreeing with me.

I may not know a lot about hockey, but since Caleb and I started getting closer, I've done some research. I think now is the perfect time to showcase my new knowledge.

"All right. You can have that if you give me a Gordy Howe Hat Trick."

A self-satisfying smile spreads across my face at his complete and utter shock. Taking a step back, he looks me up and down.

"And here I was, thinking you couldn't get any sexier."

I giggle, raising three fingers. "A goal, an assist, and a fight."

Caleb clutches his chest and pretends to tumble backward. "Holy shit, Kentucky. You did it. You actually got sexier."

"So, do we have a deal?"

"Do you know how rare it is for a college player to get a Gordy Howe Hat Trick?"

I shrug. "Big risk, bigger reward." I'm waiting for his response when some of his teammates start piling in.

"Come on, Booker!"

One of the guys tosses his arm around Caleb's shoulders and pulls him away. I'm turning my back to them when I hear Caleb shout, "You have a deal, Kentucky!"

I'm sitting in the bleachers, waiting for the game to start when Bonnie and Zola drop down on either side of me.

"Ew," Bonnie groans. "You and my brother are going to be that kind of couple?"

"What kind of couple?"

She gestures to my jersey. "The kind that flaunts their affection all over the place."

"It's a jersey," Zola laughs. "Be happy it's only that. My friends from back home are together and this one time I went to meet up with them at a bowling alley and they were full-blown making out. Like she was straddling him before the game even started."

Bonnie starts smacking her forehead.

I grab her hand to stop her. "What are you doing?"

"Trying to get the mental image of you and my brother doing that out of my head."

Zola and I laugh at Bonnie's reaction. It's only a jersey. It isn't that big of a deal. Is it?

Both teams skate out onto the ice and when Caleb winks at me, all I can think about is the tie he was wearing earlier. I wonder if he's actually going to pull it off. I don't know a ton about hockey, but a goal, an assist, and a fight seem like a lot for one person. Caleb has a look of determination as he gets in position for the puck drop.

The majority of the rink is filled with students, but a good amount of townies fill the seats too. Different chants and cheers filter through the room and the atmosphere is incredible. The excitement of the game is contagious. Every time Caleb jumps on the ice, my smile grows even bigger. He's never out for more than a few seconds, but he makes those seconds count. I glance up at the scoreboard with less than one minute left in the first period. Caleb and Jace both hop the board, Jace somehow taking possession of the puck the second his skates hit the ice. My jaw hits the floor when Jace passes the puck to Caleb and he takes the shot. Bonnie is the first to jump up when the goalie dives and misses the puck. Everyone is chanting "Booker" while I'm standing there in shock.

Holy shit! He might actually do it. Flashes of him running his fingers down his tie run through my brain. I've never done something like that before. Come to think of it, before Caleb, I really didn't do much of anything. I had sex before, but it never involved a lot of foreplay. And the dirty talk. The guys I'd been with barely made noise let alone spoke. Caleb's words turn me on almost as much as his physical touch. Being blindfolded makes me incredibly nervous, but in a good way. I trust Caleb and I know he would never do anything that would make me uncomfortable.

We're halfway through the second period when the other team scores, tying the game. Our boys don't seem fazed. The lines are switching when the ref throws his hand in the air. Jace is called for checking, resulting in a power play for the other team. Jace hangs his head as he skates to the penalty box - or, according to Google, the sin bin - as our team prepares to be down a man. The small amount of BYU fans cheer on their team as they score. Looking at the penalty box, I see nothing but rage. The second Jace is released, he skates faster than he has the entire game. Skating along another player, I think Kai, they pass the puck back and forth before Jace sends the puck through the goalie's legs.

"Is Jace really hot or is it just me?" Zola asks through a laugh.

"They're all hot," Bonnie agrees. "Well, everyone but 13. You know what I mean."

"I don't know. Number 13 is pretty sexy, especially when—"

Bonnie plugs her ears with her fingers. "Blah, blah, blah. I can't hear you."

Lowering her voice, Zola leans in closer. "Okay, but seriously, how is the sex? I might say Caleb is even hotter than Jace."

I bump my hip against hers. "I don't kiss and tell. However, I do know Jace really likes his puck bunnies. At least, according to Caleb."

Zola rolls her eyes. "Of course, he does. Doesn't matter anyway. I like the nerdy ones. I'll take a guy with glasses and a bowtie any day."

Bonnie pretends to gasp. "Does this mean you're officially done with Blane?"

Zola rolls her eyes. "You know his name is Blaze."

"Same thing."

I silently chuckle as we both wait for Zola's answer.

"I haven't heard from him since the night Caleb almost choked him out. Other than missing some good weed, no love lost there."

"Caleb did what?" Bonnie shrieks.

Neither of us gets a chance to answer Bonnie when the crowd roars to life as the players skate circles around the rink, scuffing up the pristine ice the Zamboni just smoothed out.

Bonnie nudges Zola. "What do you mean Caleb choked someone out?"

Zola shrugs. "That's what Millie said. I don't remember it. All I know is Millie and Caleb showed up to save the day and it's been silence ever since."

My heart is racing as the third period begins. So far, Caleb has only gotten a goal. He's good, but is he good enough to get an assist and in a fight in only twenty minutes? I gasp, covering my mouth in shock, when we score again. I'm not sure his name, but the only guy on our team with a man bun got the shot...and Caleb got the assist. I start laughing to myself that this really might happen. I'm on the edge of my seat for the rest of the game. The ref is about to drop the puck with thirty seconds left. Before he does, Caleb looks up and points at me in the stands. The second the puck hits the ice, so do Caleb's gloves. And his helmet. Caleb squares up against the forward, grabbing his jersey and slamming his fist into his ribs. Each guy only gets a few hits in until the refs pull them apart. The crowd cheers as we win 3-1. Oh my God. He actually did it.

Chapter Twenty-Six

Caleb

The guys continue shouting and cheering all the way back to the locker room. We kicked some ass tonight and can't wait to celebrate. Personally, I can't wait to see Millie's expression when I blindfold her with my tie. Scratch that. This is not the time nor place to get a stiffy.

"All right, all right. Settle down," coach yells over us. After a few seconds, we each take a seat. Johnson shakes his head and sweat from his hair splashes me and the guy next to him. Uproars start again until coach pins us with a stare.

"Tonight was a night. Each of you destroyed BYU and I couldn't be prouder. Now, I know I usually give a speech after each game, but I think after a Gordy Howe Hat Trick, Booker deserves the honor."

Applause erupts and I jump up, waddling to the front of the room since I'm still wearing my skates.

"Thanks, Coach." He shakes my hand before patting me on the back.

"That was incredible, but next time we could do without the dirty fight."

I shrug as some of the guys toss their sweaty towels in my direction.

I take a moment to look around at each of my teammates. We did this together. We beat one of the toughest teams in our league together. Millie definitely gave me the boost I needed, but this win feels truly amazing.

"I'm trying to find words. It's still kinda surreal that we won. As coach would say, we each made sure to remove our heads from our asses before we entered the building and now we get to reap the rewards. Let's fucking party!"

The guys all jump up, slamming into each other and cheering while Coach stands off to the side, shaking his head in disapproval. Though he couldn't hide the smile on his face if he tried.

Stripping down, I shower and get dressed quickly. I'm too anxious to see my girl and claim my reward. When she said the words "Gordy Howe Hat Trick" earlier, I almost fucked her right then and there. I know she's never been a hockey person before, so that means she had to research what that meant. It was so fucking hot. Grabbing my tie, I let it hang around my neck instead of tying it. Let her mind wander as to what tonight holds for her.

"See you at the party?" Jace asks as we walk out together.

I nod, scanning the arena for Millie. When our eyes meet, she squeals before running full speed at me. I drop my bag just in time to catch her and spin her around.

"You did it! You did it! You did it!" she shrieks as she kisses my cheeks, forehead, and nose repeatedly. "I'm so proud of you!"

It's been a long time since I've heard those words from anyone but my coaches and it takes me by surprise.

"You are?"

She nods, pressing her forehead against mine. "So proud."

My hand drifts from her lower back down to her ass and squeezes. "You know what this means?"

"That we're going back to my place to have a quiet night of cuddling?"

I laugh before whispering into her lips. "You're going to look so good tied up."

She gasps and then pouts when I lower her to the ground.

"Let's go to the party."

Her brow furrows when I put my hand in hers and pull her toward the exit. "The party? I thought—"

"Anticipation is half the fun."

Ballentine is packed by the time we get there. We have to park a few houses away and when we walk into the party, I tell one of the freshmen to move my car before they leave. Winger U has a strict rule on no hazing which we all abide by. We do, however, have a tradition of freshmen doing our grunt work. Within seconds of grabbing beers for Millie and me, she's whisked away by Zola and some other girls. I smile as I join my buddies, knowing how anxious she is for what I have in store. Contrary to popular belief, I've only been with a handful of girls in the biblical sense and none of them have ever been kinky enough to let me blindfold them. If I mentioned doing something out of the norm, they would get all skittish. Needless to say, it was never love at first sight. But with Millie...I don't know. She's pretty fucking spectacular.

I nurse my beer, wanting to be sober for later, when Jace sidles up to me.

"We fucking did it!" he shouts in my ear.

I lean away from him. "How do you already smell like a distillery?"

He shrugs with a stupid drunk smile on his face. "I pride myself on how efficient I can be when alcohol and a win are involved."

I shake my head, taking a small sip. My eyes are pinned to Millie's ass. There are way too many douchebags here for me to let her out of my sight.

Jace's gaze ping-pongs between me and Millie. "You two still good?"

"We're great. She's—"

Jace pats my back. "No need to share all the gushy details, bro. I'm gonna go find myself a bunny."

He tosses back the rest of his drink and is about to walk away when I say, "You should be careful. You're going to get an STD one day and you can't afford to lose any more brain cells."

He chuckles like an idiot as the sea of drunken students part for him, inflating his ego even more. I roll my eyes as I make my way to the kitchen to dump my drink. Someone tries to stop and talk to me, but I have my sight set on someone more important. I give them a high five, then stalk toward my girl.

"Caleb," she shrieks mid-conversation when I toss her over my shoulder without warning. "Put me down, you caveman!"

She smacks my ass as she laughs. "Sorry to interrupt ladies, but this one is coming with me."

I tighten my arm around her thighs as we move through the party, up the stairs, and into my room.

She giggles the entire time, even when I toss her down on my mattress. Her jersey rides up, exposing a sliver of her belly and I lick my lips.

"See something you like?" she teases.

I growl as I grab her legs and wrap them around me. She gasps as I press against her core.

"You're hard already?"

My hands run up her sides, under the jersey, until it's bunched up around her neck. "Have been ever since you said the words, Gordy," I press my lips to her jaw, "Howe," then her cheek, "and Hat Trick," I whisper the last words into her ear.

The laughter dies in her throat when my hands find her tits. She's wearing something that's mostly lace which leaves little to the imagination. Bending down, I bite one nipple through the fabric, causing her to buck her hips under me.

"Watching you wearing my number and cheering for me as we beat the shit out of BYU was the definition of foreplay."

She moans as my tongue darts out to lick the pebbled nipple. "This is pretty good too though, right?"

I smile against her skin as my fingers find the tops of her bra.

Her eyes widen instantly. "If you rip this bra, I'm going to be pissed. It's brand new."

"Bill me," I say before tightening my grip and tearing the fabric. It rips a lot easier than I thought it would. Millie's gaze is filled with rage and before she can tear me a new one, I lean down and capture her lips with mine. Her tongue swipes against mine as my one hand grabs her breast and the other rubs her through her thin leggings.

"Take it off," I demand.

"Take what off?" she pants.

Helping Millie to her feet, I take two steps backward. "All of it."

Her chest heaves up and down as her eyes focus on my painful hard-on.

"Now," I say, my voice more stern.

Millie shimmies out of her leggings, tossing them to the side. Then her fingers grab the bottom of the jersey which rests at the top of her thighs. She pretends to lift it and then pulls it back down.

"You're playing a dangerous game that you most certainly aren't going to win."

She lifts a shoulder. "I was just thinking maybe you would want to fuck me while I wore your number."

I deserve an award for not falling apart in that moment. Holy shit! She really is perfect. As I take the few steps to her, she lays back on the bed, sliding up toward the headboard.

Running my fingers down my tie that's still around my neck, I glance up to her for reassurance. I know we made a deal, but I don't want to push her if it's too much. She noticeably takes a deep breath and nods. I crawl up the bed, settling myself between her thighs. She instinctively wraps her legs around my waist.

"Are you sure?"

Another nod.

Her eyes are filled with heat and lust as I drape the striped fabric across her eyes. She lifts her head, letting me tie a knot - not too tight - behind her head. "Still good?"

This time it takes her a second and I'm about to rip the blindfold off her when she nods again.

Leaning back, I take a moment to admire how amazing she looks. Millie's breaths are controlled and calm. The fact that she trusts me tugs at my heart. Before Millie, if I would've thought something like that, I would've kicked my own ass. Now, it feels right.

Resting my hands on her knees, I slowly stroke them up her outer thighs, enjoying her shivers of excitement. Continuing the same path, my hands find her ass and I pause. An evil smile spreads on her face.

"Are you not wearing anything?" I ask, shocked knowing that the leggings she wore tonight were incredibly thin.

"I am. It's just a thong."

My fingers dig into her ass as I press my dick against her.

Letting go, I lift the hem of the jersey to find the teeniest tiniest scrap of black lace. The same lace that matches her bra that is now on my floor. Grabbing the flimsy string that holds this tiny excuse for underwear together, I tear it away before her mouth even opens.

"Caleb Booker!" she scolds. Her hands instantly go for the blindfold, but I grab them and pin them above her head.

Her breathing turns slow and shallow. "Do you have any idea how delicious you look right now?"

Sliding my hands down her arms, I kiss every inch of her skin that I can reach.

"Don't move your hands," I tell her as my face sits inches from the most beautiful pussy I've ever seen. I know she can feel me on the bed, but I'm careful not to touch her. I don't want her to know what's going to happen next. I sit there until she calls my name, curious what I'm doing.

Only then do I grab her thighs and shove my face between her legs. My mouth instantly finds the small bundle of nerves and I hold down her hips to keep her body from moving. She struggles as I continue sucking while shoving two fingers inside her. Her moan echoes through my room, only urging me to move faster.

"Caleb, wait, Caleb—"

I knew waiting would get her pent up, but I didn't think it would happen this quickly. She explodes over my hand and mouth and I lap up every single drop she has to give. Her thighs tighten around my head and it's then that I decide that if she squeezed too hard, this would be a great way to die.

"What just happened?" she asks through labored breath.

She can't see me, but that doesn't stop me from sucking each finger that was in her clean.

"I was having my dessert."

Running my hands up her belly, she sucks in a breath when my fingers tug and pull on her nipples. Fuck, her tits are perfect. I can't get enough of them.

When she tries to move her hands, I say, "Tsk, tsk, tsk. I said don't move."

"Please," she begs. "I need to touch you."

Grabbing a condom out of my side drawer, I put it on and line myself up with her center. Dragging my aching cock up and down her wetness has her panting like crazy.

"Caleb, ple—"

Her plea turns into a scream when I thrust all the way in. I suck in a harsh breath and everything is silent for a moment. Giving her a moment to get comfortable, I pull out slightly only to thrust back in even harder.

"Fuuuuuuck," I moan. "You're so tight."

"Again," she pants. "Please. Again."

I chuckle to myself as I grab one of her legs and place my other hand just below her throat. Picking up speed, I watch her tits bounce beneath my jersey and her hands fist into the pillows above her head. Millie picks her hips off the bed, meeting my thrusts. It makes hitting that spot inside her even easier. I hoist the leg I'm holding higher and what I'm guessing is an involuntary scream bubbles out of her.

"Caleb, I'm gonna—"

"I know, baby. Me too. You want me to come in that tight pussy of yours?"

"God, yes!"

Millie lets go of the pillow, grabbing onto my shoulders. I groan as her nails dig into my skin at the same time as she tightens down on me. Tingles travel up my spine, but I hold off, determined for her to come again before I do. I am a gentleman after all. Reaching between us, I use my thumb and forefinger to pinch her clit. She spams beneath me, screaming out my name and scratching those sharp nails of hers down my back. The twisted part of me hopes she draws blood. I want to have those scratches forever. Millie is still coming, but I can't hold on any longer. I fist the sheets next to Millie's head, focusing on keeping my body upright as she milks me dry.

Finally, I collapse on top of her. My lips find her throat when she starts giggling.

"That- that was..." Millie never finishes the statement, instead grabbing my face and kissing me.

Chapter Twenty-Seven

Millie

Another day, another stupid horny guy who thinks he's so funny when he repeatedly asks for samples. I'm handing a customer their change when a group of guys stride past the store. My eyes recognize Raphael and that's when I remember I was supposed to message him about the payment plan for my car.

"Can you take over for a second?" I ask Becks.

She shrugs which I take as a yes.

Wiping my hands off on a rag, I run out the door.

"Raphael!" I shout, waving my hand back and forth. It's then that I realize I probably look crazy. I take deep breaths, trying not to die, when he says something to the group he's with and walks back to me.

"You good?" He chuckles at my disheveled state.

"Yeah. Totally." I take a final deep breath and stand back to my full height. "I wanted to tell you that I get paid tomorrow, so I can get you at least two hundred."

His face pinches in confusion. "Two hundred for what?"

"Um, my car?"

Raphael's gaze darts around the street as he rubs the back of his neck.

"Look," he gets out his wallet, thumbing a couple bills and trying to hand them to me. "Here's your money back."

"Wait, what? I'm super confused."

Raphael drops the bills in my hand as he sighs. "I figured Caleb would've told you by now."

"Told me what?"

Caleb

I just finished some homework and am about to go lie down when I hear a loud door slam. One of the guys probably pissed off a puck bunny again. At least, I think that until my bedroom door is flung open and one pissed off looking Millie storms in.

"You entitled, arrogant, idiotic—"

"Who pissed in your cereal?"

Apparently, that was the wrong thing to ask because she uses both hands to push me. When she backs up and turns for the door, dollar bills flutter to the ground.

"Woah!" I grab her just before her hand wraps around the knob and pin her back to the door.

"Let me go," she demands, fighting against me.

"What is your deal?" Grabbing her hands, I lift them above her head and then pin her hips with mine. "And did you just toss money at me?"

I have no idea what is going on and why she's so mad, but I haven't done anything to warrant this. At least, not recently.

"I talked to Raphael."

And now I know what I did.

I close my eyes and sigh. Maybe I can play this off without her knowing.

"Talked to him about what?"

"About what?" She fights my hold and I press down harder on her wrists. "About you paying to get my car fixed, you idiot!"

"I'm an idiot because I wanted to help get that hunk of junk fixed?"

That definitely wasn't the right thing to say. "That hunk of junk wouldn't have needed to be fixed if it weren't for you. And that money I gave you is my down payment. I don't have all your money now, but I can get you more after a few paychecks. Now, let me go."

I laugh. Is she kidding right now?

"If I let you go, are you going to try to run away again?"

"Of course, I am! I don't want to be anywhere near you."

I roll my eyes and adjust my grip. "That's not the right answer."

She pushes her hips against mine, I'm assuming in an attempt to get free, but all it has me doing is stifling a groan.

Her breathing finally slows. "Why? I could've paid for it myself. Why did you have to interfere?"

Resting my forehead against hers, I breathe her in. She smells like whipped cream and cherries like she always does after work.

"I felt bad," I admit. "Your bumper was hanging on by a thread and I knew you couldn't afford to fix it right away. That's why I had Bonnie tell you about Raphael. He's a friend and I knew he wouldn't refuse my money."

Her mouth pops open. "So you admit it was your fault."

"What?" I shake my head. "Fuck, no. That's not what I meant. I meant you wouldn't be in this mess if you didn't hit my car."

Millie's jaw clenches and she growls, actually growls, at me.

"You are beyond infuriating, Caleb Booker."

"Back at ya."

Slowly, I release her. My hands falling down as I take a step back to give us both some space.

"I'll pay you back," Millie says after a few seconds of silence.

"I don't want your money."

"And I don't want your charity. Just tell me the total cost and I'll pay you back."

I know Millie doesn't make a ton of money at that ice cream shop. I also know that Millie isn't exactly rolling in extra cash - her words, not mine. I didn't pay for her car out of charity, I paid for it because I knew she wouldn't be in this situation if it weren't for me. I know I didn't hit her and she insists she didn't hit me, but one of us is wrong.

"Look," I scrub a hand down my exhausted face. "I was just trying to do something nice, but if you feel like you need to pay me back, the total was fifteen hundred."

Her mouth opens and then freezes. Like her body is buffering, not sure what to say after hearing the real price.

"Um, yeah. Okay. I can totally do that. It-it may just take a little longer than I thought to pay you back. But I can do it. I will do it. There's always random shifts for people to pick up."

I start full belly laughing.

Her brows furrow. "Why are you laughing at me?"

"Oh, Kentucky." I cup her face and pull it to mine. "I'm not taking any of your money."

I press my lips to hers before she can protest.

I'm leaving class when someone grabs onto my backpack, jerking me backward.

"Where you heading off to?" Beaver asks. "We're all heading to Oister for lunch."

I shake him off me. "I'm good. Got plans."

"What plans?" one of Beaver's friends asks. I don't even know his name, so I have no idea why he's questioning me.

"I'll catch you guys later."

I'm walking away when I hear Beaver yell, "Whipped." I ignore him until he lowers the volume of his voice. "No pussy can hold me down."

I know he's kidding. He's just messing around with his friend. But he's talking about Millie. My Millie. Inhaling slowly through my nose, I try to remain calm.

Yeah, fuck that.

Beaver's a lot bigger than me. Taller and broader. He could probably kill me with his pinky finger. I don't care. I grab his collar and pull him to me.

"Say something like that again. I dare you."

He puts his hands in the air, making sure not to touch me. He doesn't want a fight. I don't really want one either. I like Beaver. But he crossed a line just now and he needs to know that.

"Take your hands off me, Booker. It was just a joke."

"Not about my girl. Don't say shit like that about her ever again."

Prying each of my fingers from his shirt, he takes a step back.

Beaver and I have been on the same line for a while now. He watches my back and I watch his. We know each other's cues on and off the ice. Like when the other is about to explode in the worst way possible. After a tense moment, Beaver nods his head in agreement.

"Sorry, man. Was just screwing around."

My heart rate slows down and I scrub a hand down my face. "Shit. I'm sorry."

A smile forms on his ugly mug. "You really like her."

"Yeah. I really do."

The thing that's great about being a guy is you forgive and forget quickly. I was pissed as hell at Beaver for that stupid comment and the second he realized he messed up and apologized, I was over it.

Before I met Millie, I used to think guys who put their girlfriends before everything were such pussies. I now see how unbelievably stupid I was. I still want to hang out with my friends. It's even better when Millie wants to hang out with me and my friends. But I love spending time alone with Millie. The more I learn about her the more I like her. Really like her.

Just as I'm heading into Heslin Hall, the doors to Millie's class open. Students filter out as I impatiently wait. When she doesn't come out with the rest of her class, I step closer to see what the hold-up is. Through the doorway, I can see her discussing something with her Professor. She's nodding at whatever he says and then he puts his hand on her elbow. That's kind of weird. My phone goes off in my pocket and they both turn to figure out what the noise is. Millie's face lights up as the Professor drops his hand and takes a step back.

Millie runs up, placing a chaste kiss on my lips. "Hey, boyfriend."

"Dork," I tease her. Grabbing her books from her hands, I carry them in one hand and hold her hand with the other.

"Sorry about that. I just had a few questions for Professor Weckman on one of the homework assignments."

"That's Professor Weckman?"

She nods. "But I don't want to talk about class. I'm starving."

My eyes dart to the right, watching a janitor exit a room. Without words, I lead her to said room. Jackpot. It's an empty janitor's closet. It's actually pretty clean and I quickly lock the door behind us.

"Caleb," she whines, "I said I was hungry."

I drop my backpack and her books on the ground before taking her backpack.

"I know you did. But like the selfish asshole I am, I think I need to eat first."

Millie's eyes widen when I drop to my knees and quickly undo her pants, dragging them and her lace panties down her legs.

"Here?" she shrieks. "Someone could hear us."

Fuck, she smells good. "Then be quiet."

She tosses her head back against the door when my tongue licks one long, slow path up her center.

"Mm. I've been craving you all day."

At first, I'm not entirely sure she's into this. That changes when she twists her fingers in my hair, holding me to her. Lifting her right leg, I place it over my shoulder to give me better access.

Her legs shake and her grip tightens as my lips close around her clit.

"Caleb," she pants as I suck on her.

"Kentucky," I warn. "I said be quiet."

With a smug grin, I thrust two fingers into her. She gasps loudly as I curl them, then covers her mouth to muffle her sounds.

"Are you still hungry?" I ask.

She laughs, tightening down on my fingers moving in and out of her.

Snaking my hand up her shirt, I knead her tit, rubbing my thumb over her hard nipple.

Pulling my fingers out of her pussy, I grab onto her ass and bring her closer to me. My tongue licks up everything she has as she comes in waves. Her body shakes under me until she collapses onto the floor in front of me.

"All right," I breathe, my forehead against hers. "I'm full. Let's go get you something now."

Chapter Twenty-Eight
Millie

"You really should just come over. My bed is so comfy, however, my room is super warm. You should wear as little as possible. Actually, forget that. Wear whatever you want and I'll help you take it off when you get here."

I smile, holding the phone to my ear with my shoulder as I gather my notebooks. "Perfect. I'm putting on my negligee right now."

"Really?"

"No," I giggle. "The roomies and I are having a homework party."

"No offense, but I don't think any of you know the definition of the word 'party.'"

"Ha. Ha." I deadpan.

"You really aren't coming over?"

"When did you get so needy? I'm not complaining, I love the attention. It's just surprising. And no, I'm not coming over. I really have to get this paper done for Weckman's class. It's a huge portion of the grade and I'm determined to ace it."

There's a shuffle in the background and the sound of Caleb closing a door, shutting out the noise. "Okay, well maybe I could come to your party? You could study whatever a forensic science major studies and I can study you."

"You're insane. I'll call you later."

Caleb groans as I hang up the phone.

Making sure I have everything, I head down to the living room. Zola is in the recliner scrolling on her phone, Bonnie is sitting on the floor spreading out flashcards and I make myself comfortable on the couch.

Two hours later, I feel elated that my paper is done. It's then that I realize I haven't moved the entire time. Neither have Zola or Bonnie.

"Um, has anyone moved since I came down here?"

Bonnie and Zola look at each other and shake their heads. Each of us stands, a stream of cracks filling the air.

"Ouch!" Zola whines.

"Why did you guys let me sit on the floor that whole time?" Bonnie complains, rolling her neck side to side.

"The couch really wasn't that great either," I groan.

"I want a chicken wrap," Zola announces after stretching her arms above her head. "And I need to walk off this soreness. Who's coming?"

Bonnie and I remain quiet.

"Seriously? It's not that far."

I look down at my outfit then back to Zola. "I'm wearing cheetah pajama pants, a shirt with a hole in the armpit, and no bra. I'm not going anywhere."

Bonnie just shrugs. "My clothes are fine, but I don't want to leave. I'm going to have my leftovers."

"Ugh," Zola growls. "Fine, but if anyone touches my ice cream, I'll cut a bitch."

Bonnie and I just laugh because Zola angry just looks like a little kitten.

Once Bonnie heads into the kitchen, I lay down on the floor with my legs on the couch. It's a struggle to get in the right position, but it feels amazing for my back. I feel around for my phone and when I find it, pull up my message thread with Caleb.

Millie: My lower back is so sore.

Caleb: I know a good stretch for that ;)

Millie: You're an idiot

Caleb: Haha. Why are you so sore? I thought you were supposed to be studying...

Millie: I was on a roll. Finished my paper and I'm actually pretty happy with it

Caleb: That's amazing, Kentucky!

Millie: Except for the fact I was hunched over

on the couch the whole time — two hours to be
exact

Caleb: How about next time I see you, I'll give
you a nice back rub

Millie: That actually sounds amazing

Caleb: ...without clothes

Millie: *rolling eye emoji*

Caleb: Fine! I'll be the one with clothes and you
can be the one without. Better?

I don't answer. I just laugh as I toss my phone next to my head. Closing my eyes, I focus on my breathing and just relax. Until my phone starts ringing.

"I will be keeping my clothes on, thank you very much," I say, holding the phone to my ear.

"Um. Okay?" Zola says and I cover my mouth.

"I thought you were—"

"Obviously. Look, I actually need you."

I roll over and sit up at her words. "What's wrong?"

She hisses and then exhales sharply. "I think I rolled my ankle. I was walking down the steps outside Loewen Hall and tripped on something. Well, now it hurts to put pressure on it."

"Shit," I jump up, grabbing a sweatshirt and pulling it over my head. "Where are you?"

"Still on the stairs. It's humiliating. Can you please come help?"

"Already gone." I click the end button and then run into the kitchen to get Bonnie.

I share the story with Bonnie as we drive over to where Zola fell. I pull up onto the curb near the staircase and we both jump out. I want to cry for Zola when I see her curled up in a ball on the steps, rubbing her ankle.

When Zola sees it's us walking down the step, she whines, "I just wanted a chicken wrap."

The ER was insanely busy and the wait took forever. Bonnie, trying to be a good friend, went up to the front desk to ask why Zola hadn't been seen yet and that just happened to be at the same time some guy rolled in on a gurney with a chunk of metal sticking out of his leg. Bonnie quickly apologized to the nurse and we all continued waiting. Three hours later, Bonnie and I wheel Zola in her hospital provided wheelchair back to her room.

"This is so embarrassing," Zola mumbles, her hands covering her face as she lies on a rubber mattress.

"It could be worse," Bonnie says.

Zola drops her hands and narrows her eyes. "How the hell could it be worse?"

Bonnie shrugs. "You could be pregnant."

"What?" Zola shrieks.

I roll my eyes. "Nothing. Let's just wait until the nurse comes in before we get upset."

"I'm already upset," Zola whines, covering her face again. "And I'm so hungry."

While we're waiting, Zola continues sulking, I scroll around on my phone and Bonnie paces the room.

"What do you think this does?" Bonnie asks, holding something with a tiny flashlight on it.

"I have no idea. Stop touching stuff," I chuckle.

"What about these?"

I chuckle at the green bag she's holding. "I do know that one. It's an emesis bag."

"And what's that?"

"It's to throw up in."

She yelps, dropping it on the floor.

I'm still laughing when the nurse knocks on the door.

"Can you tell me exactly what you were doing when you hurt your ankle?"

We all turn our attention to Zola whose cheeks are tinted pink.

"Um, just tripped. Is it bad?"

"It would help us determine the course of treatment if we knew exactly what happened."

Zola throws her head back on the pillow and groans. "I was checking a notification on my phone and missed the step. Okay? I tripped over nothing and then tried to catch myself, but obviously didn't."

I gently smack Bonnie's arm when I notice her biting her cheek, trying not to laugh.

"I just wanted a chicken wrap," Zola whines.

"All right. We need to get an X-ray of your foot just to be sure, but I'm pretty sure it's just a sprain. Rest when you can, ice twenty minutes on than twenty minutes off, wear a compression wrap, and elevate your ankle when you can. We can also give you some crutches to help you move around for the next few days while it's sore."

After her X-ray concludes that she has a sprain, Bonnie and I take Zola back to the apartment. Zola struggles with the crutches, but we're both right next to her, ready to catch her if she falls.

"Where do you want to set up camp?" Bonnie asks.

Zola's head darts left to right, debating on trying to climb the stairs or not.

"I guess the couch is fine."

Zola hands me her crutches while Bonnie helps her lay down, covering her with a blanket.

"Why don't you get some rest? I have to run out, but can you watch her, Bonnie?"

"It's a sprain," Zola says. "I'm not an invalid."

Bonnie and I look at each other and once Bonnie nods in agreement, I turn and head out the door.

Chapter Twenty-Nine

Caleb

"I'm starving," Kai complains.

"We were just at the dining hall," Buzz says.

"Yeah, but that food isn't as good as the food in Oister."

Oister is the student complex in the center of campus. The bottom floor is a mini-cafeteria with made-to-order food stations and the top floor is used for campus activities and events.

"You guys are morons," I mumble.

We continue our walk across campus when I fish my phone out of my pocket and frown. Zero notifications. I'll never admit it to the guys, but I've pretty much been checking my phone every ten minutes since I last spoke to Millie.

"Hey," Kai smacks my arm.

Putting my phone back in my pocket, I smack him back.

"Isn't that your girl?"

I follow his gaze and don't even bother to hide my smile.

"Whipped," Buzz mumbles.

Walking ahead, I shout back, "You have your entire life to be an idiot. Why not take today off?"

I jog toward Millie before Buzz can respond.

"Kentucky!" I shout over the crowd.

She stops what she's doing and looks around, but still doesn't see me. I take the opportunity to double back around and she gasps when I wrap my arms around her from behind.

"You dumbass," she smacks my hands that are splayed out on her stomach. "You scared me."

I chuckle, holding her tight to me and kissing the side of her head.

"What happened to you today? I didn't realize homework was an all day thing."

Millie sighs and I grab her hips, turning her around. "What's wrong?"

"Zola tripped going down the steps, so she, Bonnie, and I spent the afternoon in the ER."

"Shit, is she okay?"

She nods. "Just a sprain. But she was on her way to get lunch when she fell and she was so upset about it. She kept saying how all she wanted was a chicken wrap."

"Anything I can do to help?"

A devious smile appears on her face as she drapes her arms around my neck. "Well, I actually was on my way to Oister to see if someone could still make her a chicken wrap even though it's dinner time. I know they'll have them for lunch tomorrow, but that's not the point. I just feel really bad. Plus, all we ate in the hospital was vending machine food, so I know when she gets up she'll be hungry."

Leaning down, I kiss the corner of her lips. "You are an amazing friend, you know that?"

Not wanting to let me go, Millie pulls me closer, capturing my lips. It's an innocent kiss, just our lips touching. But the second she begins moaning, I'm desperate for more. I think I actually wince when she pulls away.

"I bet there's a janitor's closet somewhere," I tell her. I've been missing her all day and that little kiss alone gave me a semi.

She chuckles, shaking her head and pushing away from me. I reluctantly let her go and intertwine our fingers together as we walk down the hill and through the double doors.

"Come with me," I say, dragging her to the food station in the very back.

"Zeke! My man!"

He looks up from the grill, a huge smile on his face. "Caleb, what's going on?"

Pulling Millie close, I put my arm around her shoulder. "My girl needs a chicken wrap. Can you hook her up?"

He shakes his head. "It's dinner time."

"Please?" she asks. Millie steps closer to the glass separating us. "My roommate fell and hurt her ankle earlier when she was on the way here. I kid you not when I say she's been talking about having a chicken wrap for the past five hours."

Zeke's gaze bounces back and forth between us.

"I work tomorrow. Have her come in and I'll make her one."

Millie sighs heavily. "Please? I know this would make her so happy. She has to be on crutches. Well, she doesn't technically have to be. It's only a sprain, but she's really upset about it. Pretty please?"

Millie clasps her hands in front of her, batting her eyelashes at him.

303

Grabbing the back of her shirt, I pull her back to me. I don't care if it seems territorial. The only guy she's allowed to bat her lashes at is me.

Zeke shakes his head. "Give me ten minutes."

I follow Millie out of Oister, one hand holding hers, the other holding a bag with a chicken wrap in it. She's almost giddy that she was able to get the wrap for Zola which is kind of adorable. It's then I remember the eyelashes. Releasing her hand, I smack her ass and then jump away quickly.

She gasps. "What the hell was that for?"

"I saw how you were looking at Zeke. Those bedroom eyes are only supposed to be for me," I tease.

Millie takes two steps to me, running her hands up my chest and around my neck. "I was just being friendly."

My free hand grabs onto her waist, sliding to rest on her lower back.

"I could've used that friendliness a little earlier today. I was so lonely," I gripe.

She pulls her lower lip between her teeth, giggling at my dramatics. "You were very helpful with the important mission of getting Zola her wrap. I suppose I do owe you. What do you want?"

This time it's me she's looking up at through those thick lashes and, fuck, I love it. I love—

"I assume you want to hang with your roomies tonight?" I ask, interrupting my own thoughts.

"I think so," she says, nodding. "I wasn't kidding when I said Zola was pretty upset and I don't want to leave her hanging."

"Tomorrow?"

She tilts her head to the side, brows pinched. "Don't you have practice?"

I wave her off. "Not until later."

"Okay." She leans up on her toes, her lips trailing kisses from my jaw up to my ear. "What do you want to do?"

Without meaning to, I growl and tighten my grip on her. "You. All of you. Naked and begging for me."

Her hands slide down my body as she pushes away, taking the bag with her. "Call me tomorrow," she says, backing away from me, "and I'll let you know if I'm free."

Before I can answer, she spins around and skips away. I don't move an inch as I watch her ass sway back and forth. God, she's perfect.

Chapter Thirty

Millie

I probably look like a dork, but the second I drop my paper in Professor Weckman's inbox, I smile with a sigh of relief. It feels as if a huge weight has been lifted off my shoulders. I'm on cloud nine as I head back to my apartment, but freeze at the sight in front of me. A rusted Oldsmobile sits in our parking lot and I know it wasn't there before. My smile slowly fades away when my eyes land on the extremely faded bumper sticker.

"Holy fucking shit."

I run the rest of the way, flinging my front door open to only find my mother sitting on my couch. No. What? How? Why? I can't even form a coherent thought. She sits, legs crossed and her fingernails drumming on her knee like she's being inconvenienced right now.

"I've been waiting for you. Where have you been?" She demands more than asks.

My jaw is still on the ground when I remind myself I need to answer her. I need to get her out of here. Where she is, my father isn't far behind.

"What are you doing here?" I finally ask.

Her shoulders slump. "Millie. Aren't you happy I'm here? I came to visit you. I missed you."

"Does your phone not work?"

A quirk of her brow tells me she's getting impatient. "The strangest thing happened. Every time I called, it went straight to voicemail. Then when I went to leave a message, it said your mailbox was full."

It is full. With messages from her and Dad. Ones I haven't listened to but haven't deleted because I don't want them to be able to leave anymore.

I divert my gaze. "Is he here?"

"Honey, I came to see you. I missed you—"

"Mom." I sigh heavily, "Is he here?"

Finally, she stands up and approaches me. "Your father has been working very hard at his sobriety and all he wants is to make amends with his daughter."

I bark out a humorless laugh. "I fucking knew it!"

She acts shocked, placing her hand on her neck and gasping. "Language, Millie."

"Learned from the best. I knew you didn't come to just see me. It'd be too good to be true. How did you even get in my apartment?"

"Your roommate with the curly hair let me in. She was waiting with me but then had to leave for class. Honestly, she was watching me as if I was a thief trying to steal your recliner with a hole in it."

I shake my head, exhausted with her being here already. "Bonnie wasn't watching you to make sure you didn't steal anything. She was probably wondering why it took you months to visit my apartment. It doesn't matter. You need to leave."

"Excuse me?"

"I said you need to leave, Mom. You can't just show up here, insult my apartment and roommates, and expect me to show Dad mercy just because he donated his sperm."

Her eyes widen, but I continue talking before she can say anything. "You want to believe he's sober? Fine, you can live in your own world of delusions. But I choose reality. Like the reality of my fifth birthday. Do you remember that? Dad was sober and promised to get a clown for my party. Instead, he spent the money on booze and showed up as the clown himself. He reeked of whiskey and cigarettes and fell into my cake. I lost a lot of friends that day."

"Millie—"

"Or what about when I was thirteen? He randomly showed up as I was getting picked up for my first date ever. I was so excited to go to the movies, but Dad told my date that he had to be careful not to get me pregnant since I just got my first period. As you can probably guess, I wasn't asked out by anyone for a long time after that. And those are only two of his shining moments."

"Millie, would you just hear him out? I get that he made mistakes. We all do, but," she walks around me and opens the front door, "I think you need to give him the benefit of the doubt. He is your father."

I open my mouth to tell her to leave when a guy with a scruffy beard, fedora, and baggy clothes stands in my doorway. He stubs his cigarette out on my stoop, a cloud of smoke still surrounding him. His face has more wrinkles than I remember and when he smiles, I see he's missing a front tooth.

"Hey, kiddo."

"Dad?"

My heart plummets into my stomach. This has to be some horrible dream. I pinch my arm, wincing at the pain. The disappointment that this is all real overwhelming me.

He shrugs. "I don't look that different. Do I?"

I nod. "You do, actually. Constant drinking and chain smoking can do that to a person."

He scrubs a hand over his face. "Millie, I—"

"I'm going to tell you and Mom what I want. And for once in my life, I need you both to listen."

I wait to make sure neither of them are going to object. Mom looks like she's about to, but thinks better.

"I want you both to leave. I want you to stop calling. Dad, as much as I want to believe you're sober, I can smell the rum. Mom, your breath isn't much better. I truly believe you two are soulmates and need each other. But I don't fit into that equation. Maybe one day if you decide to put your daughter before your own selfish needs, then we'll talk. But for right now, I need you to get out of the apartment I paid for with no help from either of you."

I'm proud of myself for keeping calm. Not raising my voice or getting angry. For a moment, I think my words sunk in and they are actually listening.

"You need money?" Dad asks. "I got money. I can help pay for things and stuff for you. This bookie owes me money."

"Dad," I sigh, "I don't want your money. I just, I need you both to leave. I have never asked either of you for anything, but I am now. Just leave. Please?"

And because the universe is twisted, Caleb chooses this exact moment to appear.

"Everything okay, Kentucky?"

"Who are you?" Dad asks, eyeing up Caleb like a real father would.

Caleb looks to me before answering and when I shake my head, he doesn't say anything. He just walks around, taking my hand with his. My mom frowns at our joined hands and I take that as our cue. I pull Caleb into the apartment with me.

"Goodbye," I say, closing the door.

I should cry. I should feel sad and upset. I don't, though. I feel...relieved. I've spent my entire life being mad and hurt about my parents, but I don't care anymore. I don't care that Dad prefers drinking himself to sleep instead of talking to me about my day. I don't care that Mom would rather spend the night at some random guy's apartment than read me a bedtime story. I don't care anymore. Because I've finally realized something. I'm not the problem. They are.

Chapter Thirty-One

Caleb

I'm holding Millie to me, hugging her tight as I run my hand up and down her back. I have no clue what just happened, but I do know she needs this.

"Kentucky? Are you okay?"

She nods her head and I hold her tighter. Millie says something, but it's muffled by my chest, so I pull back.

"What?"

Her shoulders sag. "Those were my parents."

Shit. Grabbing the back of her neck, I pull her to me and brush my lips against her forehead.

"It's okay. I'm okay," she says barely above a whisper.

"Are you sure?"

She nods again, running a hand through her hair. "I actually think I am. I needed that."

Millie closes her eyes, inhaling through her nose and exhaling through her mouth. "Shit. I think I really do feel better."

"Really?" I ask, running my hands up and down her arms.

She nods, a slight smile on her face. "Yeah. I know people usually don't say this kind of stuff about their parents, but it kind of feels like closure. I said what I needed to say and now I'm ready to move on with my life."

Wrapping my arms around her, I pull her into me. My chin rests on her head and I have the biggest smile on my face. I'm one lucky son of a bitch.

Millie said she wanted to shower and change clothes, so while she was upstairs, I ordered us takeout.

"Smells delicious," she says as she bounces down the steps. She definitely seems in a better mood. Almost lighter. Millie instantly goes to see what kind of food I got us and I take the opportunity to wrap my arms around her from behind and breathe her in.

"Yes, you do."

"I'm too hungry right now," she groans, shimmying away from me.

I jerk back, feigning hurt. "Are you telling me hungry trumps horny?"

Millie turns around and pops a fry in her mouth. "Every time."

We eat in comfortable silence on the living room floor with the television playing in the background. I want to ask if she's okay. I want to ask if she wants to talk about what just happened with her parents. But I don't want to push her.

Her eyes are glued to the show when I nudge her foot with mine. "You know you can talk to me about anything, right? I'll never judge you."

"I know that," she says softly.

"If you need to vent, I'm all ears. If you just need someone to sit and be with you, I love sitting. And if you need advice, I'm sure I could find someone to give you some."

She tries, but fails to hide her smile. "You're an idiot."

"Yeah, but I'm your idiot," I tease.

She's only silent for a few moments before heavily sighing. "My Aunt Cora helped raise me."

"Mom's or Dad's sister?"

"Neither. She was actually my neighbor. I have no idea why I called her my aunt, but she felt like family. She was such a good stand-in mom that it broke my heart she could never have her own kids."

Resting my hand on top of hers, I ask, "Where's Aunt Cora now?"

"Saint Theresa Funeral Home. She passed when I was a junior in high school."

My heart breaks for her. The girl who just wanted a family. Fuck, just wanted a mom.

"Shit. I'm so sorry."

She smiles, but it's sad. "Thanks. She had a brain aneurysm that burst while she was sleeping. The doctor said they thought it was quick. She didn't suffer, which is all you can hope for, I guess. I don't think I've ever told someone about her before. I think you might be like my safe space or something."

My hand cups her face, wiping away one lonely tear.

"Aunt Cora was an amazing woman."

"Who raised an amazing woman."

You would think after such a heavy conversation things would feel intense and overwhelming. It actually feels the opposite. I feel even closer to Millie and I love that. I love that she trusted me with such personal details of her life. I am honored to be her safe space. After we're done eating and throw all the trash away, she lays her head in my lap and I stroke her hair as a new movie comes on.

"That feels amazing," she practically purrs. So I don't stop. "I forgot to tell you. I turned in my Weckman paper. I feel pretty good about it."

"That's amazing, Kentucky. I'm proud of you."

"You are?" she asks, sitting up and looking at me.

"Are you serious? Of course, I am. I know how hard you worked on that assignment."

I grunt when she tackles me, causing us both to fall to the ground. Her lips are on mine as she giggles in excitement. I quickly silence her when my tongue touches hers. Sliding my hands around her waist, I dip under the hem of her shirt. I can feel her goosebumps under my fingertips as I rub small circles on her lower back. I'm hard in a second and roll my hips against hers. She gasps, so I do it again. The noises she makes are intoxicating.

"More," she pants.

Millie's hand finds its way between us and is undoing the button on my jeans when the front door opens.

"Shit," Millie says, quickly and awkwardly trying to push herself off me.

Zola just laughs and shakes her head. "I'd say get a room, but—"

"We just got carried away."

I chuckle as Millie attempts to defend our actions. Groaning from the hard-on I'm now stuck with, I sit up and kiss Millie's cheek.

"I'm her safe space," I tell Zola, clearly glowing with pride.

Zola laughs us off. "Just so you know, Bonnie should be home soon and I think she'd prefer not to see her brother sporting a woody in the living room."

Millie squeaks, covering her face in embarrassment. I, however, laugh at Zola's taunt as I grab a throw pillow off the couch and place it over my lap.

"Don't worry," I say, "I was just about to carry Kentucky up the stairs. Real caveman-style."

"Just make sure you don't get any blood on the floor when you hit her over the head with your club. It'd be a bitch to clean up."

Millie sighs. "You two are awful."

Chapter Thirty-Two

Millie

The rest of the week was pretty mild compared to how emotionally draining Monday was. From finally confronting my parents to telling Caleb about Aunt Cora, I enjoyed the little breather. I was excited to hang with Caleb this weekend. I forgot, however, that he has an away game so now I'm moping in bed.

"Why aren't you dressed?" Bonnie's leaning against my bedroom door, arms crossed against her chest. She's wearing ripped jeans with a Winger U t-shirt and her hair is in pigtail buns with yellow and blue ribbons.

I'm laying in bed in a sleep shirt and joggers with no intention of moving anytime soon. "This is me dressed. I have big plans tonight of scrolling on my phone until I get tired and sleeping through the entire weekend."

"That seems a bit dramatic," Zola adds as she strolls in, decked out in similar clothes.

I grunt as I force myself to sit up, letting my legs dangle off the mattress. "Why do you both look like Winger U cheerleaders?"

"How else are we supposed to let the Puffins know we aren't there for them?"

"I must be really tired because I have no idea what you two are talking about."

Zola looks at Bonnie and shakes her head. "Her boyfriend's been gone for less than two hours and she's already malfunctioning."

"Shame," Bonnie adds.

"Wait. You guys are going to the game?"

"Ding, ding, ding, we have a winner," Zola announces in a voice mimicking a game show host. "And what has our winner won?"

"A seat in the back of my car if she can be ready to go in twenty."

I stripped out of my PJs and into leggings and Caleb's jersey before Bonnie and Zola even left the room. Bonnie had to finish getting ready, so Zola helped me pack my overnight bag. Once everything was loaded in the car, Zola climbed in the back with me and started on my makeup.

Some glitter on my eyes, red lipstick on my lips, and yellow and blue rhinestones glued on my cheekbones.

Three hours later, we are checking in at the hotel where the guys just happen to be staying. As much as I want to text Caleb, I refrain, too excited to see his reaction when he skates out on the ice and finds me in the stands. I'm hoping this surprise is the good kind. Game time is soon, so we drop off our bags in the room Bonnie booked for us, which we are all splitting, and rush to the arena just down the road.

A sea of black and orange surrounds us as we make our way in. The three of us link arms, holding tight so we don't lose each other.

"Go Puffins!" someone in a bedazzled jersey yells and the rest of the crowd joins in.

I try to blend in, but the yellow and blue jerseys make that impossible. We find our seats quickly and I'm relieved to see all the other Royals fans. I'm not sure if it's because she's pure magic or because she's Caleb's sister, but my eyes widen in awe as Bonnie leads us down to the front row. I'm practically jumping out of my skin in anticipation of seeing my guy.

"Let's go Royals," someone chants and we all clap along with him.

"Let's go Royals!" *Clap, clap, clap-clap-clap.*

The lights begin flickering around us and the entire arena comes alive. Once the Zamboni drives off and the doors close behind it, black and orange lights illuminate the ice as both teams skate out.

Cheers ring throughout the building and when I spot number 13, I bang on the boards and start screaming, "Go Booker!"

Since it's just warm-ups, no one is wearing a helmet, so I have an unobstructed view of Caleb. His expression turns from serious to confused to downright excited as his eyes land on me. My face is burning up as he skates toward us, slamming into the board.

He bangs his gloved hands against the glass and gestures for me to turn around. Proudly, I spin around, showing off the name Booker across my back. When I turn back, Caleb is clutching his heart, skating backward.

"I didn't think it could be done, but Caleb Booker is officially whipped," Zola says loud enough for everyone around us to hear.

I roll my eyes the same time Bonnie says, "And thank God it isn't because of some puck bunny."

Caleb

She's here. My girl showed up to surprise me and is wearing my jersey. With every warm-up shot on net, I find myself glancing back to her seat, making sure she's still here. That this isn't some dream. Holy shit, she's actually here.

"Whipped," Jace whoops, skating circles around me. When he gets close enough, I smack him upside his head.

Flexing my stick. I whip the puck toward Rodriguez and it goes wide.

"I've seen better hands on a digital clock," Beaver shouts. I roll my eyes. Dumbass thinks he's hilarious.

Jace laughs at his stupid joke, dropping to the ice with me for stretches.

"She drove out here to see me play," I say with the smile that is now permanently tattooed on my face. I lean down into a deep stretch, loving the feeling of Millie's eyes on me. Only me.

"Don't fuck it up," he taunts.

Kai skates up to us, spraying us when he stops. "You guys going to take part in warm-ups or too busy with pillow talk?"

I chuckle, standing up and bumping my fist with Kai's. "Jace is jealous he doesn't have anyone in the stands wearing his jersey."

Kai and I laugh while Jace mocks us. "It would be a crime to lock this down."

He gestures to his body and Kai and I just laugh harder.

Jace, Beaver, and I skate up to center ice. I'm trying to put my game face on, but I can't stop smiling. Millie's here to see me play. Fuck, that's a good feeling.

"You good?" Beaver hollers over to me.

"Never better."

The second the puck drops, the Puffins take possession. I hear Beaver curse, skating backward to get back in control. I'm heading down the ice when I'm checked from behind, sending me to the ground.

"You should probably be paying attention to the puck and not eye fucking the audience," one of the Puffin players taunts.

I jump up, turning around and pushing him off me.

"Watch your mouth," I warn, but am pushed back when a ref skates up.

"Back off, boys."

"You're not gonna call that shit?" I gesture to where I was just laid out on the ice and the shithead just skates away.

Before I can even find the puck, Puffins go five-hole and the buzzer sounds.

"Dammit," coach mutters when I skate past the bench.

"Fucking weasel," Kai mutters about the asshole who checked me.

He's jumping over the board as I'm climbing back to the bench.

"Ref isn't any better," I inform him. "Keep your head up."

Usually, when our games start out like this, it's a bad omen.

Good thing Kai listened when I told him to keep his head up. A Puffin skated full force at him, slamming him into the board after he passed the puck. Shockingly, the ref didn't see anything. This game is fucking rigged. After a few shifts of no action, I'm rushing the ice with Jace by my side to the lonely defenseman. Nothing better than a 2 on 1 advantage. A little sauce pass over the defenseman's stick and a fat one-timer by Jace and we're back in the game. With me skating left and Jace skating right, we circle back in front of the goalie at full speed, only to launch ourselves into the air and at each other at the last second. We're both laughing like idiots as our chests collide and we fall to the ground. The crowd goes crazy at the celly we decided on when coach placed us on the same line.

At shift change, I hop the board and squirt some water on my face. My eyes scan the crowd and I sigh in relief when they land on Millie. Every stop in play or break I get, I can't help looking for her. Making sure she's still here. Yes, I have a supportive family and they're great, but I've never been with someone who is proud of me for me. Someone who cares about what I care about. Typically, they see my hard-earned abs and figure that's all I'm good for. Millie is different. I knew that the second she stepped out of her car on move-in day.

Full of sass and attitude and sexy as ever.

"Booker," coach snaps me out of my daydream. "You here with us?"

I nod once. "Yes, sir."

"Then get the hell out there!"

I feel our momentum deflating more and more with every shot on goal the Puffins get. They're out for blood today, making sure to only mess with us when the refs aren't paying attention. Sometimes even when the refs are paying attention. I guess it doesn't matter when you have the refs in your pocket.

"Ref," Beaver yells from behind me, "Are you pregnant? Because you missed the last two damn periods. Call a penalty for fucks sake!"

"You want me to call a penalty? Fine, I'll call a penalty." The ref shoves his hand in the air. "Number 33 for unsportsmanlike conduct."

The section of yellow and blue in the stands boo and yell as Beaver skates toward the ref. Kai shows up out of nowhere, pulling him back and pushing him toward the sin bin.

I look over just in time to see coach break his clipboard in half.

This has never happened before. We have never collectively lost our shit during a game. With Beaver out, we're down a man and totally hosed. Coach is cussing up a storm and every one of our men, me included, is sucking wind. These shitty refs are just as dirty as the Puffins and it's clear to everyone that we're going downhill fast.

Sweat drips into my eye and I wipe it away just in time to watch the Puffins score a shorty. It's pathetic and I feel bad for Rodriguez. He's an amazing goalie, but something is off with him tonight. Something is off with all of us tonight.

The last minute of the game is the most painful. The Puffins are toying with us. Fancy stick handling and shitty passes. They laugh the entire time and as the seconds disappear, so does our chance at winning. I hate to say it, but when the buzzer sounds, it's a relief.

Chapter Thirty-Three

Caleb

The locker room is dead silent when coach walks in. Everyone staring down at the ground, not wanting to talk about what just happened.

"We lost," Coach starts and the room collectively sighs. "It fucking sucks, but it happens. They were chirping all night and you guys let it get to you. Learn from tonight. Do better. In regards to the hotel, every employee there knows you are my responsibility. I expect you all to be in bed by midnight. We have an early ride back to campus tomorrow and I don't feel like dealing with a bunch of hungover assholes in the morning."

Someone off to my left chuckles and coach turns his glare on him. "Who here would like to enlighten Cardone on what happens if I am woken up in the middle of the night and forced to deal with drunk players?"

Ouch. Cardone stepped in this one.

Jace clears his throat and stands up. He experienced Coach's wrath firsthand sophomore year and has never been the same. "Coach will not only wake you at the ass crack of dawn the next day, he will make you sit next to him on the bus ride home while he describes in detail his favorite movies and television shows. And yes, most of them are old as fuck and you will not have heard of them. Once we get back to school and you think it's all over, at the next practice, he will have you running suicides until he's satisfied."

Cardone's mouth drops open in horror as Jace sits.

"Oh, and one more thing," he stands back up, "Coach makes you the water boy for the next few weeks. How'd I do coach?"

Coach has a shit-eating grin and nods in acceptance. "I'm impressed, Bennett. Now, sit back down and stop looking so smug."

Jace bows like he's just completed the performance of his life and everyone but Cardone chuckles at him.

"8 a.m." Coach reminds us just before he heads out of the locker room.

The guys are somewhat in slow motion as we shower and get changed. Tonight's loss sucked. There were about a thousand things we could've done differently, but everything truly started going downhill once Gomez took that bullshit boarding penalty. I feel like we wouldn't all be so butthurt over this L if it were any other team. The Puffins are all dickbags and having to shake their hands after the game was painful.

I'm still sulking like an emo teenager when I push out of the locker room. My mood instantly changes when someone who looks scarily like my girlfriend but has rhinestones on her face comes running toward me. I drop my bag on the floor and catch her when she launches herself at me, wrapping her legs around my waist.

"Rhinestones?" I laugh into her neck.

She sighs, "Shut up. It's called 'school spirit.'"

Millie pulls back, looking down at me with the biggest smile.

"You came," I whisper, not wanting her to know how desperate I am.

She nods. "I did. And even though you lost, you played great. You were easily the hottest one out there."

A bark of laughter escapes my throat.

"You look beautiful," I tell her, loving the hint of pink in her cheeks. "But the dirty side of me is thinking something entirely different."

"Oh yeah?" she asks, grinding her hips into me. "And what's that?"

I lower my voice so I know only she will hear, then reach up and rub my thumb over her lower lip. "That I can't wait to see what this lipstick looks like smeared over my dick."

She shivers and goosebumps break out all over her. I love how just my words can turn her on.

"We can totally skip the afterparty," she says.

"Oh, we're definitely skipping the afterparty."

"Just admit it," I say with a cocky grin once we're in the elevator, "you came all this way because you missed me."

Millie rolls her eyes. "More like I was just bored and looking for something to do."

I quirk an eyebrow at her in challenge. "You sure about that?"

"Absolutely positive," she says before sticking her tongue out at me.

"You're going to pay for that," I tease.

Bracing herself against the wall, her eyes dart from mine to the elevator door, waiting for the chance to escape. Hoisting my hockey bag on my shoulder, I bend down and scoop her over my other one.

"What are you doing?" Her shriek is mixed with a laugh.

When the doors open, I rush us out and toward my room. Millie's laughter echoing through the hallway.

"Put me down, you Neanderthal!"

I only let her slide down my body once we reach my door. I remain close, so she has nowhere to go, while I pluck my room key from my pocket. Once we're inside, I toss my hockey stuff down and pin her to the wall with my hips. The second the door clicks shut, darkness takes over. Neither of us move to turn on the lights as we inch closer. The air turns heavy around us. Millie's breaths become shallow, her tits grazing my chest with each inhale.

"Okay, fine," she whispers. "I came because I missed you."

A smile spreads across my face as I run my nose up and down hers. She leans forward, trying to find my mouth, but I duck and sink my teeth into her neck.

"Caleb," she pants, arching into me.

I lick a path from my bite up to the shell of her ear. "Walk over to the bed and get naked."

She sways a little as I back away but instantly complies. Millie is such a headstrong warrior, but I love it when she lets me dominate her. It's such a turn-on for both of us. She turns to walk away when I grab onto her wrist.

Her brow furrows in question when I add, "Take everything off but the jersey."

This time she doesn't turn around, just steps back a few feet before shimmying her pants down her legs. I loosen my tie and start unbuttoning my shirt when she reaches inside the jersey and takes off her bra like some illusionist.

"Now what?" She licks her bottom lip, patiently waiting.

"Panties too."

Millie bats her eyes like she's so innocent. "What panties?"

A hungry growl rips through me and I can't take it anymore. In two long strides, I grab the nape of her neck and pull her lips to mine. She gasps in surprise and I take the opportunity to shove my tongue in her mouth. Curious if she's telling the truth, I slide my hand down her body and in between her thighs.

"Christ, Millie."

She's completely bare for me. That coupled with her wearing my name tonight for everyone to see has me about to come in my pants. I press my thumb on her clit as I shove one finger inside her. Millie's hands grab onto my shoulders as I add a second finger.

"Oh my God!" she shouts.

She's dripping all over my hand and I have to resist the urge to toss her on the bed and fuck her senseless right now. Millie is big on foreplay. Actually, I am too. Don't get me wrong, I love every second my cock is inside my girl. But getting her all amped up, wound so tight she needs me for her release, is the fucking sexiest thing in the world.

"Damn, Kentucky," I say as my other hand slides up under the jersey and tugs on her hardened nipple. "You should see how good you look right now."

Millie's mouth opens, but only moans come out when I move my fingers faster. Her legs shake and her nails dig into my shoulders, trying to hold on for dear life. Millie's face scrunches together and I know she's so close. She's almost there. Just needs a little push over the finish line.

Leaning in, I whisper in her ear, "Come for me, baby."

I press down on her clit and she falls apart. Quickly, I remove my hand from her shirt and grab her waist, holding her to me so she doesn't fall.

"Caleb," she moans, "Caleb, please."

"Please what, baby?"

Millie's fingers tug on my hair as she kisses me breathless. Her tongue explores every inch of my mouth and I hiss sharply when she grabs my hard-on.

"Millie," I warn.

She attempts to undo my pants when I grab her hands and hold them behind her back.

"You're being mean," she taunts with a smile.

"You think I'm being mean?" I move close enough to her mouth to where she thinks I'm going to kiss her then command, "Get on the bed and spread yourself for me."

She crawls on the bed as I remove every article of clothing. The sight of her lying on my bed with her knees bent and spread for me is the most beautiful thing I've ever seen.

Millie's body shakes in excitement as I run my hands up her thighs, moving them even further apart.

"I love every single inch of your body."

Licking my way up her inner thigh, I place a small kiss on her clit.

"Please, I need…" she pants, arching her hips up in search of more.

"You need what?" I ask again then lick one long, slow stroke up her center.

"I need your cock," she pleads and I smile against her skin.

I press my lips to her hip bone, stomach, breast, collarbone—

"This is torture." Millie squirms beneath me and I let her push me off, leaning back on my knees. She joins me with a wicked smile. "I want to ride you."

I groan low in my throat, loving when Millie voices what she wants. I scramble off the bed to grab a condom from my jeans. After placing it on, I arrange myself so I'm leaning against the headboard, then grab her hips and help her straddle me.

Reaching underneath the jersey, I grab her tit, kneading it, and ask, "Is this what you want?"

When she doesn't answer immediately, I smack her ass, quickly massaging the red spot I know is there.

"Yes," she shrieks the second I pull her down onto my dick.

"You're so," I moan, struggling to form words. "You're so tight, baby."

Millie's eyes flutter shut and her mouth pops open as she takes all the pleasure she needs.

"Oh, wow. I love your cock."

I can't hold back any longer. I can't take it. I grip her hips and thrust up into her faster and faster each time. She leans back, grabbing my knees to hold herself up. Every inch of her body is on display for me. Her pinched brows telling me she's close to coming all over my dick. Her tits bouncing with every pump of my hips. Her beautiful stomach I can run my hands down. All leading to the most perfectly tight pussy I've ever encountered.

"Reach down and rub your clit for me, baby. Tell me how good it feels."

She does as I say and I swear she's going to push my dick out of her with how hard she's squeezing it.

"You're so deep," she cries.

Sitting up, I wrap my hand around her throat and pull her to me. Her breath is hot and her lips are warm and with a final smack to her ass, she explodes. Her body is still shaking and as I ride her orgasm with her, my legs tense as I find my own release.

Chapter Thirty-Four

Millie

I'm lying next to Caleb on his bed, his hand rubbing up and down my thigh, struggling to regain my breath. He has a sheet draped over his lap and I'm still in his jersey that stops mid-thigh.

"Don't you have a roomie?" I ask through a chuckle.

Caleb sighs, "Yeah. Jace. But he's not leaving the afterparty anytime soon. There's nothing puck bunnies love more than to tend to a broken spirit."

"Ew," I laugh but am somewhat relieved. I would've been pretty mortified if Jace walked in on what Caleb and I just did.

He turns to look at me, a dazed expression on his face. "You look absolutely stunning. I'm so happy you're here."

I turn on my side, facing him. "You sure you wouldn't rather be partying downstairs with your teammates?"

"Ha," he barks out. "God, no. I'd much rather hang out with my girlfriend than those smelly assholes. I would rather sit and stare at a pot waiting for it to boil than go out to a party if it meant that I could spend time with you."

If this was an Anime cartoon, I would have little heart emojis in my eyes right now.

"That is the sweetest thing anyone has ever said to me."

Caleb reaches up, and brushes a strand of my hair behind my ear. I don't think I've ever felt like this before. Caleb makes me happy. He makes me feel good and safe and...loved.

From a fun road trip with my roomies to spending time cheering on my boyfriend, the weekend was a nice break from reality. And now that it's Monday and I'm back in class, reality sucks. I'm sitting in the back of the classroom, biting my fingernail and staring at the paper Professor Weckman just handed back. In big, fat red numbers, the 80% mocks me. There's no way I barely scraped by to get a B. I researched for weeks and put my all into this assignment. I knew how important it was. Thumbing through the pages, I'm confused when I don't see a lot of red marks. How did I not get a better grade with barely any revisions suggested?

The second we're dismissed, I quickly gather my belongings and rush to the front. I need to talk to him about this. I know a B isn't necessarily a bad grade, but I feel I deserved better. At least deserved to know why he gave me this grade.

"Professor Weckman?" He's packing up his satchel when he stops and looks up with a smile.

"Miss Bardot. How can I help you?"

I hold up my paper with a smile. "I was wondering if you had a moment to talk about my grade."

He shrugs his shoulders, pursing his lips. "I was a bit surprised. Usually your work is more thorough."

"More thorough, how? I've been working on this assignment for weeks and what really confused me was the lack of corrections."

The professor continues to gather his things, not stopping to acknowledge my concerns.

"Um, if I'm holding you up from somewhere, I can come to your office hours this week. When are they?"

I grab my phone from my back pocket so I can write down the times but pause when he sighs.

"I'm afraid my week is full. I'm sorry, Miss Bardot. Let's think of this as a lesson, shall we? College is a time for fun, but you also need to make sure any extracurricular activities you partake in don't overshadow your homework."

Extracurricular activities? All I do is go to work and study. Okay, I also find time for Caleb, but I still don't agree.

Professor Weckman swings his bag on his shoulder when I make my final plea.

"Please. Professor, is there any way to make up with an extra assignment or redo this one? I feel very strongly that I did my best."

He tilts his head, taking in my desperation. "Like I said, my week is completely full. I am, however, meeting a friend for dinner and drinks later at The Midnight Lounge. If you would like to stop by, I can get there early and we can discuss your concerns then."

A bar? That seems highly...unethical.

My eyes dart around the room and that's when I realize we're alone. Everyone emptied out while we were talking.

"Um, I don't know if that's a good idea."

"I'm sorry you feel that way. But like I said before, Miss Bardot, I do not have any other time. You will need to accept the grade you received."

He turns his back to me, heading for the door.

I know a B isn't the worst. I know I can still kick-ass the rest of the semester and be fine. But I don't want to just be fine.

"What time?" I find myself saying before I can chicken out.

The Midnight Lounge is just off campus. I grab my phone out of my pocket, dialing Caleb to pass the time as I walk to the bar. It goes straight to voicemail so I send him a text instead.

Millie: Heading to talk to my Professor about a crappy grade. Wish me luck

Caleb: Wish you luck in the form of a dick pic? I would totally do that for you...

I giggle at his message. What an idiot.

Millie: I think I'll just settle for words of affirmation, but I'll keep that in mind

Caleb: Good luck! The team and I are going on

a run, but I'll call you later

Pulling the door open, the light instantly darkens. The restaurant is more of a swanky bar. All dim lighting and close quarters. I grip my backpack straps, feeling off. This just seems weird. Don't get me wrong, this place is gorgeous. But I should be here with someone like Caleb, not my professor. I find him sitting near the end of the bar and make my way there. Everyone here is dressed in ties or dresses and I'm in leggings. It's actually kind of funny how out of place I look. Maybe that's some weird omen that I shouldn't be here.

"Millie, you made it." Professor Weckman gestures to the barstool next to him. It's only once I'm sitting down I see a glass of white wine in front of me. And register that he called me Millie. Not Miss Bardot. I don't think he's ever called me by my first name.

"Am I in someone's spot?" I ask, pointing toward the glass.

"Oh, no. I figured you would like it. I know girls like to feel classy when they're in public."

Shivers run down my spine and not the good kind. Carefully grabbing the glass's stem, I slide it away from me.

"Um, I don't really drink."

Professor Weckman swallows a bit of amber liquid. "What? Come on. You're a college kid. Live a little." When I don't move, he continues. "Just try a taste. The bartender said it's delicious. Their most popular one."

I smile to be polite, but it's strained and uncomfortable. Reaching around, I grab the paper out of my bag and set it on the bar as I sit down.

"I was—" I start to say but Professor Weckman shakes his head.

"I just got out of work mode. Let a man have a drink first."

My laugh is awkward and I think the bartender can tell because his brow furrows when he looks between us.

"I just figured you were meeting people and my assignment is the whole reason I'm here, so we should talk about it."

Professor Weckman swallows a large gulp. "Look," he leans closer, resting his hand on my knee. "Your paper was fine. It wasn't anything spectacular. I know you can do better. Maybe you have too much on your plate and have been too distracted lately."

Every word he's saying is going in one ear and out the other. I can't process anything he's saying. Only the fact that his hand is still on my knee. Why is it on my knee?

Swallowing the sand in my throat, "Can you please remove your hand from my leg?"

His eyes dart down and he looks surprised. "Oh, didn't even realize that was there."

A burning sensation forms behind my eyes and I regret ever coming here. This was a horrible mistake. Screw the grade, I need to get out of here.

"I think I should go," I tell him, sliding off my stool.

His arm darts out, caging me in against the bar. "What about your paper? I'm sure we could work something out to help get your grade back up. I mean, that is why you're here, isn't it?"

"I, um," I stammer, "I think I'll just keep the grade I have. It's time for me to leave."

We're in a stare off. I clench my fist to keep from shaking, but the truth is I'm absolutely terrified. Professor Weckman has always been welcoming and fun in class. I've enjoyed this year and was shocked when he made a 2 1/2-hour class seem fun. I don't know who this man is, but it's not that guy. This guy is scary and threatening and I don't think I've ever felt this uncomfortable in my entire life.

Finally, he sighs in disgust, removing his arm from the chair. "I knew it."

My curiosity gets the better of me and I hear myself ask, "Knew what?"

Swirling the small amount of liquid in his glass, he laughs humorlessly. "You're no different. Just like every other student who is looking for a handout. Refuses to do the work and then gets mad when they get punished. You act so innocent, but I guarantee your hands are plenty dirty."

My entire body convulses as I run out of the building before tears start pouring down my face.

Chapter Thirty-Five

Caleb

"You need to get your ass back to the gym," I taunt Kai who lags behind.

I keep my breath even as I quicken my pace. We're not racing, but I can't let Kai get ahead of me. He's been on my ass for weeks about my speed on the ice. I'm about to yell something again when a familiar head of purple hair darts out of one of the restaurants up ahead.

"Kentucky!" I shout and she stops in her tracks but doesn't turn around. Her head twists side to side like she's looking for somewhere to run. I speed up and grab onto her elbow before she can disappear.

She jerks away quickly and I place my hands up in surrender.

"It's me. It's me, baby."

That's when I see her red-rimmed eyes. Why the fuck is she crying?

"Millie? What happened? I thought you said you were meeting with your professor?" I look back to see if anyone's with her and that's when my heart drops. A blackhole opens up in the pit of my stomach and I pray to God she isn't going to say what I think she's going to say. "Millie, who was in there with you?"

Her hands are shaking as she brings them to her face, wiping the tears from under her eyes.

"I- I don't understand," she sobs.

I pull her into my chest, cradling her head. I have no idea what happened, but I'm going to kill whoever made her like this.

I notice a few of the guys hanging back, waiting to see if I need help.

"Millie," I pull her back, guiding her chin up to look at me, "I need you to tell me what happened."

She takes a slow, deep breath. "I had questions on a paper and when I asked Professor Weckman about it, he said he was too busy to talk about it but could meet me tonight. I knew it was a bad idea, but—"

I don't let her finish. I make eye contact with Jace, slowly letting Millie go.

"Wait here," I tell her.

"Caleb—"

I push the double doors to The Midnight Lounge open, scanning the area for Professor Weckman. I've heard his name around campus. Even before I met Millie. He's newer to the university but is popular with the students. The female students in particular. It takes a moment for my eyes to adjust to the dark lighting, but I find him quickly. Sitting at the bar drinking. And there's a glass of wine next to him. I clench my fists and inhale deeply before walking over and taking the stool next to him.

I gesture to the wine. "Date ditch you?"

Out of my peripheral, I see him smile, taking another sip. "Something like that."

Making eye contact with the bartender, I push the filled wine glass toward him. "He doesn't need this anymore."

Professor Weckman has the fucking nerve to laugh like this is all some joke.

"You're Booker, right?" That's when I look over at him and his smug expression. "Right wing? I've heard of you. Mainly because I'm the faculty sponsor."

I don't let it show on my face, but holy shit! That definitely makes this situation more complicated. But I really don't care.

"Millie Bardot is my girlfriend," I inform him.

His forehead creases. "I'm not sure I know who that is."

"That's odd because she said she just met with you not even five minutes ago."

He nods slowly like he knows he's busted. Then he starts to laugh again.

"Come on, man. You're a good looking dude. You know what it's like."

He takes a swig of what's probably whiskey. Pretentious douche.

"And what is it like?"

"These girls throw themselves at me every day and then act like I'm the bad guy when I invite them out for a nice drink. She's just another dumb bitch who—"

I have no idea what his next words are because my fist is too busy flying into his nose. I feel the crunch of cartilage against my knuckles as he goes down like a sack of potatoes. I jump off my stool and lean down, punching him again in his stupid mouth. *Laugh at that, fucker.* I cock my arm back to land another blow when I'm hooked under my arms and yanked back.

"Calm down!" Jace yells in my ear as I fight against his hold.

"Get out of here!" the bartender yells.

"We gotta go," Kai says, pulling Jace and me to the exit.

Even though I know I'm royally fucked, I don't even try to hide my smile. I don't give a shit who you are, you aren't going to talk about my girl like that.

"Oh my god! Caleb!" Millie shouts the second she sees me. She grabs my hands, examining the cuts and blood.

"You should see the other guy," I joke.

"Cut the shit," Kai says.

He and Jace break into a jog to rejoin the team.

Millie and I don't talk the entire walk back to my place. I know coach is going to be pissed I ditched our run, but I'm pretty sure that's the least of my problems. Millie leads me to the kitchen sink, turning on the water and running a washcloth under it. She dabs at my cuts, never meeting my eyes.

"I really just wanted to talk to him about my paper," she says barely above a whisper.

"You don't have to talk about it if you don't want to," I tell her. I want her to know she's safe and this is a safe space. Millie tosses the washcloth on the counter before bringing my knuckles to her mouth and kissing each one.

"He touched my knee."

"He fucking touched you?" I growl.

"No. I mean, yes he did. But his hand was only on my knee for a moment before I called him on it. He acted like I wanted to be there with him. In the bar. Like I didn't try to meet with him during office hours or in class or something." She can't bring herself to look at me and it absolutely kills me. "He said some really awful things. I don't know what I did wrong. I didn't do anything to...I didn't ask for this."

"Baby." Placing my forefinger under her chin, I gently guide her to meet my gaze. "You didn't do anything. I'm so fucking proud of you right now."

She blinks and a tear falls. "What? Why?"

"Because you told him to stop. You said something and got out of there. This was not your fault and I need you to know that."

"Are you going to get in trouble?" she asks, looking at my bruised knuckles again.

"Don't worry about me. I probably do need to do some damage control, so..."

I let my sentence fade away. Honestly, I have no idea what to do right now. I don't know how to help her or make this better.

Chapter Thirty-Six

Millie

Caleb insisted on driving me home. Neither of us spoke the entire way. When he parks in my apartment's lot, we both continue to just sit there like zombies.

"Okay. Well, thanks for the ride," I say, unsure of what to do next. Back at his house, it seemed like he was trying to get rid of me. And now, everything just feels...off.

I wait a minute to see if he's going to say anything and when he doesn't I open the door and step out.

"We'll talk later," he quickly adds before I shut the door.

I nod in understanding and sulk back to my apartment.

I feel numb. Like I'm not fully processing what just happened with Professor Weckman. When I open the front door, I find Zola and Bonnie laughing at something on TV. They both instantly turn to me. I can see their mouths moving, but I don't process what they're saying. Bonnie grabs my hand and guides me to sit down on the couch next to her.

"What happened?" Zola asks, crouching down in front of me.

So I tell them.

Zola's usual happy and chirpy personality is nowhere in sight. She looks like she wants to grab the scissors from the junk drawer and go find where the professor lives.

"What the actual fuck?" Bonnie yells.

"I don't know what I did. I mean, I didn't do anything. He's my teacher."

Wrapping her arm around my shoulders, Bonnie pulls me in for a hug while Zola comfortingly rubs up and down my arm.

"Caleb's fist looked bad," I mumble.

"Good. I hope he broke the Professor's stupid face," Zola says.

"Oh my God." Suddenly, it hits me. I stand up and start pacing around the room. "Oh my freaking God. Caleb hit a faculty member. He's going to be so screwed."

"Caleb will be fine," Bonnie reassures, but I can't stop now. I'm on a roll.

"Professor Weckman has control over my grade. He basically called me a whore. He's going to tell everyone and then fail me on top of it. I'll never be able to step on campus again. I might as well drop out now and move to some obscure town no one has ever heard of. Maybe in Idaho? I've never met someone from there and I like potatoes—"

"Hey!" Zola shouts, causing me to stop in my tracks. She stomps over to me and cups my face in her hands. "You are not leaving. You did nothing wrong. That slime ball used his position and took advantage of you. Do you hear me? You did nothing wrong."

When I don't nod, she repeats herself. "I want to hear you say it, Millie."

"I did nothing wrong," I mutter.

"Louder," she demands. I've never heard Zola this intense before.

"I did nothing wrong," I say slightly louder.

"I said louder!"

"I did nothing wrong!" I finally scream.

The air is heavy and thick for a few moments before Zola pulls me to her chest. Bonnie joins and I'm being crushed between the two of them.

"We got you," Bonnie says. "We'll help you get through this."

"But—"

"No buts. We're family and you aren't going through this alone," Zola adds.

Fuck, I love my roommates.

The next day, I don't go to classes. I barely got any sleep and can't bear to see anyone. Well, other than my roommates. I looked like shit and I knew it. Puffy eyes from crying, lips destroyed from me gnawing on them, and chipped nail polish because my hands felt like they had to be doing something. Zola and Bonnie were so sweet last night. They helped me move my mattress into their room and even though it didn't help with my sleep, it was a really sweet idea.

I hadn't heard from Caleb yet. I know it's still early in the morning, but it was weird how we left things. I didn't like it. I'm lying on my mattress, that is still on Zola and Bonnie's floor, staring up at the off-white ceiling. I should at least get up and brush my teeth. Maybe get dressed? Gah! Everything feels like such a big task and I have no energy.

I flinch when the door is flung open. Zola stands in the doorway, hand on hip, looking down at me.

"What do you think you're doing?"

"I think it's called wallowing."

Zola shakes her head. "I think it's called getting up and getting ready for the day."

"I don't want to," I tell her. But my voice is small.

Zola walks up to me and crouches down so we're on the same eye level.

"What happened to you is shit. But you control how you react to it. You control what you do next. Not Professor Pencil Dick. Do you hear me?"

"Yeah," I mumble.

Standing up, she yells like a drill sergeant, "I said, do you hear me?"

Finally, I push myself to a sitting position. "I said yes. Just stop screaming. I have a crying headache."

"Well, while you brush your teeth, I'll get you some Advil."

"It feels like too much," I say quickly before she's out the door.

Her brows pinch together. "What's too much?"

"Everything. Moving. Brushing my teeth. Eating breakfast. It just feels like too much."

Zola grabs my hand reassuringly. "Just take it one step at a time. First, you'll get up. Then once you're up, we'll decide your next move."

Pulling on my hand, she helps me up. Once we're both standing, I take a deep breath and Zola smiles.

"See? One task is already complete. What's next?"

"My breath does stink," I murmur, trying not to breathe on her.

Zola chuckles. "Then let's get you to the bathroom."

Zola holds my hand the entire seven steps we take to the bathroom and all but shoves the toothbrush in my mouth.

She turns to leave, but I stop her. "Thank you. Really. You're a great friend."

"I learned from the best," she says with a wink.

Six completed tasks later and I'm standing on the sidewalk outside a ranch-style house giving myself a pep-talk.

"I can do this," I mutter to myself. "I did nothing wrong."

Inhaling through my nose and exhaling through my mouth, I move my feet toward the house.

"I did nothing wrong," I repeat with each crunch of gravel beneath my feet. Before I can chicken out, I make a ball with my shaky fist and knock on the pale yellow door.

An older lady with graying hair opens the door. She removes the glasses from her face as she takes me in.

"Can I help you?"

I did nothing wrong.

"Hi. My name is Millie Bardot. I'm a student at the University."

She starts shaking her head. "This is highly inappropriate to visit me at my home. You need to—"

"Please?" I beg. "I just need to speak with you for a few moments."

"Then you need to call my receptionist and make an appointment like every other student who needs to speak to me."

"Dean Winters, I know I'm risking a lot by coming here but I need to speak to you. I'm going to continue talking until you either stop me or shut the door in my face. The other day, I brought up a concern I had to Professor Weckman about a grade I received. He said he would only speak to me if I met him after hours and off campus."

"Not another one," Dean Winters whispers as she shakes her head again like she doesn't want to hear this. Needing to get my story out,

I start talking faster.

"I met him at a bar and he instantly was inappropriate. I knew it was a mistake, but I needed to talk to him. He bought me a drink. I'm underage and didn't take it. I didn't want it. He said horrible things to me and he tried to touch—"

"That's enough!" Dean Winters raises her voice and suddenly I feel like a toddler being scolded. "Not only is it unacceptable for a student to show up at my house, but then to make accusations about one of the professors on campus? That is outrageous and will not at all be tolerated."

"I'm not making anything up," I insist. "He was crass and—"

She holds her hand up in front of her face, silencing me. "I am done with this conversation. I will not have you going around spreading lies about faculty members. Not to mention you're claiming this inappropriate action happened off campus, yet here you are. At my house. Off campus. With absolutely no proof I might add. Seems to me like maybe you are the issue."

I open my mouth to protest when she continues. "And if you choose to ignore my advice, you should think long and hard about if you like attending school here."

With that, the door is slammed in my face. I don't move for at least five minutes. I'm too stunned. How does she not believe me?

How does *she* not believe me? Once my legs start working again, I walk straight home and climb right back under my blankets. I never should've gotten out of bed this morning.

I'm in my room, staring at my phone plugged into the charger when I hear a knock at my door.

"Come in."

The hinges creak as Bonnie opens the door. With a smile, she grabs my desk chair and sits down across from me.

"I heard what happened with the Dean. How are you?" she asks.

I tear my eyes away from my phone to answer. "I don't know. I'm okay. Kind of. Not really."

"Can I do anything for you? Zola had to run out, but she wants to help too. Neither of us are stealthy, but we could YouTube some karate moves and go kick Professor Weckman's ass for you. Now for the Dean, it'd probably be frowned upon for us to take down an old lady, but I'm not above blackmailing."

I laugh. Actually laugh. "Thanks, but no thanks. No need for both Bookers to be in trouble."

"Did Caleb already talk to his coach?" she asks.

Glancing over at my phone again, I shake my head. "I don't know. I haven't heard from him."

Bonnie smacks her left ear a few times. "I must have ear wax or something stuck in there. What did you just say?"

My phone screen remains dark. Like it has since the second I stepped out of Caleb's car. At first, I turned it off, wanting to shut the world out. About two seconds after that, I realized Caleb wouldn't be able to get a hold of me if I did that. And he said we would talk later. It's been almost 48 hours. Isn't that later?

I scrub a hand over the back of my neck. "He's, um, he's probably just busy and stuff. With school and hockey and things."

"Things?" She raises one eyebrow like she can't believe what she's hearing.

"Yeah," I mutter. "Things."

Bonnie stands up, runs downstairs to grab something then comes back to my room. She hands me a can of beer and some candy.

"What's this?" I chuckle.

"Provisions. I have to go run an errand, but I'll be back shortly."

Chapter Thirty-Seven

Caleb

My bedroom door is flung open as Bonnie storms in. "I know being a dumb jock is a stereotype, but you really live up to it."

"What are you talking about?" I ask, pulling my headphones off.

"Millie, you dumbass!"

"Bon-Bon—"

"No!" she shouts. "Don't *Bon-Bon* me. Where the fuck have you been the past two days? Millie is a mess and I just assumed her boyfriend would want to be around and help her through this. Do you even know what happened with the Dean?"

"Bonnie, you need to calm down."

I regret the words the second they leave my mouth.

She picks up a textbook off the floor and throws it at my head, missing by only a few inches.

"What the hell?"

"Why are you nowhere to be found? Why are you not by Millie's side right now? What the hell is wrong with you?"

This time she picks up a shoe and cocks back her arm. I grab a piece of white paper and wave it in the air, pretending it's a flag.

"You're such a dipshit," she says, dropping the shoe back on the floor.

"I wanted to give her time."

"Time to what?" Bonnie's looking at me like I have a dunce cap on.

"I don't know. I had no idea what to say and Millie wanted to go home, so I assumed she wanted to be alone. Wait, what happened with the Dean?"

"Why are men so stupid?"

I stare at her blankly.

"It wasn't a rhetorical question. I genuinely want to know why you think she would want to be alone right now."

I open my mouth, but nothing comes out.

Bonnie's shoulders sag and she finally stops yelling. "You need to talk to her. She's my friend and you hurt her. She's crying because she thinks you don't want her anymore."

"Why would she think that?"

Bonnie pinches the bridge of her nose like talking to me is exhausting. "Her professor made a move on her and the fucking Dean doesn't care enough to do anything. And yes, you defended her, but then you just left her to deal with the aftermath herself. She doesn't need space, Caleb. She needs her boyfriend. She needs you to reassure her that you aren't going anywhere and that you are going to stick by her side no matter the consequences."

"Of course, I'm going to. I have a meeting with coach later today."

"Well, maybe tell her that."

I flinch when she slams my door behind her.

I'm 99.9% sure what is about to happen. It still doesn't stop my palms from sweating as I knock on coach's office door.

"Get in here," he shouts, knowing it's me.

I sit in the chair opposite him, his desk the only thing separating us.

Coach refuses to look at me, staring at a folder on his desk. Neither of us says anything for the first few minutes. I think about starting the conversation, but the second I open my mouth coach pins me with a death glare.

"You're a good player. Have a good head on your shoulders. Yes, you sometimes draw stupid penalties, but so do the other guys. What they don't do is go attack the fucking team sponsor."

His last few words grew in volume until he was screaming.

"Professor Weckman sponsors the Royals and you go and smash his face in for a chick? What the hell is wrong with you? Did you even think before you walked into that bar? If I remember correctly, you were supposed to be running with the rest of the guys, not screwing your life up."

I'm about to defend myself when coach slams both hands on his desk.

"It is not time for you to speak. The dean has approached me and you're off the team. End of discussion. I have no idea what was going through your head, but I think the dean is willing to hear you out to avoid expulsion."

He reopens the file on his desk, shaking his head in disapproval.

"All this for a piece of ass. What a shame. Go clean out your locker."

I clench my jaw so hard, I'm afraid my molars might crack.

"Coach—"

"I said," he shouts over me, "clean out your locker."

I stand up, but pause when I'm at the door. He looks like he's going to hit me when I turn around.

"Did you lose your hearing in the fight? I said—"

"Coach," I interrupt his rampage, "I respect the hell out of you. It would be an honor to be like you one day. But if you insinuate one more time that my girlfriend is just a piece of ass, I will have to smash your face in."

He sits back in his chair, stunned at my reaction.

"I'm going to say this as respectfully as I can, but I'm not sorry in the least bit. Professor Weckman is a predator and a creep and hit on my girlfriend. He lured her to that bar and when she wasn't taking the bait, said pretty awful shit to her. I will never apologize for defending her against someone like him. Someone who uses their job and power to get what they want. Now, I will go clean out my locker."

I never leave a ton of stuff here after the game, so most of my things are already in a pile when coach rounds the corner.

"Broken nose, hematoma around his eye that doctors say will take a while to go away, and a contusion to his jaw."

I freeze at the list of Professor Weckman's injuries. I have to tamp down the desire to smile. I love hearing that the creep looks like that and I don't feel bad in the slightest.

"That's all you did to him? I thought I taught you better."

I turn to him. "Coach?"

"If what you say is true—"

"It is."

"These are serious allegations, son."

"I know that, sir."

Coach takes a deep breath. "You're still off the team, but don't clean out your locker just yet."

Chapter Thirty-Eight

Millie

Bonnie and Zola are the most amazing people I've ever met. The past few days, I've been a shut-in but, thanks to my roomies, I have plenty of Ben & Jerry's to comfort me. They've tried to talk to me and help me out, but I've been stuck in a daze, my mind replaying everything that went down with Professor Weckman. And then there's Caleb. He put his entire college career on the line for me, but I haven't talked to him since. He said we would talk later. I didn't imagine that, did I?

"People have their theories," Bonnie told me after she got home yesterday. "Some people said Professor Weckman is part of an underground fight club."

"That is the dumbest thing I've ever heard," Zola added.

"That was the best one. The worst was that the Professor got attacked by a bird or swan or something."

"A swan?" I choked out a small laugh.

Zola gasps. "Don't make fun. When I was younger, a swan chased me around the playground and I thought I was going to die."

This makes my smile grow. Slightly.

Apparently, there are rumors around campus about Professor Weckman's messed up face, and as much as I love my roommates for trying to make me feel better, I'm just plain sad. I have no idea how I got myself into this situation and I haven't heard from my boyfriend in over 48 hours. I just don't know what to do.

Someone knocks on the front door as I'm shoving my face full of Chunky Monkey. I ignore it. Another knock follows and I continue to pretend no one is there. I'm not in the mood to talk to anyone who isn't my roommate. When the jingle of a key sliding into the lock gets my attention, I watch the doorknob turn only to find Caleb. His face falls instantly as he closes the door behind him. He takes a step like he wants to come to me but then thinks better of it.

"I haven't heard from you in two days," I mumble before eating another bite.

Caleb's shoulders sag. "I really need to hug you. Or touch you or something. I fucking miss you so much."

"Did you take care of damage control? Was that what you were doing the past 48 hours?"

Caleb takes one step closer. "I didn't know what to do. I didn't know how to act. When I saw you crying on the sidewalk, I wanted to kill whoever did that to you. And when I saw Professor Weckman, it took every ounce of strength I had not to beat him into nothing. I don't know if I would've stopped if I hadn't been pulled off him, but I don't regret it for a second. I thought maybe my reaction might've scared you and you needed time. I didn't want to make your situation worse."

"I really needed my boyfriend," I say through a sob. I try to hold back the tears, but one slips out.

His eyes shine with unshed tears as he asks, "And now? Do you still need me? Or is it too late?"

Grabbing the blanket on my lap, I toss it off and set my ice cream down before running and attacking Caleb in a hug. He cradles the back of my head, holding me to him as his lips kiss the side of my head.

"I'm so sorry, baby. I really thought you would want space, but that was such a stupid thought. I promise not to be that stupid again."

My shoulders shake with laughter. "I needed you. I wanted you."

"I know that now. God, I'm so sorry I'm such a dumbass. Can you forgive me? I'll even get down on my knees and beg if that helps."

A smile appears on my lips for the first time in days. "Depends on what you plan on doing while you're down there."

Caleb's lips brush against my cheek. "There's my dirty girl."

I wrap my arms around Caleb's waist, pulling him tight to me. I inhale deeply, taking the time to memorize his scent. I've missed it so much.

When he starts pulling back, I tighten my grip. "I'm not done yet. Can you just hold me a little longer?"

"Baby, I could hold you forever."

We stay in the entryway hugging for a solid five minutes. And it's the best five minutes of the past few days. Caleb and I cuddle on the couch as I share the entire story. Every icky detail. It makes my skin crawl and I hate that I fell into that kind of position.

"It's your turn now," I tell him.

His brows furrow. "My turn for what?"

"To tell me what your coach said. You got in trouble, didn't you?"

Caleb brings a spoonful of ice cream to my mouth.

"Open up."

I open and lick the spoon clean. It's weirdly sexy and cute at the same time.

Caleb groans, setting the ice cream on the floor and snuggling into me.

"I'm off the team."

"What?" I sit up straight, staring down at him. "They can't kick you off the team! You're amazing. I get you hit a professor, but he had it coming. You can't be off the team!"

"It's no big deal."

"No big deal? What are you talking about? Caleb, talk to me."

"Weckman was our faculty sponsor. Clearly, he talked to the dean first."

"Oh my God. No. I'll talk to the dean again. Bonnie mentioned something about blackmail, which is totally out of the question, but—"

Caleb pats my laugh. "Slow down, killer. I talked to coach and told him what happened. He asked why Weckman didn't have more injuries."

This makes us both chuckle.

"He said he'll talk to the dean about not expelling me—"

"Expelling you? Caleb! You can't—"

"Relax, Kentucky. I'm not going anywhere. Plus, I wouldn't change a damn thing about what went down. Now, come over here."

Leaning down, I snuggle back under his shoulder as he fixes the blanket to cover both of us.

"Actually," he speaks up, "that's a lie. I would change the amount of damage I did to him. I let the guys pull me off him too early."

The next morning, I wake to Caleb's goofy sleeping face. He drools in his sleep and it's hilarious. He stayed with me all night and held me close until I fell asleep. I rest my hand on his chest, feeling his heartbeat thump, thump, thump. I can't believe when I met him, I didn't know how amazing and incredible his heart truly is.

"I like waking up to you," he mumbles, squinting one eye open to look at me before closing it. He wraps his arms around me, pulling me on top of him so I'm straddling him. "I like this even more."

"I really needed last night," I admit. "You being here and being with me. I really needed it."

"Me too." His hands rub up and down my thighs as I lean down and lightly kiss his lips.

"Have you talked to the team yet?" I ask, nervous of his answer. He didn't seem too eager to talk about it last night.

He nods. "Yeah. I did. I told them what happened. Kai and Jace explained what they walked in on."

My entire body deflates. I liked his teammates and I like to believe they liked me. But that was before I got Caleb kicked off the team.

"I'm so sorry. They probably hate me. They totally think you should break up with me, right? That's the only logical thing to do."

I shriek when Caleb's hand collides with my ass.

"That's for bringing up the topic of breaking up. Now, don't do it again. And the guys aren't mad at you. Why would they be?"

"I got you kicked off the team. I'm not even saying this to boost your ego, but you're a great player. They're going to suck without you."

"As sweet and true as that is, you didn't get me kicked off the team. Weckman did that the second he thought he could put his hands on you."

I sigh, "Really?"

"Really. I hate to break it to you, but you're part of our dysfunctional family now. And there is no way of getting out of it."

Tears spring to my eyes and I lean down and kiss Caleb.

Chapter Thirty-Nine

Millie

I was adamant about not going to the hockey game tonight. Caleb is still suspended and I have no school spirit. I planned on curling up under a giant blanket and going to bed early. At least I was until Caleb busted into my room and practically put my clothes on me. Once I was dressed, I was still complaining about going when he said he was done listening to my excuses, threw me over his shoulder like I weighed nothing, and then waved goodbye to my roommates. Bonnie and Zola just smiled and let it all happen. Traitors.

"I still think this is a horrible idea," I say to him once we find our seats. The arena is packed tonight because WU is playing their arch-nemesis, WSU. Caleb wraps his arm around my shoulders, pulling me against him. He kisses the side of my head making me feel even worse. I know it's killing him that he's not playing tonight. And if the guys lose? It'll be all my fault because I got Caleb suspended.

"Hey," Caleb grabs my chin, forcing me to look at him. "If you really want to leave, we can. But I think we should stay. The game is going—"

A throat clearing echoes through the rink and I turn my attention to the ice. I feel paralyzed as the entire arena fades away. Professor Weckman stands on a red carpet rolled out on the ice with a microphone in his hand. He's smiling at the crowd and part of me wants to vomit. The other part of me wants to high-five Caleb when I see the bruises around his nose.

"What the fuck?" I whisper.

Professor Weckman taps the microphone a few times before speaking into it again. "Hello? Can you all hear me?"

Cheers erupt from around Caleb and me, but we stay silent.

"Settle down everyone," he says through a fake laugh. "Settle down. Tonight we are here to watch two incredible teams. Captains?"

He looks over both shoulders as Kai and the WSU captain hop over the bench at the same time. They meet at the carpet, each standing on opposite sides of the Professor.

"I really don't want to be here anymore," I mumble.

"Everyone, stand please," he announces.

Everyone stands, making the bench shift underneath us. Caleb grabs my hand, pulling me up with him.

"Caleb, I really want to go," I say louder this time so he can hear me over the crowd.

He leans in, "Do you trust me?"

I don't hesitate. "Of course, I do."

"Then just wait. If you want to leave after the puck drop, we can. I promise."

Wait? Wait for what? I don't want to have to see Professor Weckman's face for longer than I have to.

"Captains? This is going to be a clean game—"

Professor Weckman is interrupted when Kai leans in and says something to him. Kai takes his glove off and gestures like he's saying "Give me." The professor, confused and unsure, hands the mic to Kai who instantly skates away with it. Professor Weckman tries to go after him but stops the second he realizes the carpet is only so big.

"Good evening!" Kai shouts. "Who is here to see a kick-ass game?"

The entire rink roars and cheers so loud, I think I may be going deaf. Kai laughs, a big smile on his face, loving every moment of this.

"What is he doing?" I yell over the crowd.

Once the cheers die down slightly, Kai starts speaking. "Well, that is unfortunate. I would like to formally apologize to all of the amazing fans here tonight."

Weckman yells something at Kai, but he just shakes his head and skates further away. I swear, if it was possible, steam would be blowing out of the professor's ears right now.

Kai sticks his tongue out, skating in random circles, just out of reach.

"This is our wonderful faculty sponsor, Professor Bradley Weckman. Give the crowd a wave, professor."

Kai waits and the professor does as he's told.

Even from here, I can see the danger in Kai's eyes.

"See, the great professor has hurt one of our own."

I gasp, bringing my hands to cover my mouth.

Kai chuckles darkly. "And we protect our own. As a result of the University sitting on their lazy asses and doing absolutely nothing to a teacher who is lording his power over innocent young women, this is the Winger U hockey team's first ever protest."

Murmurs surround me and I still can't figure out what the hell Kai is doing.

"A protest? What does that mean? Caleb?" I turn to him and he has the biggest smile on his face.

"I once again apologize," Kai continues, "because we will not be playing tonight. Or any night for that matter until something is done about Professor Weckman. However, if you all stick around, you can watch one killer practice."

Kai skates over to the other captain and fist-bumps him before dropping the microphone at Professor Weckman's feet. My mouth still hangs open and I am not sure I'm fully processing what just happened. A bucket of pucks is dumped on the ice and both teams hop the board. The teams mix together as they mess around. Some of the fans disperse, but a good amount of them stay to watch. A member from WSU's team skates over to Weckman and shoos him away before grabbing the red carpet and tossing it off the ice. I have no idea what is being said, but Professor Weckman is stomping away, his hands flying all over the place. When my eyes find Caleb's coach, he's holding his clipboard in front of his face, trying not to smile.

Caleb's hand tightens around my shoulders and that's when I finally realize what happened.

"You did this," I say to him. His eyes are still on the ice, but his smile gets even bigger. "How? Why? You didn't—"

"I wish it was all me." Caleb is watching his team with pride. "The guys actually thought of the plan. Said if I can't play, then no one can."

"Caleb, this could get you guys in major trouble. I appreciate the gesture, but—"

"But nothing," he interrupts me. He turns to me and cups my cheeks. "Kentucky, we are all behind you 100%. That douche will not get away with what he did to you. And if the dean still tries to look the other way, we'll do something even bigger."

"Caleb."

Caleb leans his forehead against mine. "You are one of us. We protect our own."

Twisting my fist in his shirt, I pull him to me. He moves closer, towering over me and deepening the kiss. I hold onto him for dear life and realize my feelings for him. Caleb put his entire hockey career, his entire life, on the line to stand up for me. His teammates, who he sees as family, are standing up for me. They did this for me. I've never had someone in my life like that. Someone who would run headfirst into a fight for me. Someone who would risk everything for me. His tongue swipes against mine before he bites my lower lip and pulls away. I remember we're in public and instead of kissing him for the rest of eternity, I open my eyes. He stares down at me and I have no idea how to explain it, but he's looking at me differently. Like he...

I shake my head and start giggling. "You're really not going to say it, are you?"

"Say what?"

I gently smack his chest. "You know what."

He turns his attention back to the ice, placing his arm around my shoulders again. I shimmy away and grab his face to make him look at me and only me.

"Stop that. You know you love me. I know you love me. You wouldn't have potentially imploded your life for me if you didn't love me. Now, tell me you love me God dammit!"

His shoulders shake with laughter as he places a gentle kiss on my nose.

"Only if you tell me first."

Chapter Forty

Millie

I tighten my grasp on Caleb's hand. I'm not sure if I can do this. We're standing close to the entrance for Professor Weckman's class and I don't know if I can go in. After the protest, the dean immediately took action. Winger U is known for their sports teams and if the hockey team just stopped playing, the university would have lost millions in donations. The dean's hand was forced and although there was probably a better way to go about it, Professor Weckman was fired without severance.

The moment Kai announced to the arena that Professor Weckman was a known creep, other girls started coming out and telling their stories. There were a few girls who weren't doing great in his class and he exchanged good grades for...certain activities. Others said they started flirting and they thought it was fun until he would threaten them. Tell them they had to do what he wanted or he would reveal the messages and pictures shared between them. Hearing all this truly disgusted me. As happy as I am that he is gone, I know how many students, who were once in the dark like me, loved him.

"We can stand here as long as you need, Kentucky. No rush," Caleb says.

That's a lie. According to the clock above the door, class starts in exactly one minute.

"That's not true. You have practice and you cannot afford to miss it."

He shrugs. "Call it even for the dean calling me being kicked off the team a suspension."

"Yeah, but Coach told you to—"

He rolls his eyes, "Keep my shit together. Blah, blah, blah. You're deflecting."

"What if everyone hates me and throws tomatoes at me the second I walk through the door?"

He chuckles. "You think they went to the cafeteria, asked for whole tomatoes, and brought them to class just to throw them at you?"

I roll my eyes which makes him laugh even more.

"Millie. This is completely up to you. It is your decision. If you don't want to go inside, we can do whatever you want. We could go bungee jumping or streaking across the football field. Or you could go in there with your head held high and show everyone how tough and badass my girlfriend is."

The hand on the clock ticks and that's when I make my decision. Giving Caleb a quick kiss on the cheek, I walk down the ramp and through the door with shaky hands.

I don't know what I expected, but when I open the door, everyone is busy still finding their seats. A few people stop, pointing to their friends and giving me all their attention. I'm a frozen statue, trying to decide if I should turn around and run back home.

"Miss?" I jump at the shaky voice. The new professor is an older man with gray hair and smile lines. "Class is about to start if you'll take your seat."

I nod, holding tight to my backpack straps. I lower myself down in a seat, still acutely aware of everyone.

A girl with vibrant green hair, who I've never spoken to before, sits down next to me.

"You're Millie, right?"

I nod, not able to look her in the eyes.

"Thank you."

What? My gaze instantly finds hers.

She must note my questionable look because she continues, "Thank you for having the balls to do what a lot of us couldn't."

"Us?"

She nods. "Us. You're a fucking badass and I'm not sure if you noticed, but all of us are in awe of you."

She holds her fist up and I bump it with mine. My body relaxes as a slow smile spreads across my face as the professor dives into his lecture.

Those girls weren't pointing and staring at me when I walked in because they were pissed. They were happy I said something. I spend the rest of class smiling like a total idiot and for the first time since Professor Asshole was fired, I truly feel like everything can go back to normal.

Epilogue - Millie

"Caleb."

When he doesn't respond, I glance up from my phone to find him swaying from side to side at his desk with his headphones on. He's such a dork. I love it. I grab the closest thing, one of his dirty shirts, and toss it at his head. He instantly freezes, slowly turning around to me with a death glare.

"Did you just throw my dirty clothes at me?" he asks, pulling his headphones off.

I wave the book I'm reading in the direction of his phone. "Your phone keeps going off and it's driving me crazy. Just answer it."

Standing up, Caleb walks over to where I'm lying on his bed.

His tongue darts out while his eyes scan my body. "You look so fucking good right now."

Oh, I forgot to mention I'm wearing one of his hockey shirts and only that.

"Is that one of your dirty books?"

I roll my eyes. "You're ridiculous. Just because it's a romance novel doesn't mean it's dirty."

"As long as you picture me as the main character, I'm good with it," he teases. "What's it about?"

I shrug, turning the book over to look at the back cover.

"Two people fall in love only to realize they were each other's childhood nemesis. It's a romantic comedy by a new author. Her name is Tatum Moore."

"Never heard of her."

"Never heard of an author who doesn't write about hockey? I'm shocked," I mumble.

"What was that?"

"Nothing," I giggle.

Caleb leans down, but I place my foot on his chest to stop him. "We made a deal. No touching until you finish your homework."

He groans. "You're killing me, Kentucky."

He wraps his hand around my foot, trying to pull me closer to him, but I kick him away while laughing. When his phone goes off again, I yell at him to turn it off.

Caleb walks over to his dresser where his phone is charging and grabs it. "Yeah, yeah. Don't get your panties in a knot."

"What panties?"

He stares down at his phone in confusion.

"What's wrong?" I ask.

"Some number messaged me like seven times in the past few minutes."

"Your other girlfriend getting jealous of all the time you're spending with me?" I tease.

Caleb fake laughs. "I can barely handle you let alone another girl."

"I take pride in the fact that I can keep you thoroughly entertained."

Caleb walks over, falling on the bed next to me.

"Check this out."

The texting thread is full of videos. He scrolls to the top and clicks the first one.

"Holy crap!" I sit up straighter, taking the phone out of his hand to get a better look. "That's me."

"And me. I think this is when you hit me."

"When you hit me," I correct.

I'm about to press play when he yanks the phone back. "If this is a video of the accident and we find out that I'm right, it's not going to change anything between us, right?"

"Right," I agree. "I love you and all, but you're wrong and I'm right."

I grab his phone again and click play before he can say another word. The video was taken in the back seat of the car at the stop sign opposite me. I think the person filming meant to record everyone singing or dancing or whatever, but you can see my car clear as day.

My eyes pop out of my head at what I see next. The camera shows the person in the driver's seat waving the other cars on. After replaying and zooming in, you can see me looking down before going. I remember I was skipping the song that was playing on my phone when I saw her wave me on and that's when I went. But when we zoom over to Caleb's car, you can see him fixing his hair in the rearview mirror before going. And then we crash.

"So," Caleb says, setting his phone down on the bed, "it was both our faults?"

"I thought she was waving me on and you thought she was waving you on. So we both went."

Caleb scrubs a hand down his face. "Holy shit."

"We were both wrong? That seems highly unlikely. Are you sure you were actually paying attention? Let me see the video again."

I go to grab his phone when he tosses it away along with my book before tackling me back onto the bed. I try to fight him off, but he grabs my wrists and pins them above my head with one hand.

"Caleb," I laugh, "get off me and give me your phone."

"Not a chance." His fingers walk up my thigh and stop once they meet the hem of his shirt. "You know, I was thinking about it and I've done enough homework for today."

I scream when his fingers attack my ribs, but am silenced when his lips land on mine. I shrug out of his grasp and wrap my arms around his waist, pulling him even closer.

"I was just thinking," he says.

When he doesn't continue, I prompt him. "And?"

"And what are you doing this summer?"

My fingers trace patterns on his back. "Considering it's more than a few months away, I have absolutely no idea."

"What do you think about spending the summer with me?"

He's about to kiss me again, but I place my hand on his chest to stop him. Is he serious?

"Spend the summer with you? Like you and your family?"

He nods. "We have a summer house and more than enough room—"

"Because I take up so much space?" I tease.

"Yeah, you and your big—"

I place my hand over his mouth. "Be very careful of your next words."

When I slowly remove my hand, he says "Big heart. Your big heart."

"Nice recovery."

Caleb wraps a piece of my hair around his finger. "I'm serious. I can't imagine a summer without you. Just say yes."

His lips suck on that spot on my neck that he knows makes my knees weak.

"Just say yes," he whispers.

"Okay. Yes."

His head shoots up. "Wait, did you say yes?"

I laugh at his surprise. "Yes. Did you think I would say no?"

"The perfect fucking woman and you're all mine."

Pushing off the bed, I hold my arms in the air, waiting for him to help remove my shirt when his door is flung open.

Caleb instantly jumps off me and blocks Jace's view.

"Are you kidding me? I locked the door," Caleb shouts.

Jace shrugs. "I know the code. Can you spot me a twenty?"

I can't see his face, but I can almost see the steam coming out of Caleb's ears. Grabbing my book, he chucks it at Jace.

"Hey!" I scold him just as Jace closes the door, saving himself from getting hit in the face. "Why did you throw my book?"

"It just happened to be right next to my foot."

I gently push him away. "Next time, I'm throwing you across the room."

"Oh yeah?" His brow quirks up. "I'd like to see you try."

He must see the challenge in my eyes because the next thing I know, I'm on my back with him between my legs.

"I love you, Kentucky."

"I love you, too. And I can't wait to spend the summer with you."

Acknowledgements

Even though I call myself a writer, I have been staring at this blank page for the past ten minutes, trying to articulate my feelings. I think I just have to dive in and hope for the best.

First off, I would like to say a giant thank you to the Bookstagram/Booktok community. I was incredibly nervous about choosing to self-publish, but all of you were so welcoming and incredible, it gave me a boost in confidence to keep writing. I've always had a love/hate relationship with social media, but ever since I started writing, it has helped me meet some truly amazing people.

This book would not be seeing the light of day if it were not for my beta-readers. Thank you for all your feedback! It was monumental in making Caleb and Millie who they are.

To all of my close friends whom I consistently bugged about grammar, sentence structure, and random questions, I cannot say thank you enough for continuing to put up with me.

Choosing an editor is a tough job. You want to make sure they understand your voice, what you're trying to say, and how you're telling it. Laura Cifelli was the perfect editor for The Power Move. Not only were her ideas perfectly aligned with the story, but she was beyond helpful in brainstorming with me. Even if it was how to clean out my dryer vents.

A huge shoutout to Yummy Book Covers. This is my second cover they have done and I could not be more obsessed with their artwork. Thank you to Enni and her partners who were so patient with my indecisiveness and helped bring my characters to life.

Finally, thank you to my loving husband. I could not have finished this novel without you helping wrangle our beautiful children so I could find time to write. Your love and support are the reason I can now call myself an author. If it wasn't for you, my novels would most likely be hiding away in my Documents folder for no one to ever see.

Milton Keynes UK
Ingram Content Group UK Ltd.
UKHW011503151223
434437UK00004B/281

9 798986 545523